SWEET DEATH
COME SOFTLY

Also by Barbara Whitehead

The York Cycle of Mysteries
Playing God
The Girl with Red Suspenders
The Dean It Was that Died

Historical fiction
The Caretaker Wife
Quicksilver Lady
Ramillies

SWEET DEATH
COME SOFTLY

Barbara Whitehead

St. Martin's Press
New York

Library of Congress Cataloging-in-Publication Data

Whitehead, Barbara.
Sweet death come softly / Barbara Whitehead.
p.   cm.
ISBN 0-312-08900-7
I. Title.
PR6073.H543S92   1993
823'914—dc20   92-43892   CIP

First published in Great Britain by Constable & Company Limited.

First U.S. Edition: March 1993
10 9 8 7 6 5 4 3 2 1

Lovingly dedicated to my aunt
Mary Curtis Ash
whose energy and zest for life
have always been outstanding

Author's Note

All the characters in this book are completely imaginary both as people and as members of institutions. Benn's factory, although reflecting aspects of all the confectionery factories of York, is not based on any individual one of them.

My thanks go to the York confectionery industry and to all those people connected with it who have advised me; they have been most generous with their time and knowledge.

SWEET DEATH
COME SOFTLY

1

Lena Lindgren, blonde, beautiful and three-quarters Swedish, walked into St Helen's Square early on New Year's Eve. It was in that hush that falls on the busiest city between the end of the working day and the beginning of the evening's revelry, but today was even quieter than usual. The night was damp and chill. For once, the open paved space was completely empty except for the brilliant Christmas tree, which had been placed in the centre of the pedestrianized area and was covered with coloured lights. A road led enticingly from each corner of the square, and a fifth, narrower road, Stonegate, went from the higher side. All round were shops, cafés and historic buildings, notably the old church of St Helen and the Mansion House. Under the blackness of the night sky the illuminated square looked like a stage set waiting for something to happen, for the first actors to arrive, for the heroes and heroines, the citizens of the city, the first and second murderers, to make their exits and their entrances.

Floodlights beamed out from the top of Betty's Café on one side and from the building which had once been Terry's Café on the other side.

Light flooded the Mansion House on the lower side of the square, the official residence of York's Lord Mayor. It was a moment for appreciating its Georgian architecture, the red-brick dignity ornamented with pale pilasters, the small-paned windows, the beautiful proportions.

The square seemed to be holding its breath.

Lena Lindgren, wearing sugar-almond coloured T-shirt and anorak, blue jeans, white towelling-type socks and expensive leather-topped Reebok trainers, looked round slowly and thoughtfully and then walked to the place where the little crooked street called Stonegate entered the square.

She turned her back on the stately Mansion House and looked up Stonegate. The buildings there crowded their steeply pointed gable-ends together on each side. Their jettied upper storeys overhung the road so that the houses crouched and leaned towards one another like something out of a fairy-tale.

Above their roofs she could see the golden floodlit central tower of York Minster, which seemed to look down into the ancient street like a benevolent elder brother. Still there was no one about. It seemed that to enter would break the spell in which the street lay enchanted.

Lena stepped into Stonegate and walked in the perfect stillness.

Half-way along, moving below the myriad of tiny twinkling white lights from the small Christmas trees which projected above every shop between the wreaths and garlands of holly, she reached an elbow-like crook in the road and could no longer see the Minster. The golden floodlit mass came into sight again as she neared the junction with Petergate, where the old buildings of the town seemed to huddle near the protection of the cathedral.

Then she heard the singing of several voices.

People were approaching. There was the sound of confused footsteps on the cold wet winter air. Lena stood still in the middle of the narrow road.

The singing was to a dance tune and as the footsteps grew louder and closer she could tell that there was a regular rhythm to the sound. It was not the steady clear steps of walking, but the shuffle shuffle thump thump of dancing feet.

Round the corner from Petergate came four figures linked in two pairs, dancing along, and they seemed to Lena Lindgren like four trolls come down out of the forested hills of her native country, as much part of a fairy-tale as the whole city centre was that night. They sang, 'See me dance the polka! Dum di dum dum diddle dum dee! Oh see me dance the polka!' They tacked towards her in a zigzag dance, hopping, skipping, full of bubbling merriment.

As they reached her they seemed to become self-conscious and the singing and dancing stopped. The four of them dropped hands and formed a line.

'Excuse me,' she said. Her voice was very clear and distinct, with every syllable carefully spoken.

'Hullo,' said the eldest troll.

'Hullo,' Lena answered.

'You look a bit lost. Can we help?'

8

'Excuse me, I'm not lost really. It's just that I'm on my own and not sure where to go. It is New Year's Eve and there is no one about.'

'You a tourist?' asked a second troll.

It was unfair to think of them like that.

They weren't really like trolls, not a bit.

They were four ordinary women, all, she guessed, over thirty and under sixty-five. One of the younger ones was tallish with long straight black hair that drooped over her shoulders and large brown eyes; one was stocky, of medium height with nothing remarkable about her except the size of her bosom; and the other two were short. Of the short ones the younger had frizzy bleached hair and the elder was a comfortable little woman with a cheery round face, wearing a knitted hat and carrying a large handbag.

'I am not a tourist now,' Lena explained. 'I came in the summer to the Mystery Plays and I was a tourist then. I liked the city so much and wanted to know it better so now I'm over here on a year's work permit.'

'If you're at a loose end, come and have a drink with us,' said the oldest woman, looking up from under the knitted hat like a bright-eyed bird.

'I'd like that.'

'We've been celebrating already, but you could guess that, couldn't you? We start work again the day after tomorrow, second of Jan. We're going to go on celebrating now and it'll take all tomorrow for us to get over it.'

'There's Ye Olde Starre,' said the stocky woman with the bosom, pointing to an alleyway. 'They have a good old time on New Year's Eve.'

'We can go there later. Let's start at the Punch Bowl,' said the young bleached blonde. She had her reasons.

'Come on,' said the oldest, who seemed to be the ring-leader, and took hold of Lena's hand. 'Can you do this dance? Come on! It's New Year's Eve! It's easy, follow me.' In a moment Lena had two women on either side of her, and they all began to dance down Stonegate in the direction she had come, singing 'See me dance the polka!'

They revolved in the street, stretching from side to side in a wheel. As they entered the Punch Bowl one of the staff looked at them dubiously, wondering if they were drunk.

'Only cheerful!' the eldest reassured him. 'Now, you sit there,

9

love.' She pushed Lena on to a bench behind a small round table. She took her purse out of the vast handbag. 'I'll get 'em in. What'll you have?'

Everyone wanted lager and lime. They found stools to sit on and settled round the table while the oldest woman was at the bar.

Outside the pub the temporary calm of the city had gone. A few shivering revellers were crossing St Helen's Square, avoiding the puddles, hunching their shoulders against the capfuls of rain which hurtled at them from any direction, borne by the gusty wind. Stonegate itself was now peopled by several teenagers in anoraks and jeans, the girls with long hair blown here and there as the wind wound its way among the old buildings.

The Punch Bowl was welcoming with fire flame and coloured lights and gentle music. Behind the bar the barmaid wore Christmas tree baubles at her ears for ear-rings and an eighteenth-century gown contrived out of black dustbin liners. The barman was dressed as a woman with a low-cut dress revealing his hairy chest and swelling biceps, and a rose in his short-cropped hair.

'That's Sue,' the oldest woman said to Lena when she returned with the lager and limes. She gave Sue her drink. Sue was the stocky one, perhaps fifty years old, with the vast one-piece bosom.

'That's Polly,' handing Polly hers. Polly was the one with the black hair trailing on her shoulders, and large eyes which Lena could now see were beautiful as well as brown.

'That's Betty.' Betty was the youngish one with the bleached frizzy hair. She gave Lena a saucy wink.

'That's mine, I'm Vi – short for Violet. Here's yours, love, and you're?'

'I'm Lena.' She pronounced the name as if it was spelt Lay-na.

'Happy New Year, Lena,' said everyone, raising their glasses.

'You've got a job then?' asked Sue.

'My job finished today. It was only for the month of December.'

'What do you do?' asked Betty.

'I'm trained as a secretary. I'm very quick and my typing is very good.'

'So you'll be looking for a job?' asked Vi.

'Yes. As soon as tomorrow is over.'

'We all work together,' volunteered Polly, who had not spoken until now. 'We're all tea-ladies at Benn's.'

10

'What is Benn's?' asked the Swedish girl.

'You've not heard of Benn's?' She was pierced by the astonished glances of four pairs of eyes. 'You've been in York in the summer and again now and not heard of Benn's?'

'I have not heard of Benn's.'

'Chocolate? You eat sweets and chocolate?'

'I like chocolate very much.'

'You must have heard of Terry's and Rowntree's and Craven's and Benn's.'

'Oh! This is a chocolate firm? Benn's?'

'Chocolate and other things, confectionery.'

'Yes, now I know. There are those – what are they called – Benn's Bars?'

'That's it. Everyone eats Benn's Bars. That's us. We work at Benn's.'

'The bars are our big seller,' said Betty, the one with bleached hair.

'You can't expect her to know anything about it,' said the oldest, in the knitted hat, called Vi. She turned back to Lena and explained. 'Benn's used to be a firm which only dealt in quality, specialist chocolates. We still do. But five years ago Matthew Benn – head of the firm – started making Benn's Bars, they are for sale anywhere. They are sold in boxes to all the shops who order them by the hundred.'

'Now you talk about it I remember that when I was here in the summer I could sometimes smell chocolate. It smelt like a chocolate cake baking in the oven. Did that smell come from Benn's?'

'And Terry's and Rowntree's. Craven's not so likely because they specialize in sugary sweets.'

'In a town like York if you have to have an industry it is a suitable one, making good things to eat.'

The women began to talk generally, about their families, about presents they had been given for Christmas, about work in two days' time. More people came in and sat at the other tables, and everyone looked cheerful and expectant. They all felt that special thrill of New Year's Eve. All the concerns of the old year would soon be swept away, all the broken hopes and forgotten promises, and a bright new set of dreams would be bound to be realized in the months to come, and if they weren't, well, at least tonight was going to be one to remember.

* * *

Hannah Benn had put her foot down. Matthew was not staying up to let the New Year in. Eight years was nowhere near old enough. It was nine o'clock now and that was quite late and she didn't want tomorrow ruined.

'One minute you're spoiling that boy and the next you're strict with him,' grumbled her mother.

'You would be the first to point out my error if he spent all New Year's Day fretful and whining.'

'All right, then, but who is going to let in the New Year?'

Except for the child, who had just been tucked up in bed, violently protesting, the two women were on their own in the big old house on the Mount. The gardener cum handyman and his wife, who lived in a self-contained flat over the big double garage and the vast disused kitchen next to it, had been allowed a fortnight off to visit their son and his family and they were not due back until 2nd January. The daily help had gone at five o'clock as she always did unless they asked her to stay longer. Hannah Benn and her mother Faith were in the new kitchen, where an Aga gently produced its warmth, and Hannah was in the process of making them both a cup of tea.

Now that old Matthew Benn, Faith's husband and Hannah's father, was dead, Faith was the only one of her generation left, apart from some distant relatives. As she and Matthew had had only one child – their daughter Hannah – Hannah was the only one of her generation; the relatives were even more distant in cousinship from her. She had not married, but she had a child – an unheard of event, she had been told, in the Benn family. As she had never looked into the family history, Hannah believed what she was told. Old Matthew had wanted a grandchild to carry on the line, and Hannah had obliged. Upstairs Hannah's love child Matthew, the only member of the next generation of Benns, had now fallen peacefully asleep in a room with circus wallpaper.

'We ought to be having something more exciting happening than this on New Year's Eve,' said Faith.

Hannah put cups and saucers on a tray and carried them into the long double sitting-room, where the curtains partitioned off one end, and the fireplace in use had a glowing grate full of Homefire smokeless fuel in the heart of its elegant white marble and carved Corinthian columns. Hannah straightened up after putting the tray on the coffee table and looked at herself in the mirror built into the

12

fireplace. It was too high to see more than her head, and her eye did not rest on that but travelled over the enchantment of the reflection of the charming room.

'Put the telly on,' she said to her mother.

'It is always boring on New Year's Eve.'

'Better than nothing.'

They watched for a couple of hours, then switched off the set.

Into the silent house came the sound of a far-off door bell.

'Someone at the side door.'

'I'll go.'

'Pierre Fontaine isn't due till tomorrow, is he?'

'It can't be him. I tried to persuade him to come today, or Tuesday, but no, he insisted on New Year's Day.'

Hannah could see that it was a policeman before she even opened the door into the pretty porch which looked out on to a square courtyard.

'Trouble?' she asked.

'Well, not really, ma'am. Sorry to bother you but we didn't know what else to do.'

'Well?'

'A lorry's turned up at the works.'

'On New Year's Eve?'

'That's what we said, miss. He was raising a hullabaloo because he couldn't get in.'

'Of course he couldn't get in, the silly idiot. Hasn't he heard of holidays?'

'He's come from a long way off, one of them Moslem countries. There's that squiggly writing on the side of the artic.'

'An articulated lorry? Moslem? I suppose they don't realize we shut down for a fortnight over Christmas and New Year. I'd better come down.'

She shouted to her mother and grabbed a coat.

'I'll take you, miss. There's a car outside.'

Benn's works lay next to the railway in the city centre, and as they drove there it was obvious that the people of York were getting down to a bit of serious celebrating. Probably half of them were at home with the telly on, grumbling about the programmes in between eating sandwiches and pouring the whisky. Some were having parties and dances. Most of the rest were on a pub crawl, and groups of increasingly noisy folk, young for the most part, were making unsteady progress along wet pavements and across

13

windy roads, cheerfully waving at the police car and wishing it a Happy New Year.

The gates to Benn's, both the wrought-iron front gates and the massive reinforced back gates, were shut as though they never meant to open again. The night was growing steadily colder and damper, with a chill that struck to the bone. The capfuls of rain which had been blowing on the wind were now continuous though not heavy.

The lorry driver could only muster a few words of English, none of them very suitable.

'I can't do anything about it,' said Hannah Benn.

The driver suggested forcibly, mainly in his own language, that she fetch someone to unlock the gates.

'You know', she appealed to the policemen, of whom there were several by now, 'that we shut the place up for a fortnight, put all the alarm systems on, they are connected up to police headquarters, and that's it until seven o'clock on Tuesday. No one's on duty. I can't undo all those arrangements. If we opened the gates we'd be no better off, we couldn't unload his stuff. I'm not fetching my staff out tonight because he's loused up his schedule. I don't suppose I could find them if I did try. You'll have to let him park it here and I'll pay for an hotel for him for tonight and tomorrow, and decent meals.'

That would have been all right if the driver had been willing to leave his vehicle.

'I can't make him,' protested Hannah. 'No matter how much of a traffic hazard it is.'

The lorry driver indicated that he would die rather than desert his responsibilities, he would sleep in his cabin, but if the food they sent was suitable for him to eat he would accept it.

'We've got somewhere, then,' said a policeman.

'He's from Turkey,' said Hannah, who had been looking at the driver's delivery note. 'Is there a Middle Eastern restaurant anywhere? Have you got a Moslem in the police force? Isn't there anyone we can ask?'

'I know a restaurant where they are from those parts,' said the policeman who had fetched Hannah. 'They'd know, surely.'

'Can we ask them?'

'I'll take you, miss.'

It took some time getting to the place and then longer to explain what was required, but at last they persuaded the manager to

14

come back with them, protesting all the time that his restaurant would not be safe without him on New Year's Eve. He had a lively conversation with the truck driver while Hannah and her policeman looked on. The others had left; they had more urgent things to do.

'Can you ask him if he has enough blankets? If he'll be warm enough? Or can you persuade him to stay in an hotel?' Hannah asked the manager earnestly.

'He wants to stay with his lorry.'

'What about tonight and tomorrow morning? Can you bring him some food? I'll pay for anything he wants.'

'We'll see to it.'

'I'll come down in the morning and see how he is. Will you be closed – I suppose you will?'

The manager indicated that in this emergency it might be possible to make special arrangements.

'It'll cost me the earth, I expect,' sighed Hannah.

Lena Lindgren and the group of tea-ladies had somehow got no further than the Punch Bowl. A thin voice behind Lena broke in on their conversation.

'There's something funny going on at the works.'

Everyone turned round. Lena saw an immense man leaning against the wall next to her, with a pint in his hand. He nodded a greeting to them all.

'Thought you were a long time getting here, Len,' said little Betty with the bleached hair. She then ignored him and buried her nose in her drink, in a manner that made it obvious that Len belonged to her.

'You might have dressed up a bit, Len,' said Sue. 'We see you in jeans and that sloppy jacket every day of the week. You want to get something that you can pull up over your beer belly.'

'He hasn't got owt else,' Betty remarked to her lager and lime. 'Won't dress up for nobody.'

'What's funny at the works?' asked Polly.

'There's an artic turned up. It's parked outside.'

'What, tonight?'

'Looks as if it's full of nuts or something. One of them foreigners. It's usually nuts.'

'Well, there won't be anybody turn out to let him in.'

15

'Miss Hannah was there,' Len said. 'And a load of police.'

'I say,' said Betty, 'did you know – Hannah's going to get a shock Tuesday morning, I'll say she is . . .'

'Why, what?'

'That personal secretary of hers, you know, the one who gets everybody's back up, well, after Miss Hannah left on Christmas Eve that secretary sat down and typed a letter giving her notice in, and she left it on Miss Hannah's desk, and went off. By God she was in a temper. Hannah'll be in a right hole on Tuesday.'

'How do you know?' asked Polly.

'I went round with the afternoon tea, didn't I?'

'You never bothered! Not Christmas Eve! They were all at their parties or off home. We went. We didn't bother.'

'I know you didn't bother. But I was waiting for Len. You was driving back from Bristol, wasn't you, Len?'

'That's right.'

'So I thought I'd fill time in and go round. I didn't make a full load, only one of them big teapots and a few packets of biscuits. There was hardly anyone about, only one or two here and there, but they were glad of a cup of tea. Miss Drury was the only one in the offices and she was pleased I'd come with a cup. She was typing out her notice and she was that worked up she told me all about it.'

'What brought that on all of a sudden?'

'There's been nothing but rows,' said Vi, and nodded her head in its round knitted hat.

'That's right. Nothing but rows. It's about this new countline Miss Hannah wants. Her mother doesn't, she thinks we ought to go on as we are.'

'Mrs Faith never did like the bars. When they started she was against it.'

'She never? You can't imagine Benn's without the bars, can you?'

'Faith didn't want them.'

'I never knew that.'

'There's a job for you.' Vi leaned over the table and spoke to Lena, who had been silent during all of this.

'A job?'

'Miss Hannah Benn's secretary's left without warning and she'll need someone desperately on Tuesday morning. You turn up early, before she has time to get on to one of these agencies for temps, and I bet anything you get taken on.'

'It would only be temporary, I expect,' put in Betty. 'But she'll be wanting someone there and then. Vi's right. I do the offices, I know what goes on.'

'Won't she take someone from the General Office?' asked Polly.

Betty looked appraisingly at Lena. 'I'd say she'd take Lena. She looks as if she's got a bit of sense about her. They're all young girls in the General Office apart from the bosses. All they do is them standard letters most of the time, typing in the bits where there's spaces. Hannah's work's all one-offs, it's different.'

'I will try, at least,' said Lena. 'If she says no I can then go to the agency.'

'That's the girl,' said Vi.

'What are you having, ladies?' asked Len, who was looking a bit out of it.

'Lager and limes, aren't we? You treating us, Len? Is that your New Year resolution?'

'My resolution is to stop buying ladies drinks, you'd better make the most of this one.'

It was nearly midnight before Hannah reached home again. She was grateful for the courtesy shown by the policeman – she thought of him as 'her' policeman – who had fetched her in the first place and now drove her home. They left the articulated lorry surrounded by hazard warning lights and with the driver sitting in the cab eating from a big tray of food containers.

The police car drew up at the side entrance to Oaklands, the Benn house.

'Can you come in for a minute?' asked Hannah. 'Cup of tea – glass of wine – mince pie?' Then a thought struck her. She raised her wrist so that she could read her watch by the light of the street lamps. 'Look – I don't know your name . . .'

'John Clark, ma'am.'

'You've got dark hair, haven't you?'

PC Clark looked at her in amazement. Now what was she on about? 'Yes,' he said. 'I suppose I'm quite dark.'

'John, the police force can spare you for five more minutes and I need you. You're a tall dark stranger and we haven't a First Foot. Will you do that for us?'

The young policeman did not need much persuading. He parked the car properly and walked round to the front door. Hannah had run in and roused her mother, who had fallen into a doze by the fire. Hastily she collected the things she needed. Then she ran out of the side door again, broke off a piece of the ivy which grew on the old kitchen wing, ran round to the front and found John Clark. She gave him a lump of coal, a bread roll, a twist of paper containing salt, a coin, and the rain-wet spray of ivy.

'I must get inside again quickly before midnight,' she gasped and hurried off the way she had come.

Clark had never been to the Benn house before that night. He had known which it was, of course. It had been built a hundred and fifty years ago on its corner site on the Mount, one of York's most exclusive residential streets at that time. The roof and top-floor windows looked over the wall surrounding it, so that a passer-by on foot could look up and see them. The small door opening into the courtyard, which he had passed through earlier, was up two steps off the pavement of the main road. The carriage drive had its open-work iron gates round the corner on the minor road. Through them any passer-by could see the stately façade with its Virginia creeper making the whole front a riot of scarlet in autumn and delicate green in spring and soft deep green in summer. Now the wet bare winter stems could be dimly seen in the darkness, lacing over the dressed stone. As PC John Clark stood in the cold, waiting silently, looking at the imposing front door, each heartbeat seemed to take a minute. He'd had no idea that first-footing could be so stressful, his father always did it at home. But in fact almost as soon as he had heard the distant clunk of the side door closing behind Hannah, the time came. Far off the Minster struck the hour of midnight. Usually the bells were stopped during the night hours but tonight was an exception.

John Clark waited until the sound had died away, then he stepped forward to the door and knocked. At once Faith, as head of the household, opened it. John spoke formal words of greeting and was welcomed in. He presented to the family within the house the gifts of warmth, food, money and the symbol of everlasting natural life, and everyone laughed with the release of tension.

'Come along,' said Faith. 'There's a glass for you. You mustn't refuse.'

They went in to the welcome of the fire and John Clark accepted a token mouthful of wine and a piece of Christmas cake with cheese. Afterwards he shook hands formally with Faith and Hannah and took his leave. The police force was paying him to be on duty.

Once back in the police car he reflected that it had been the best cake and cheese he had ever eaten. He'd got something to tell the family when he got home. They'd never believe him.

Throughout the city people wished one another a Happy New Year. At the wilder parties folk took hands in a drunken ring to sing 'Auld Lang Syne', finishing with maudlin tears, kissing one another as though they would never meet again in this world.

2

Hannah wished her mother would not indulge in power struggles over breakfast. New Year's Day was meant to be enjoyed, surely? Granted it was darkish and dismal outside still, although it was nine o'clock, but in their new kitchen the lights were bright and the table welcoming and the smell of food brought a sense of well-being. If there was one thing Hannah liked better than anything else it was bacon and egg, which they usually had on Sundays.

'I don't know that I want a cooked breakfast,' said her mother.

'Don't, then, Mother. I've done toast. There's marmalade and butter. There's cornflakes and tea and coffee.'

'We're at the end of the Seville orange marmalade.'

'There's three-fruit. And the Sevilles will be in in a few weeks and I can make a fresh batch of Great-grandmother's recipe.'

'And there's that man coming as well.'

'Now really! You've known for weeks that he was coming.'

'You should have refused. You should have told him we weren't interested and he had to take his idea to Nestlé or somebody.'

Matthew charged down the stairs and into the kitchen.

'Oh, scrummy!' he said. 'Bacon and eggs!'

To Hannah and her mother, Matthew brought sunshine in with him.

'You can have your granny's as well, she says she doesn't want any.'

'I'll have it since you've cooked it,' said her mother.

'What are we doing today?' asked Matthew. 'Can I play with Orlando?'

'Milk,' said Hannah, putting a glass in front of him. 'And must you wear a hat for breakfast?'

It was a cotton baseball cap of pale blue which showed up the intensity of Matthew's blue eyes, the fairness of his rosy face and the corn gold of his hair. He wore scarlet cord trousers and a pale blue trainer top. He didn't bother replying to his mother or taking off his cap. He plunged into his bacon and eggs.

'We don't need another countline,' Faith Benn said to her daughter.

'Mother, we've had this out so often. I've told you it might not happen. Pierre Fontaine is coming to stay, we're trying out his new recipe, first in the pilot plant then on to market research. Then if all goes well we will look into the finances of it and decide whether to go ahead. At this stage we can draw back. We can draw back at any stage up to the final signing of the agreement.'

'Fifteen or twenty million pounds,' said her mother. 'That's what we're talking about at 1991 prices. Say twenty million, and at today's interest rates. It just isn't feasible.'

'It's feasible if the product is as successful as Benn's Bars.'

'I didn't agree with that when your father went in for it.'

'No, I remember.'

'We should have stayed as we were, small and select, and left countlines to the big boys.'

'It's paid off, hasn't it, mother?'

'Your father was a very good organizer.'

'It's a good product. He did it for Matthew, for the future of the firm.'

Her mother did not need to speak. She had aired her opinion often enough. Matthew could have inherited a small select chocolate factory, that would have been prize enough for anyone. Countlines – the big sellers, the mass market products which shops ordered by hundreds – were a different ball game, as Matthew himself might well have said.

'Is Pierre coming? When?' asked Matthew.

'Monsieur Fontaine to you,' said his grandmother.

'He's driving up this morning.'

'Oh, utterly brilliant! Has he still got the Rolls?'

'I don't know.'

'When I have a car I'm going to have a Ferrari. Vroom! Vroom!'

'Matthew! There's no need to make those car noises at table.'

'When I grow up I'm going to invent things. I wish I'd invented Benn's Bars. Pierre did that, didn't he?'

'Monsieur Fontaine to you,' said his grandmother.

'Yes, Pierre Fontaine invented Benn's Bars, and now he's thought of another product and he's offered us first refusal.'

'It's ages since he came to see us,' said Matthew. 'I bet he's changed his Rolls.' Matthew had forgotten the cause of that last visit. He was, after all, only eight. Pierre Fontaine had last come to attend old Matthew Benn's funeral.

'Well, you'll see for yourself later today.'

'When's he coming?'

'Any time after eleven I expect. Mother, I'll have to go down this morning to see if that driver's all right.'

'What driver?' asked Matthew.

Hannah explained about the articulated lorry full of nuts which had arrived from the Middle East late on New Year's Eve.

'Can I come?'

'You can come if you like. Mother, can you see to things? Coffee and lunch? It's all ready in the fridge, just wants putting out in the breakfast room and the rolls warming and the soup.'

'What about dinner tonight?'

'We needn't worry about that yet, plenty of time. Everything's ready for heating up.'

'Are Orlando's mummy and daddy coming to dinner tonight?'

'Yes, they are, but you and Orlando will be in bed.'

Matthew thought of sulking but there were too many excitements promised for the day to risk spoiling it. 'Can I show Orlando my computer?'

'If they aren't going out. I thought you were coming with me?'

'I meant after,' said Matthew. His friend Orlando Trim lived next door, in a building which had once been the Oaklands potting sheds but had been beautifully converted by architect John Trim into a modern home. The Trims had been away for Christmas and Matthew hadn't yet had the chance to look at Orlando's Christmas presents or show him his own.

'Give Orlando a ring, dear, and tell him he can come over in about an hour. Or do you want to wait until Pierre has arrived and you've seen his car?'

This was difficult. Matthew wanted to do everything at once.

'Go with your mother and see what time it is when you get back,' advised Faith.

Pierre Fontaine arrived at eleven on the morning of New Year's Day, driving himself in his new Rolls Royce. He was a small, spare man of middle age with the liveliness of a bird, and had bright eyes of a grey which matched his hair and suit. Matthew was delighted to be proved right. He'd told his mother Pierre would have a new car. When it was garaged in what had been the bigger of the two old kitchens, now entered by large up-and-over doors on to the courtyard, Matthew danced about it, admiring the finish in Bordeaux Red, the deep deep carpets and the burr walnut fascia while inwardly deciding he would have chosen a brighter outside colour than maroon. Then he climbed in and out of the driver's position demanding to be shown the controls and to be shown how to work the electric seats, to have a go on the telephone and to make the windows go up and down.

At last Pierre came laughing into the drawing-room where Hannah was serving coffee.

'He is great fun, that little one,' he observed, taking a cup from Hannah's hand.

'Where is he now?' asked Faith.

'I sent him upstairs to wash his hands. Not that he had oil on them or anything like that, although I had difficulty in keeping his fingers out when I raised the bonnet to show him the engine, which impresses him by being six and three-quarter litres. He was the same when I was up last year.'

There was a tiny silence when he mentioned his last visit. Matthew may have forgotten but his mother and grandmother had not. Pierre Fontaine sat down and took one of the delicately fashioned Continental biscuits from the nearby coffee table.

'I do feel I'm a disappointment to Matthew in the direction of cars,' said Hannah. 'I'm perfectly happy with my Mercedes . . .'

'What model?' asked Pierre.

'It's a 190E – Father gave it to me – and I'm going to run it as long as it holds together, it's so reliable.'

Fontaine made a polite remark about Hannah's car, then had time to tell them about his journey up from Hampshire before Matthew's noisy entrance into the room.

'You must come and stay with me one day, little Matthew,' suggested Fontaine. 'You can help me take Paddy a walk round the golf links in the very early morning.'

'What kind of dog is Paddy?'

'He's an Irish setter, and sometimes he finds golf balls and brings them to me. Then you could come into the kitchen and help me make chocolates until lunch time, and in the afternoon I would play golf and you would play at being my caddie and look after the clubs.'

'Can I go to stay with Pierre, Mother?'

'We'll see.'

'Say Monsieur Fontaine, Matthew.'

'I don't see why.' Matthew sounded argumentative. 'In the factory everybody calls you Faith, Grandma, and they call Mother Hannah, and you told me that it was good for morale and created a better atmosphere, so why can't I call Pierre Pierre?'

'It's different, Matthew. At work we try to break down the barriers between workers and management and create a friendly teamwork feeling, because everybody's work is important to the whole. But you are still a little boy and it is proper for you to show respect for those who are older and wiser than you.'

Pierre Fontaine laughed at the comical face Matthew pulled.

'When you know as much about chocolate as I do, Matthew, when you invent a countline as good as Benn's Bars, I will let you call me Pierre. Until then be as *douce* as the respectful little French and Belgian boys who call me Monsieur Fontaine.'

Matthew pulled a still more comical face. 'Is your new countline better than Benn's Bars?' he asked. 'What's in it? What are we going to call it? Can I tell Orlando?'

Pierre shot an alarmed glance at Hannah.

'Matthew!' she said sharply. 'We don't mention these things to anyone outside the family and the firm, you know. At the moment we and Monsieur Fontaine are only talking about an idea.'

The bell rang at the front door. Matthew ran to answer it and came back with another boy the same size as himself, who said good morning politely.

'Orlando's come to play, Mother, may I take him to my room and show him my computer?'

A silence stretched out after the two sets of noisy feet had clattered their way upstairs. At last Hannah got up and closed the panelled door which led into the hall.

'I ought to tell you that Mother is not keen on the idea of adding another countline to our products,' she said.

Fontaine turned to Faith in concern. 'But this is superb, madame,' he said defensively. 'You will love it. Have you ever regretted Benn's Bars? This is even better. It will be a great success.'

'You are a very good chocolatier, Pierre. I don't deny that. The Special Selection I do of your recipes sells very well and of course the Benn's Bars have done and are doing big business. But that is what I object to. I would like us to stay small, carrying on the tradition as we have had it for a hundred years. We have a niche in the specialist market. Countlines are big business and I would have liked to stay small. It is easier to weather economic storms.'

'Mother points out to me the expense of installing another production line. The machines are all specially designed, as you know, Pierre. If a project fails they can't be adapted to anything else.'

'At present you are in no financial danger, madame. I have this superb new recipe, I offer it to you because we are old friends and I invented Benn's Bars, and we have agreed to test it – that does not commit you to anything. You have, as they say, first refusal. Our agreement covers the preliminaries, and if they are not satisfactory I offer the recipe to someone else and you have lost only the cost of the trials. Other producers have been in touch with me, you know. They would snap it up. I would have no difficulty.'

'We much appreciate your offering it to us.'

'So what is the problem?'

'You are right, Monsieur Fontaine. But I feel that once the trials take place we are virtually committed to very large expenditure in a period when the economy is taking a down-turn. All the same, I am pleased to see you again and to have you under our roof.'

'*Enchanté*, madame.'

'Now if you will excuse me – Hannah, I am going to see about lunch. You two can talk business.'

'All right, Mother.'

'Things are difficult?' asked Pierre Fontaine when Faith Benn had left the room.

'A little.'

'Don't worry. When you taste my new recipe you will be over the moon and your mother will forget all her opposition.'

'I've had rather an uncomfortable time since the matter was raised,' admitted Hannah. 'I don't blame her, don't think that. She has her ideas, I have mine. Even Father met a lot of opposition over

Benn's Bars, but then Father was Father and I am her daughter. It isn't the same thing at all.'

'Which of you has the casting vote?'

'The firm's now owned by a family trust. Neither of us is in outright control, though in day-to-day matters she is in charge of specialist stuff and the bars tend to keep me busy. Don't think about it, Pierre. We will proceed in the usual way and by the time we have produced samples for market research we'll have reached a consensus, don't worry about it. I intend to enjoy having you with us for a few weeks.'

'And I to enjoy being here. How are things? The factory starts work tomorrow?'

'It does. I've had a place to work prepared for you, the small laboratory kitchen where you worked last time. Tonight we're having our next-door neighbours to dinner to meet you, the Trims – Orlando's mother and father; you'll like them. Also the Works Manager and the Sales Manager and their wives, and our financial adviser. Luckily he's single and balances the table. I promise you we'll keep off talking shop. Oh drat, thinking about the factory reminds me that I've got to go down there this afternoon. I've been down once already, this morning.'

'On a bank holiday? Such devotion!'

'Not really. This lorry driver turned up last night in an artic full of nuts.' She told the confectioner about the incident. 'He's what you might call obstropolous. Wouldn't go to an hotel. But we managed to arrange to have meals sent to him. I go down to show concern for his welfare and to check that everything's all right.'

'Running a factory would never do for me. I have enough with my house, my chocolate recipes, my dog and the golf club.' Fontaine had a comfortable architect-designed house built in the 1930s in two acres of garden.

'You're a prima donna.' Hannah grinned at him.

'Don't be cheeky. Don't forget I knew you when you were in pigtails and I designed the centres for your mother's Fontaine Special Selection.'

Hannah Benn was outside the factory well before seven o'clock on the morning of Tuesday, 2nd January, waiting by the articulated lorry. The driver had been brought a good hot breakfast by the restaurant who were seeing to his meals, and at the prospect of unloading and getting on his way he had become quite friendly and cheerful.

In spite of the cold and dark the sulphur lamps lighting the road made everything there visible. The security people arrived and the great reinforced gates were swung open; the artic drove in and parked near the unloading bay to wait for the factory hands to arrive.

The security man who was to be on duty on the works gate took up his post in the cabin built between IN and OUT. The gates remained open and the single poles raised.

Hannah did not hasten away. She found herself standing near the gates, and began to ponder and think about the future, wondering if she was right in fighting for the new countline or if she should give in to her mother and forget the whole idea. She could hardly bear any more family warfare. Standing there quietly she felt as though at last, in the calm of early morning, she might be able to see through the mass of conflicting claims.

The factory, which had been unseen in the blackness, was now visible as the cleaners moved in and every window lit up. The clock on its ornate tower, specially built to her grandfather's design, was also lit up so that the approaching work-force could not avoid knowing if they were late. The single-storey extension which housed the production line for Benn's Bars was delineated as light flooded up through the glass in the row of zigzag roofs.

As the minutes ticked past more people arrived. Hannah remembered her childhood, how she had sometimes stood here with her father and earlier still with her grandfather, and how the city of York had been filled with the susurration of bicycles as the thousands of men and women arrived at the different confectionery factories and at the railway carriage-works. That didn't happen any more, or not nearly as much. There were now flexi-time schemes which staggered the rush and as car-owning had increased and as people had moved to homes farther away from the city centre they had begun to arrive on four wheels.

Cars were parking at the sides of the approach road. The workpeople arrived in ones and twos. Mopeds and motor-cycles buzzed up. People on foot walked quietly along, solitary dark figures with a few yards between them. The only sound of human voices was made by two people who were walking together, talking and laughing. Sometimes a car parked briefly to let out a passenger and then drove on. Some of the work-force still arrived on bicycles,

26

and Hannah was glad to see them. They came singly with riders in dark clothing, mostly jeans and warm jackets, the girls bareheaded in spite of the cold with their hair flying, the men with woolly caps pulled down over their ears.

The whole sound of the city, Hannah thought, was many-layered, the rumble of the railway and the major roads in the bottom registers, the nearer sounds of the cars and mopeds in the middle, and the faint but clear sounds of the bicycles forming the upper register. Hannah had never noticed before that as the bicycles travelled along the roads they made a noise as if they were closing up an endless zip-fastener, with the regular light thump of the pedals giving a rhythm. She realized that she had been standing for a surprisingly long time; the sky had perceptibly lightened and in the grove of trees her grandfather had planted near the gates birds began to chirp and twitter to one another, forming the top notes, penetrating the rest of the sounds like the tinkle of triangles.

By a quarter to eight, when the great gates clanged shut, there was enough light to see that a slight ground mist had developed so that the factory seemed to spring up, crisp and isolated, from a nothingness of soft grey. The air was cold and frosty and Hannah's breath on it was a cloud outline issuing from her lips like ectoplasm. From the factory also cloud outlines formed where heat and steam were radiating upwards, for the boilerman had let himself in with his own key through the small boiler-room door at four o'clock. Hannah fancied that the building was a great beast gently breathing out these clouds which showed on the frosty depths of air.

As time went by two people separately walked their dogs past Hannah as she stood meditating on her future. The postman went along on his walk. A paperboy worked his way down a line of houses opposite the factory. In one of them a pretty young woman in a pink house-coat leaned towards her living-room window and watched her husband set off to work.

Hannah could perceive now the faintest of odours, a mere suggestion on the wind, almost a private scent which crept to her alone, like the scent which once in *The Wind in the Willows* had said to Mole, *dulce domum*. For Hannah it was a delicate teasing of the nostrils which said, chocolate. *Dulce domum* for her too, for she was a Benn and this was Benn's, and Benn's, she was determined, would go on into the future.

27

She was going to press for the new countline, if the research proved a success. If it were not, another recipe, another formula, would be. One way or another, she was going to build on the success of Benn's Bars. She wanted to carry on her father's work into the future. His death and the consequences of it constantly reminded her of the finite quality of life and the short span of personal ambition – but it made no difference. She intended to steer the firm forward, to decide policy and priorities.

The thrill of living ran through her veins and she knew how much she would enjoy the work, how the heat of the competitive battle would exhilarate her, how she would return home each night tired but borne up by the excitement of it all.

Inside her the conflict was resolved. Now this day must be faced. At home her mother and Matthew and Pierre Fontaine would be getting ready to come down with her to the factory for nine o'clock. Clapping her hands together to get her circulation going again, Hannah began to walk to the place she had parked her car.

3

Lena Lindgren was sitting in the small entrance foyer, between the rubber plant and the Swiss cheese plant, when Pierre Fontaine walked in at the formal front entrance door on her right, followed by Faith, Hannah and Matthew Benn. She looked up at them but they did not notice her and she did not speak. Faith Benn's secretary, who appeared to be in a state of near distraction, had suggested that she wait there and promised to mention her to Hannah.

Lena saw a small, spry man and two plumpish women. Both the Benn women had an air of authority. Faith's hair was in thin grey plaits round her head in an old-fashioned style, she wore no make-up and her clothes, though expensive, were simple and tweedy. Her figure was definitely motherly. In Hannah the family plumpness was as yet only a suggestion of softness round her body. Her hair was beautifully cut so that the short straight dark brown emphasized the attractive shape of her head. Her clothes were also simple and expensive, but unlike her mother's they were definitely smart.

The three swept through the foyer, past Lena, and out again through double doors immediately on her left, with Matthew dancing beside them. His bones promised length; he would be a tall and handsome man one day. He was again wearing his favourite scarlet corduroy trousers, blue jumper and pale blue baseball hat.

Apart from Lena the foyer was now empty, because the small reproduction Victorian sweet shop, which was a charming feature on the wall facing the entrance door, was closed. Lena learned later that its shutters were open daily between ten and four, with a suitably dressed lady in attendance who answered enquiries from visitors to the factory in addition to looking after the shop.

After a second or two Lena got up and discreetly followed Fontaine and the three members of the Benn family through the double doors. She had already been into the wide carpeted corridor in which she found herself, with its photograph-covered wall to her right. On her left were two doors, one marked 'Board and Seminar Rooms' and the next marked 'Directors' Offices' with, underneath, the names 'Faith Benn' and 'Hannah Benn'. Closing the corridor ahead of her was a wide door marked 'Reception and General Office', and next to it, breaking the otherwise plain photo-hung right-hand wall, was an archway with a screen of plastic strips.

Lena stood waiting near the door the group had entered, which was labelled 'Directors' Offices'. This led into the room where both Faith's and Hannah's secretaries worked, and the two directors had their own rooms opening off this, one on either side. Each of the three rooms was carpeted and had a window looking out on to the front of the building, where Hannah's grandfather had planted a small formal rose garden.

'Shall we take a look at the factory?' Faith said, in her deep, positive voice. 'You wanted to, Pierre, and it might be best to do that first. Later Hannah can settle you in your quarters. We've a meeting this afternoon which will keep us busy.' She took off her coat and put on a white overall with the name FAITH over the breast pocket, and tucked a white mob-cap over her grey hair and its antiquated plaited style. 'Hannah, have you got an overall for Pierre?'

'Just for you.' Hannah, for once the biddable daughter, took it from the hands of Faith's secretary and passed it to him. 'We had your name embroidered on it, and here's a hat.' Fontaine looked very dashing in the white open-mesh trilby and he carefully placed the white mesh hairnet, which dangled at the back, round the nape of his neck. Matthew had inserted himself into a small white boiler suit and replaced his baseball cap with a white version.

'Who said you were coming round?' asked his grandmother, but with an indulgent smile.

'But I can, can't I, Grandma?'

Ann, Faith's secretary, spoke quietly to Hannah to say that there was an urgent letter for her, and instantly Hannah knew that something was wrong.

'I'll see you at coffee time,' she said hastily to the others, as they left the office and walked towards the screen of hanging plastic bands which separated the office corridor from the factory proper. They hardly noticed her defection. Faith was about to enter the realm where she was queen and where Pierre had designed the jewels in her crown, and Matthew wanted to be where the action was.

Hannah remained. Turning round and moving back to Ann from the open door, she asked, 'Where's Jean?'

Ann picked up a letter and passed it to her.

The next door along was to Reception and the big open-plan General Office. This office was staffed by the bulk of the clerical staff for all departments. A hush had fallen on the people there as soon as the most junior clerk had pushed her head round the door, used her ears, and said, 'They've come!'

Now they were all listening as hard as they could to discover what would happen next, because by now the whole factory knew that Jean Drury had left a furious letter of resignation on Hannah's desk, last thing before knocking off work for Christmas. Someone had tiptoed to the door of the General Office and propped it open with a tin normally containing Benn's Speciality Assortment. The directors' door was still ajar.

'Bloody hell,' Hannah exploded, loudly enough to be heard by the whole of the adjoining open-plan office. 'Bloody, bloody hell. That's all I needed. Bloody woman.' She banged her fist on the surface of a desk in temper. Then she ripped the letter of resignation in pieces and threw them on to the floor.

The sharp sound of tearing paper came to the fascinated listening ears. Then the most junior clerk crept over and moved the tin, before closing the door very slowly, not making a sound. The

General Office staff and Elfrida, the receptionist cum switch-board operator, looked at one another with expressions full of satisfied shock.

When Hannah flung open their door heads were down and they were all working conscientiously at their word processors. She threw a scathing glance round the office, then banged the door as she went out again.

'There isn't one of them who could do Jean's job,' she announced to Ann.

'I couldn't possibly help out, I'm sorry, Miss Hannah,' Ann said quickly, rightly interpreting the gleam in Hannah's eye.

'You'll have to get on to a bureau for temps,' she was told.

'There is a girl waiting outside, wanting to see you to apply for office work.'

'You know I don't take my personal secretary off the street! Good Lord, whatever next!'

'You might at least see her,' said Ann.

'The women are all on eggs at present,' Faith remarked to Pierre Fontaine, 'and they will be for another fortnight. We produced enough of the Special Selection to see us through.'

They were standing in the large hall-like room in the factory which was devoted to making the Selection, one of the most constant tasks in Faith's part of the work, and other chocolates as required. In front of them the production lines were spotlessly clean and motionless. They were not large lines or large machines, but on ten of them the ten chocolates of the Selection with their ten different centres were produced. Some had pastel-coloured centres deposited from moulds then covered with chocolate by a machine known as an enrober, which draped them with a robe of rich dark chocolate. Other machines formed chocolate shells into which the smooth-flowing centre was filled by the next machines in the line. Still other centres began life as a continuous sheet of praline, fudge, caramel or toffee which was then divided into squares or rectangles or other shapes and finally also enrobed with chocolate, or dusted with fine sugar or crusted with chopped nuts.

Fontaine looked round the tidy place and approved of the shining floor and the general air of order.

They walked to the end and Faith picked up one of the boxes of the Selection which were neatly stacked waiting to be packed into larger containers and then go to the storage area known as TC1, an area which was once Tennis Court Number One, for employees' recreation. She passed the box to him. 'You might like to test them, Pierre, to see if we are still upholding your standard. It does make them an expensive line, but we do our best, and people seem willing to pay for the quality.'

'People will always pay for quality.' He lifted the lid, removed the soft pad of many-layered fine paper and the brown shiny glasine sheet printed in gold with an index showing a picture of each sweet against its name, and at last uncovered the Selection itself. First he inhaled the aroma of top-quality chocolate which drifted up. Then he spoke the names as if they were old friends long missed. 'Alpine Truffle, Parisienne Cream, Nougate Supreme, Pistachio Cup, Lemon Snow, Yoghurt Surprise, Café Delight, Mint Bombe, Curaçao Liqueur, Marzipan Melody. All present and correct. I will let you have my verdict later,' he said, slipping the shallow box into the pocket of his overall. 'Now let us look at the eggs.'

The Easter eggs were being produced in the next department. Benn's made only one type of egg, that created by moulding two hollow halves of an egg shell in chocolate, placing a number of pieces of their confectionery in one half according to the egg being produced, then slightly heating the rim of the matching half-shell before sealing the two together to form a whole egg, finally to be wrapped in shiny metallic foil paper. They were then boxed in any one of a number of fancy boxes depending on size and content of the eggs, from little boxes decorated with lambs and fluffy chicks to vast boxes with a luxurious glimpse of the egg through a window, in the centre of satin bows and a tasteful ring of spring flowers beautifully colour printed.

Outside the window on this 2nd January the sun was now shining from a blue sky on a world cleansed by the rain of the previous two days, but cold and frosty so that underfoot muddy patches had become crisp. The women working on the production line looked warm and cheerful, chatting together as their fingers flashed, picking up whatever chocolates they needed for the egg they were working on and placing them in one half of an egg before they sent it on its way to the next girl, who placed the second half on top of it and then passed it on to the next who neatly wrapped it in foil (Benn's had tried wrapping machines but the breakage rate had been too high). At last it went to the girls who assembled boxes, dextrously gluing the fancy cardboard shapes together with the egg held firmly in the centre.

'Do you enjoy making eggs?' Fontaine asked one of the women.

'Oh yes, it's a change, isn't it?' she said. 'I like a bit of variety.'

'That's it,' remarked Faith. 'On the bars you and Hannah are so keen on it's day in, day out, making the same thing, on the same production line, round the clock, twenty-four hours of the day for fifty weeks in the year. I and my staff rarely do any job for more than a few weeks and often production is organized day by day, almost hour by hour if we get a rush order that somebody's wanting urgently. Many a time, particularly with boiled sweets, we get an urgent order on a Monday and we have to rearrange schedules to fit it in, but it might well be on its way by Friday, made and boxed and off to Germany or Turkey or somewhere. The eggs don't go overseas of course, they're too fragile, as you know, Pierre.'

'It must make for constant interest,' said Fontaine.

'We certainly don't have time to get bored. The eggs are only for a few weeks in the year but the staff enjoy making them. In summer, although everyone else has stopped doing it, we still have deliveries of fresh fruit coming in. I remember when in the old days everyone used fresh fruit straight into the factories and the whole of York was scented with raspberries or strawberries or apricots as they came off the railway. Nowadays all that fruit processing is done elsewhere and we only get the fruit product ready for flavouring. I stick to the old ways as much as I can. I also produce short-life lines for special customers with the fresh fruit.'

'No one without your short runs and flexibility and highly individual customers could do it, though.'

'No.' Faith looked proud as she agreed.

The trolley appeared with the morning tea, driven by Polly, the tall tea-lady with beautiful brown eyes and long black hair. At present the hair was tucked out of sight in an orange-coloured mob-cap. The first line, on the smallest eggs, stopped work; the women clustered round the trolley with their own mugs to have them filled, examined the food on offer critically, and a spate of talking broke out.

'We'll go, shall we?' said Faith. 'Let them have their tea-break in peace.'

The four tea-ladies worked round the factory, beginning with those staff who had started earliest and finishing with the offices, which began work last.

In the executive area, Hannah had decided that it would do no harm to see the girl who had turned up so opportunely for a secretarial post.

Lena walked in, and made a good impression at once. She looked sparkling clean, energetic and intelligent, and judged on another scale, very attractive. She had a lot of white-blonde hair framing a lovely face with wide blue eyes. When she replied to Hannah's greeting her enunciation was clear and every syllable was beautifully pronounced. Hannah suddenly decided that her own speech could do with a lot of improvement.

In response to questioning Lena mentioned a typing speed so fast that it resembled the speed of light and professed intimacy with all and every make of computer, word processor and software. Hannah did not believe anyone could be that perfect.

'Will you do a test piece of copy typing?' she asked, and produced a report which she knew was full of technical terms and trade words unfamiliar to most people, let alone people who were three-quarters Swedish. 'Two pages will do.'

The report was handwritten, but it was clear. It had been typed on the last working day before Christmas by Hannah's former secretary so there was no need for the typing, but it was a handy example. Hannah read Lena's references and CV, then beckoned Ann and went through into her own office, while the girl clicked away on the WP on one of the two secretaries' desks.

'Check these references,' Hannah instructed Ann. 'At least, check this one for Britain. If she is any good we'll check the Swedish ones later.'

Lena worked quickly and the task was carried out perfectly, technical words and all. Hannah congratulated her.

'It is only a skill I have naturally,' said Lena.

'But the language is not your own.'

'Every Swedish child learns perfect English,' said Lena.

'Then, next, will you type a letter for me from this audio tape?'

This test also was passed with flying colours.

'Do you do shorthand?' Hannah was beginning to wonder if she had discovered a prodigy. If so it would be very pleasing, very pleasing indeed.

Lena took down a letter in shorthand and typed it.

'Could you take shorthand notes of a meeting and produce minutes?'

Lena was sure that she could.

'You do realize, Lena, that if I do take you on it would only be as a temp – only a stopgap until the vacancy is advertised properly?'

Lena allowed a look of sadness to flit across her face, but then brightened and asked if she would be able to apply.

'Well certainly, if you've been all right in a temporary capacity ... Now, tell me about yourself, Lena. I've read through your references and they are certainly very good. What made you decide to spend this year working in England, and why in York? Most people in your situation want to go to London.'

'Ah, you see my grandfather was from York.'

'Really? How interesting.'

'I believe he even worked in a chocolate factory, although I don't know which one it would be.'

'How did he come to leave?'

'During the war he was a British soldier in Norway, he was also a prisoner of war, and then after the war he came on holiday touring Scandinavia and met my grandmother and fell in love, and settled in Sweden, because my grandmother was Swedish and her parents were old and she did not want to leave them. My grandfather was called Samuel and my mother was called Samantha after him.'

'Do you remember much about him?'

'No, no. He died before I was born. So once I came to England as a tourist to the York Mystery Plays, and now I am here to work for a year.'

'Have you any relatives in the city?'

'No, my mother told me there were none.'

Hannah reflected that it was an asset to have a good-looking secretary, and Lena reminded her of someone she had seen in an old black and white film, late one night when she was half asleep – who was it? Oh, Mai Zetterling, that was it, she was a Swede too, wasn't she? Aloud, she said, 'Did you enjoy the Mystery Plays?'

'Oh, very much, I so much admire the pop star Poison Peters, and he gave me his autograph. I said his name was like the French for fish and he drew a little fish, it is on the margin of my play programme, I have it safe at home.'

'How interesting,' said Hannah. 'Well, Lena, we will see how you do. Can you start now, at once?'

'Yes, Miss Benn, thank you very much.'

'Hannah, please, or if you want to be formal, Miss Hannah. I shall call you Lena.'

'In fact,' said Lena, 'it is pronounced differently, it is said like this, "Lay-na."'

'Lay-na,' Hannah said carefully. 'I will remember. Now for the rest of the morning Ann can show you where things are and what there is to do. You can buy lunch in the canteen. This afternoon there is a meeting which I would like you to attend and take notes, then we can see how you manage with minutes. It isn't a board meeting or anything like that, so if you get in a muddle it won't matter too much.'

'But I shall still want someone permanent,' she said belligerently to Ann. 'Draft that advertisement for me.'

By the time coffee arrived in the directors' offices the maintenance men were already having their lunch hour in the canteen. There were twenty of them in dark green overalls with green caps, two supervisors, electrical and mechanical, in red with red caps, and the maintenance manager in white.

Except for Betty, who had not yet returned from the offices, the tea-ladies had finished their rounds, balanced their takings and cashed them, and were helping the dinner-ladies for the last bit of time before they knocked off for lunch themselves.

'Are you coming out with us tonight, then, Polly?' one of the maintenance men asked the black-haired girl. The other men had finished eating and some of them had gone over to the social club which was next door to the canteen for a quick game of table-tennis or pool.

'You know I'm not, Kev. I'm going steady with Bri.'

'He's away tonight, though, isn't he? Delivering to London.'

'Just because he's away that's no reason for me to go out with you.'

'You didn't used to be so fussy.'

'What's past is past, Kev. Let's forget it. I'm not going out with you no more.'

'You want to watch it, Polly. I could tell Bri about you and me.'

'You couldn't tell him anything he doesn't know.'

'You've never told him about . . .'

'I tell him everything, don't I?'

Polly put her nose in the air.

'It's all Bri, now, is it?'

'That's right.'

'By God, Polly, you'd better watch it. I don't think I like you going out with that Bri. I could knock you down when I think about it.'

'Don't you threaten me, Kev. Bri's more your size than I am.'

'Break it up, you two,' put in Sue, who had overheard some of this. 'Come here, Polly, we need you. There's these salad dishes to fill up before we have our lunch. Go on, Kev, you play with the lads.'

The first of the next batch of lunchers had begun to trickle in.

Betty was the only one of the tea-ladies to make coffee as well as tea and that was only for the executive suite. Tea and only tea was the choice on the trolleys, it made for a much simpler operation, but there was a small coffee-maker in the seminar room and on it Betty made coffee every morning for the Benns, their secretaries, any guests, and this morning for Pierre Fontaine.

Like everyone else they clustered round, waiting, chatting and looking to see what there was to eat.

Ann, Faith's secretary, always chose tea from the trolley instead of coffee. She had found a spare mug for Lena. Faith, Hannah and Pierre had china cups. Matthew had a small mug with a scene of ducks round it and half milk and half coffee inside.

When they were served Ann and Lena went into the secretaries' office to drink theirs and the others stayed in the seminar room.

'It is strange that the directors are women,' Lena said. 'Is that man one of the directors too?'

'No, he's only a visitor. He'll be working here for a few weeks, I expect. You're right in one way, Lena, I don't suppose there are many other women at the top at present in confectionery. But the work-force in the industry is two-thirds women and there have been lots of women at the top before.'

'It is a tradition, then?'

'Yes, in a way. I don't know about Terry's but Rowntree's was started by a woman called Mary Tuke, a Quaker, who kept a little grocer's shop at the end of Coppergate. Later, the Tukes took up the making of cocoa. They say the Quaker influence had something to do with it, drinking cocoa instead of getting drunk for a penny and dead drunk for twopence, as you could in those days.'

Lena wanted to know what Quakers were so Ann had to explain their religious beliefs.

'They were good tradesmen, they founded dynasties on cocoa. And at Craven's, when the owner died and his widow couldn't sell the business, she decided that rather than give it up and put about a hundred people out of work she'd carry on herself. She had three children to support as well. In the Craven's board room they still have the supervisor's chair she used to use.'

'How interesting,' said Lena.

'All the York confectionery firms started in the centre of the city, near the river. It was tidal then, and they used it to bring in the raw materials – sugar, gum arabic, nuts, cocoa beans, condensed milk. Now we're the only one left, they all moved out as road transport took over, and built themselves new factories farther out of town. We did move a bit, as far as here from the old place, but we're still the most central, actually.'

'It is easy to get to from my lodgings.'

'Where are you staying, Lena?'

'You say my name "Lay-na",' explained the girl, and after that the talk drifted to domestic subjects.

Ann could have told Lena that the paternalistic impulse had played its part too, the desire to provide decent working conditions for the employees, plus sports facilities and the opportunity for intellectual development with library and theatre projects. Rowntree's, numerically the largest and most powerful of the firms, had created a whole model village.

Benn's had taken advantage of a bit of land close to the railway and in 1935 had built its red-brick two-storey block surrounded by trees, rose gardens and tennis courts.

The river, once the lifeblood of all this activity, now ran unused by them, but the firms did not forget their origins. Craven's still made Mary Ann toffee named after the woman who saved the firm, Terry's commemorated the year of their founding in their 1767 chocolates, Rowntree's had just celebrated the centenary of their present site; and Benn's too found their strength in the sense of continuity.

*   *   *

'But of course I want to see the Benn's Bars,' said Pierre Fontaine as he drained his coffee cup. 'It gives me great pleasure to feel that I have a part in all that production, all that automated machinery working so miraculously on its own to produce that lovely foodstuff.'

Hannah laughed. 'Stay with Granny,' she said to Matthew. 'I'll be back soon.' She put on a white mob-cap and tucked every hair inside.

As they walked along she said, 'We won't actually go on the shop floor, Pierre. I've had a walkway built along one side, sealed off from production. When we start the new countline I'm going to install shower rooms and lockers so that the workers in both will shower and change into sterile uniforms on their way in and change back into mufti on their way out. They won't have the tea trolleys any more either, there will be a rest room with machines for drinks and food.'

Pierre pulled a face.

'I don't suppose they'll like that part of it,' Hannah answered his look. 'I don't like food from machines either. Vi, our oldest tea-lady, serves them in here and she's very popular, but fortunately she's due to retire in a couple of years so I won't have to make her redundant. It's the way things are going generally in the industry. In recompense I think there will be a special pride involved in working on the countlines. They'll certainly earn more money.'

They walked along the covered walkway near the side of the Benn's Bars production line. By now all the processes had started up again after the annual break. The ovens were baking the foundation biscuit on which the bar was built up and it was emerging smoothly and continuously. The filling for the bars moved along in a continuous thick sheet through ovens and cooling processes, then was placed on the sheet of biscuit and cut into pieces which passed through a curtain of liquid chocolate that fell like a brown robe over each filling before they moved on through a machine which tweaked each bar to give it a pattern on top and through another which cooled the chocolate.

Three men were strolling up and down the throbbing production line, keeping an eye on the smooth progress of the bars. At the end when the bars had passed through the cooling chamber a little bevy of youths were waiting, several on each side, to finish checking by human eye the perfection of the product which had already been checked by machine. At every stage there was provision for the automatic disposal into waste bins of any imperfect bar.

Other men supervised the wrapping machines, which needed as much attention as all the rest of the line put together.

In the air were the pipes leading to vats of semi-molten ingredients. Indicators of temperature and pressure on the pipes were glanced at regularly by the men on the line. From inside the shut-in walkway hardly a sound could be heard.

When they reached the end of the line Hannah and Pierre walked into the freedom of the packaging area, where the already wrapped bars were packed by the dozen and the hundred and the hundred thousand into boxes, which were then shrink-wrapped to form large cubes, which were placed on pallets and taken off towards the enormous new storage building known as TC1.

'Well?' she said, turning to him at last.

'It makes me proud,' said the middle-aged man at her side.

'Let's go to your quarters now – I must start work myself as soon as you have settled in. I'm dying to have a taste of Recipe 179 when you've made some up.'

'If you don't mind taking your lunch hour from twelve to one,' Ann had said to Lena.

'I do not mind at all.'

Ann showed her where the canteen was and Lena said she could manage perfectly. She queued up for a salad and took her tray to the table where by now the four tea-ladies were sitting together.

'Come on, Lena,' said Sue, the middle-aged woman with the large bosom. 'There's always room for a little one.'

'How are you getting on?' asked Polly of the black hair.

'She's in with the nobs,' announced Betty, who had winked knowingly at Lena as she served her with coffee an hour or so before. 'Miss Hannah's secretary no less. What do you think of that?'

'I am only temporary,' said Lena. 'They are going to advertise but Miss Hannah says I can apply if I am satisfactory as a temp.'

'Well, if you can stand the racket,' Vi put in. 'Before Christmas Hannah and Faith were having the most awful rows, that's why Jean Drury left.'

'They have been very polite this morning,' Lena said.

'Hannah swore something alarming when she read Jean's letter, so I heard from the General Office,' said Betty, nodding her bleached curls wisely.

Lena, who had also heard the swearing, said nothing.

'She had a phone call from Brandt's this morning,' went on Betty. Brandt's was a big Continental firm who were looking out for a base in the UK, ready for European free trade.

'What did they want?'

'They've been on at her before, haven't they?' asked Sue and Polly.

'They wanted a take-over as usual.' Betty was quite willing to tell all she knew. 'They got the brush-off once, but they're back again with a better offer, so Elfrida told me. Look, she's just come in. Hey, Elfie!'

Elfrida came over to their table. 'I haven't got time to fraternize with you lot,' she said. 'I'm having lunch with that new bloke from Sales.'

'I was telling them about Brandt's being on again with another take-over bid,' Betty said.

'Well, I didn't hear much. Do you think I've nothing better to do on the switchboard than listen to calls? All I heard was that one of their directors was coming to see her.'

'Go on then, off to your fancy man,' and Sue gave the switchboard operator a slap on the rump.

'Stop it, Auntie Sue,' complained Elfrida, but she smiled over at the new man from Sales and joined him in the queue by the counter.

'Nothing but excitement in this place.'

'I don't know that I fancy being taken over.'

'Rowntree's seem to have settled down now, they're happy being Nestlé,' said Vi, picking up her large handbag and looking in it for a handkerchief.

At two o'clock the meeting took place in the seminar room. Present were Martin Legg, suave and elegant, the Sales Manager; David Rexell, a stolid sort of man, the Works Manager; Bruce Swallow, head and sole member of the Design Studio, who had been afflicted by polio as a child and had been left with a limp; Sally Binson, folding her hands capably and firmly on the table edge, in charge of Dispatch; Paul Change, visibly tense and nervous, Personnel; and Hannah and Faith. In a corner at her own small table sat Lena, ready to take notes. Matthew had been shut out of this event and had been sent outside to play with strict instructions as to what he might and might not do. Pierre Fontaine had already begun work on preparing a small trial batch of Recipe 179.

'The usual after-Christmas meeting, ladies and gentlemen,' said Faith, who was taking the chair. 'You have your agendas in front of you. A look at the sales figures first, Martin, and a report please of the effect of the different packages and advertising, so that we can form a few guidelines for next Christmas. We'll have a meeting a fortnight from today to finalize our next Christmas production when we've had a chance to evaluate this one. Then Easter – if you can give us a breakdown of orders to date, Martin. I'd like a discussion of the new designs and how you feel the public are responding to them so far. We'll monitor that and carry those considerations on also in our next. Then a quick round-up from all of you on the Christmas period and suggestions for improvements. Any current problems can be mentioned last, but briefly I think, because they can be dealt with individually afterwards.'

Martin Legg handed out copies of his report on the Christmas sales, and moved over to the standing board on which he had already placed various charts and graphs.

He uncovered the first in the series.

'We can see by this, Mrs Faith, Miss Hannah, Miss Binson, gentlemen . . .'

'Well, Matthew,' said Faith as Hannah swiftly drove the whole party home at the end of the day's work, 'what did you do with yourself this afternoon?'

'Helped Pierre, but first I bombed about,' replied Matthew, who had persuaded his mother to take his bicycle in the boot of her car that morning. 'Bombed about the car-park, bombed about the front drive and the rose garden and bombed about the works entrance.'

'If I'd known,' Hannah expertly slipped round a stationary van, 'you wouldn't have been allowed your bike at all. What possessed you to go round to the works entrance? Those big lorries going in and out. It wasn't safe. Don't ever do it again.'

'I was careful, Mummy. When that big artic was going I stood and watched him. That foreign man. He said goodbye to me.'

'It's the last time you have your bike down at the factory. I thought you only had a ride round the rose garden at lunch break.'

'Won't again, Mum, honest.'

'You won't,' replied Hannah. The bike was in the boot of the car and home was where it was going to stay.

'How did you get on, Pierre?' asked Faith, breaking the awkward silence.

'Very well. Didn't you see me putting tins in the back of the car? Hannah kindly had all the ingredients I asked for ready and waiting so I was able to make up the first trial batch. We will have a grand tasting tonight. You, *chère* madame, will be the first to try it.'

Faith said nothing but she could not help but look pleased.

'Was the chocolate all right?' asked Hannah.

'Splendid. Exactly as I asked.'

'You must thank Mother for that, she was in charge there.'

'Rich and dark and beautiful,' said Pierre, putting his fingers to his lips and throwing a kiss into the air.

'You couldn't use chocolate of that quality on a countline,' said Faith.

It was fortunate that they were nearly back at Oaklands, because suddenly the atmosphere became tense.

Hannah had driven in at the front gates, which were standing open. She stopped at the front door and her passengers got out, Pierre taking his several tins with him. Then Hannah drove round into the stone-paved yard at the side and parked in the garage cum old kitchen, fastened the doors, went back down the short drive and fastened the gates, and at last entered the house. She reflected as she stood for a moment in the hall that she could tell that the Goodwins were back. The electric light bulb which had blown, in the left-hand fitting, had been replaced; an enticing smell was coming from the kitchen; the letters were in a tidy four-square pile on the hall table; and as she closed the gates she had noticed that they were no longer squeaking. Soothed by the sense of order, she went upstairs to shower and change for the evening, then she gave Matthew his tea and bath, read him a story, and tucked him up in bed before dinner.

Polly, the tall tea-lady with the long black hair who had served the Easter egg production line, had left work at the end of her day and set off to walk home. The tea-ladies finished as soon as they had cleared up at the end of their afternoon round, so their hours never

43

coincided with those of anyone else on the staff except – in Polly's case – Kev, one of the men on maintenance. He drew alongside her in his car and, leaning over, wound down the window.

'Give you a lift, Polly,' he said.

'No thanks.'

'Go on. Won't hurt you to have a lift. Bri wouldn't mind you having a lift.'

'He would, you know.'

'Come on, love, get in.'

'I'm not your love and you're causing a traffic hold-up, Kev.'

'Come on in then.'

'I'm walking.'

Polly felt rain in the wind. She said nothing for a while as she walked her determined way along the pavement and Kev drove very slowly alongside her with the car door slightly ajar.

'If you don't get a move on some policeman's going to have you for dangerous driving,' she said to him bitterly at last. 'Kerb crawling, that's what you're doing.'

'I'm only offering a lady a lift home.'

The sulphur lights were on now, fighting the gathering darkness. Polly shivered.

'Oh, all right then,' she said suddenly, and climbed into the car.

4

It was not until 4 January that Pierre Fontaine disappeared.

At seven o'clock that night, when Hannah and Faith were sitting at the dinner table waiting to start eating, his absence really became noticeable. At a quarter past they decided to start without him. At eight o'clock they finished their meal and Pierre's was set by in the kitchen to be heated up again in the microwave on his return. At ten o'clock Hannah made the bedtime hot drink for Faith. At half-past ten, the only person still awake in the large house, she decided to ring the factory. At ten-forty, having tried Pierre's extension without result, she finally raised an answer from the security man.

'Miss Hannah, his Rolls is still here. I can see it through the window; it's in the car-park where he put it this morning. I haven't seen him since then.'

'Lock your door, Stan, and go to see if he's still in his workshop. If he's really absorbed he might have forgotten the time.'

Ten minutes later Stan rang back.

'No one there and the light's off, Miss Hannah.'

She didn't see what else she could do. Pierre was a grown man quite able to look after himself. Perhaps he was even then walking back through the frosty darkness. Perhaps he had accepted an invitation – gone off somewhere – and would turn up at the end of a convivial evening. After a bit of thought she decided to leave side and front doors unlocked and go to bed. The risk of burglars was a slight one – at any rate it was preferable to making Pierre ring for admittance in the small hours. She wished she had given him a key.

In the factory the only sound was the distant rattle and whirr of the production line as it made Benn's Bars by the hundred and the hundred thousand. The only other place in the whole factory which bore evidence of life was the security man's office by the front gate, where Stan was whiling away the quiet night with a soft porn magazine chosen from his pile of miscellaneous reading.

When the Benn family arrived at the factory next morning Pierre Fontaine's car was still parked outside the office entrance and there was still no sign of him. Faith and Hannah went up to his work area and looked around helplessly. Things were not untidy, but neither were they put away as they would be at the end of a normal working day.

Back in her office, Faith said, 'I wish that nice policeman were here, our First Foot.'

'Police Constable John Clark? Yes, we need someone.'

It was not often that the two Benn women missed husband and father as much as they were doing at this moment.

'I'm going to ring the police station,' said Hannah.

The call was taken by the man on duty. 'Missing person? . . . Adult? . . . Male? . . . In good health?'

'As far as I know.'

'We don't carry out an investigation in those circumstances, madam. Adults do go off. It's their right if they want to do that. They go off all the time. The Salvation Army is your best bet. They trace missing persons and ask them to get in touch, but it's up to the person themselves, the public don't realize that.'

After a few more minutes of this Hannah slammed down the receiver. 'I'm getting nowhere,' she said. 'All he said after all that was that he would put Pierre on the Missing Persons List. I expect in most cases what they say is fair enough, but not in these circumstances. I think I'll have to go down and see them.'

Her mother had been playing with the pens on her desk. 'Let me try,' said Faith now, as her daughter turned away and stared furiously out of the window. They were alone.

'This is Benn's factory,' Faith said in winning tones down the phone. 'On New Year's Eve we were helped by a young policeman in this area – PC John Clark. We were very impressed by his handling of a delicate situation. Could we have his help again? It's only a small matter, but if he happened to be on duty . . .'

'He's out on patrol, I can radio to him, madam, and I'm sure he will give what help he can.'

'There you are, you see,' said Faith, as she put down the phone.

In a couple of minutes the white police car with the red stripe down the side drew up outside the front entrance.

'Look, there's a jam sandwich,' said Ann in the secretaries' office, where she was looking out of the window as she waited for Faith to summon her.

'Jam sandwich?'

Ann looked at the Swedish girl impatiently. 'Jam sandwich. Police car painted white and red. Don't they teach you colloquial English at your Swedish schools?'

'They teach us correct English,' said Lena, joining her at the window. 'We don't usually eat white bread and jam.'

'I wonder what they've come about.'

One policeman stayed in the car while PC John Clark went in at the front door, looked around, and headed instinctively in the right direction, towards the directors' offices. He tapped on the door, which was opened by Lena, who looked at him appreciatively. She liked tall dark men.

'I've called to see Mrs Benn,' he told her and she showed him into Faith's office.

'Dishy,' she remarked to Ann.

'I thought you didn't know any colloquial English?'

The three in Faith's sanctum looked at one another appraisingly. They had met in the strange atmosphere of New Year's Eve, and this was the cold light of a Thursday morning in January. To the

46

two women PC Clark looked as he had then, pleasant, friendly and dependable. To him they also looked as they had before, exotic, different, powerful, like no other women he had come across.

'I believe you wanted help?' asked PC Clark of Faith, who had come forward to greet him.

She explained the situation.

His first inner reaction was that of the constable on the desk who had answered Hannah's telephone call; but as he stood quietly listening his instinct told him that this did not fit into the usual pattern. He had lived in York all his life and his father and brother worked at one of the much bigger confectionery firms, so he knew all about the intense secrecy and security measures surrounding a new recipe which was a potential winner. It was not a matter much discussed, but everyone realized that industrial espionage was more than a possibility and was particularly to be guarded against during the development period of a new product. He realized, therefore, why Faith and Hannah were so concerned. It was not the disappearance of a colleague so much as the horribly uneasy feeling of a possible breach of security and the loss of a secret which could be worth untold millions of pounds.

'Can I see the place where he worked?' he asked.

Once there, looking round from the doorway without touching anything, he found more reason for concern. This was obviously the workshop of a tidy man, but there had been no preparations for a long absence. He turned to the two women who were waiting behind him.

'I think we ought to have CID in on the problem,' he said. He closed the door. 'Can you lock this?'

Hannah locked it and gave him the key.

As he left the building PC Clark looked out for the good-looking blonde secretary, but he didn't see her.

Speaking on the car radio to the Clifford Street police headquarters PC Clark asked for CID, and got Detective Inspector Dave Smart.

'Sounds as if we'd better take a look,' said Smart. 'I'll send someone out. Can you wait on a minute?' He put the receiver down and looked at his loaded desk. There were reports to write and forms to fill in and he felt he ought to get through them. He went and knocked at the door of Detective Chief Inspector Bob Southwell's office.

'Come in,' said Bob. When Dave Smart went in, both the DCI and Detective Superintendent Joseph Birch lifted their heads from the documents on the desk, which they were obviously discussing.

'Oh,' said Dave, and hesitated.

'It's all right, Dave. We're not having a high-level conference, you can interrupt. What is it?'

'Benn's – the chocolate factory, you know, sir . . .' Dave was still diffident about butting in when the problem might be nothing at all.

'Yes – they make Linda's favourites, the Fontaine Special Selection. What is it?'

'My wife likes them too,' put in the DS, not realizing that there was any urgency about Dave's mission. 'Particularly the lemon one. Lemon Snow, they call it. She often says she'd like a box with nothing else in but those.'

'Linda particularly likes Yoghurt Surprise,' said Bob Southwell. 'I always go for the Mint Bombe.'

'My favourite is the Curaçao Liqueur,' Dave broke in, by now desperate to terminate this conversation on the Fontaine Special Selection. 'Benn's have a visiting confectioner, and he's vanished,' he went on very loudly. 'He was working on a new recipe, very hush hush, an industrial secret. He's vanished from a locked and guarded factory and his car's still there.'

'I rather like the Alpine Truffle myself,' murmured the superintendent, going back to the document he had been reading. He was trying to clear up various matters in advance of his imminent retirement. Everyone had known it was on the cards for the last year or so and at present he was bringing himself round to announcing the date; he could not put off the statement much longer. Applications would have to be invited from those anxious to fill his shoes.

Bob leaned back in his chair so that its rear legs dug yet another dint in the thermoplastic tiles. He was a tall thin man, almost bony. The large lenses of his glasses tended to reflect windows and other lights and obscure the expression in his eyes, but looking at him now Dave knew well the keen light-grey gaze which seemed to see through trivia.

'Well, we know, Dave, don't we, that there are usually three reasons for someone to disappear.'

'They want to, and we tell the relatives to get in touch with the Sally Ann.'

'Right in most cases. But there are other possibilities as you know full well. Suicide, well concealed. Murder, and a hidden body. Kidnapped and held to ransom.'

'Four reasons, counting the voluntary one, sir, which is usually because of another woman or a financial problem.'

DCI Bob Southwell nodded in agreement. 'True. So this might be anything or nothing. Who put in the report?'

'PC Clark, sir.'

'John Clark?'

'Yes.'

'He seems to be a good officer. Fairly new. I've come across him.'

'He's still there, Bob, waiting outside the factory, hanging on to the radio for further instructions. The missing man's workplace has been locked and he has the key. He can't go on sitting there for ever, he's supposed to be out on patrol.'

'Who's available?'

Dave hesitated. 'I've got a lot of desk work to clear up. Rollo's out on that mugging in Coney Street.'

'Any of the DCs around?'

'Jester, sir.'

'Our James?' There was a pause. 'Might be good experience. Send him up. Ask Clark to hang on for a few minutes, we'll have Jester out as fast as we can.'

James Jester had to put up with a lot of teasing in the force. He was a gangly lad with red hair and burning ambition. It was when it was discovered that he carried a magnifying glass that the teasing started, although he kept protesting that he only carried it because he collected stamps. The lads in the station had clubbed up and bought him a Sherlock Holmes hat for Christmas and told him it would be useful to collect stamps in, and was he writing a monograph on the ninety-seven different varieties of perforations?

He looked apprehensive now as he stood on the other side of the desk to his DCI and the super.

Bob Southwell gave him his instructions. 'It might be anything or nothing,' he said again. 'PC Clark will report to you. You then go into the factory, see the top management and do a recce. Gather all the facts you can, come back and write a report. If necessary you can leave a uniformed man there – ring Mr Smart to arrange someone – but it probably won't be necessary. OK?'

James Jester nodded and gulped. He'd never been sent out on his own like this before, not to anything that might be important. He left the room with Dave and paused for a moment by Dave's desk in the outer office, still speechless.

'You'll be all right.' Dave was reassuring. 'Keep your wits about you. Go on, then, we haven't got all day. Take one of the plain cars.'

In the station everyone then forgot about the disappearance at Benn's. There were other things, real crimes, to think about.

James checked carefully. He'd got his notebook, ballpoint pens and one or two pencils. Some plastic bags, large and small, for objects which might be evidence. The much-derided magnifying glass was in an inner pocket – he didn't care what anybody said, it was going to be useful one day. He got out and walked over to the white and red patrol car, and John Clark reported to him, before the two uniformed constables zoomed off, once more on patrol.

'I'm sorry to have to ask you to say it all again,' James Jester was apologizing some time later to Hannah.

'That's all right. You're asking different questions.'

'I'd like to speak to the security man.'

'He's off duty now, in fact he'll almost certainly be asleep. Ann will give you his address. We're a small concern, Mr Jester, we only employ three hundred people – give or take a few, obviously it varies a bit – so we know each other very well. Although we have a personnel manager, we also have an office directory here on each desk giving a résumé of the staff classified under departments. The copies on Mother's desk and mine give both names and addresses.'

'Perhaps I could have a copy,' said James. 'We may need to ask around to find out who saw him last.'

'You will treat it as confidential.'

'Of course.' Jester went on, 'This man was staying at your house, Miss Benn?'

'Yes. We have known him many years. He was an old friend of my father's.'

'You expected him home last night? He said nothing to suggest he wouldn't come?'

'We expected him'

'You hadn't seen him in the afternoon?'

'No, I hadn't seen him since lunch time. We ate together. Had you seen Pierre, Mother?'

'No.'

At that moment Matthew burst into the room. He stopped in his tracks and looked inquisitively at James Jester.

'Matthew! Who let you in here? You're supposed to be helping the maintenance men, aren't you?'

'Boring,' said Matthew.

'It's not boring at all. You were helping with the energy efficiency programme. Saving the world isn't boring.'

'Changing light bulbs is boring,' said Matthew. 'Who's he?'

'Matthew!' said his grandmother.

'My son,' Hannah introduced him to Jester, who felt that he had called her Miss when he should have called her Mrs. But the secretary who brought him in had said 'Miss Hannah'. Perhaps she wasn't married. James Jester's ears tingled a bit.

'We are trying to become more energy efficient,' went on Hannah. 'Today the maintenance men are changing all the light bulbs they can to those low-energy ones. We already have a lot of fluorescents in the factory and they're very good, and those small D-shaped lights in the corridors, but today we're concentrating on the other lights where we're still using tungsten. Most of them are being changed to those Wotan lamps. Some of them we can't change, of course, where we need a different, intense light, so those are going to be halogen or they will remain tungsten, depending on the use and conditions.'

'It's a very good idea,' said Jester, making a mental note to put forward the idea at work. The force was always asking for suggestions to improve efficiency, and energy efficiency was efficiency, wasn't it? If they saved money on the electric bill there would be more to spend on overtime.

'So you need to question our night security man.' Hannah reverted to the matter in hand. 'Be quiet, Matthew. In fact you'd better go out of here. Mind, you know the rules, you are not to go anywhere near production unless there is an adult with you. Ask on the egg-packing line if they'll let you help with the packaging. You're good at making boxes, or you can help supply the girls on the line. Don't forget you'll be in the care of the overseer if you are there and must do as you are told immediately.'

51

Matthew went.

'I'd like to examine Mr Fontaine's place of work.'

'You've got the key?'

Jester produced it.

'I'll take you up in a minute.'

'We'll need Mr Fontaine's home address. Can you tell me what family he has?'

'None. He's a bachelor. Never been married, no children. He has a housekeeper who comes in by the day, a part-time gardener, and a dog. The dog stays with the housekeeper when Pierre is away, and the house is locked up.'

'He will have relatives – brothers, sisters, elderly parents, perhaps.'

'He has, but they're mostly in Belgium,' Faith put in.

Hannah gave Pierre Fontaine's address to Jester. At that moment the rattle of the tea trolley was heard outside. Betty put her head round the door and asked, 'All right to do the coffee, Mrs Faith? Ann says you're in conference.'

'Everything stops for coffee,' and Faith indicated to Jester that the interview was suspended for the statutory quarter of an hour.

Left alone, later, in Pierre Fontaine's workplace, James Jester looked around him excitedly. This was the stuff that dreams were made of. From this ordinary looking scene a man had vanished. Inside a locked factory with security staff on the door, he had dematerialized, and he, James Jester, was determined to be the one to find him. He tried to keep his imagination in check, to stop it picturing dead bodies, dramatically discovered by Detective Constable Jester.

What had he been taught? The first things to check in a case of disappearance. The missing person's home and ask his family. Check his bank account for unusual withdrawals, deposits or different pattern to normal. Check his Access and Visa cards likewise. His passport?

The workplace so filled with James Jester's romantic imaginings was not much bigger than a suburban kitchen. There was the usual apparatus for cooking, a range of electric hot plates and gas rings set into the worktop, with a stainless steel 'parking plate', for hot pans, in the worktop beside them. A fairly standard set of sparkling white fitted cupboards. Good sensible working lights at strategic points. A large centre table with electric points set in it, a large commercial-size food processor and a large set of first-class Avery scales occupying part of the top. A couple of stools. A notepad and pen on a corner of the table near one of the stools. A pile of forms nearby held down by a rolling pin. Various ingredients standing about in packets and boxes. Tray upon tray of some kind of confectionery, covered in chocolate, looking as though a big batch had been made and set out to cool. A very large refrigerator and two or three workmanlike stainless steel sinks, with stainless steel saucepans upended on the draining boards, and a few kitchen tools standing soaking in a bowl of water.

The floor was covered with what looked like rubber tiles. Jester poked them experimentally with his toe and felt them give in a firm sort of way. Squatting down he could see under the table, and his heart rejoiced to see a wastepaper basket which had obviously not been emptied. Slipping a fine clear plastic glove on to his hand he tiptoed over and slid the contents of the basket into the largest of the polythene bags he had brought with him. The objects thus retrieved did not look promising. Mostly they were screwed-up pieces of paper, but there was a discarded ballpoint pen, and a plastic carrier emblazoned with the name of a local store. As he carefully labelled the bag he felt a thrill of excitement.

From this vantage point in the middle of the workplace he looked round, wondering what would be visible from this new angle. Kneeling down he scrutinized the junction between fitted cupboards and floor, where in a normal house there are usually cracks and crevices between things and under things. This, however, was in an industrial setting, a factory producing food, and the joint was carefully sealed and not even a crumb or a scrap of paper could be seen.

The workplace had a homely air, in spite of its clinical qualities. James looked behind the door, where there was a coat hook, but nothing was hanging there. He wondered about this. He was tempted to break a bit off one of the tempting array of chocolate-covered bars and eat it, but he did not. Neither did he get out his magnifying glass. As long as the room was locked, fingerprints and suchlike could be left to the team who would undoubtedly come out if suspicion of foul play strengthened. With all the cleanliness he doubted if there was much to find. At least he had safeguarded against the accidental destruction of the contents of the wastepaper basket.

After locking Exhibit JJ1 inside the boot of his car, Jester asked Faith Benn if he could be allowed to go over the rest of the factory, to get an idea of the layout and the possibilities.

'There's one thing I must say,' Faith said. 'My daughter gave you one of our visitors' overalls when you were going up to see Pierre's work area, but you shouldn't have gone out to your car in it.'

'Oh, I'm sorry.'

'Hygiene is really very important indeed. The white coats are only for inside the factory and must be taken off before leaving, even if only for a couple of minutes. I really ought to make you take that one off and put a clean one on. Nor are you wearing the hat.'

Jester had felt ridiculous in the soft white trilby with the hanging hairnet at the back. It was worse even than that stupid Sherlock Holmes hat. He'd taken it off and stuffed it in his pocket. Now he took it out again, guiltily, and put it on.

'That's better. I'll ask Matthew to take you round, if you don't mind. Hannah and I are both very much behind in our work with all this upset.'

Matthew, who had become bored with the Easter egg boxes and had returned to his mother's office, looked delighted.

'Now, you are not to ask Mr Jester questions, Matthew, only to answer them. Mr Jester is going to look for Monsieur Fontaine for us, because we don't know where he's gone and we're rather worried about him. You are not to say anything – anything, do you hear me? – to anyone at all about this. If anyone mentions Monsieur Fontaine to you, you say you don't know where he is today. If anyone asks you who Mr Jester is, you say he's a friend of Grandma's. Now is that absolutely clear?'

'Yes, Granny,' said Matthew.

They had a lightning tour of the factory with Matthew talking all the time non-stop. Fortunately Jester noticed that the talk was all about the place itself, the products and the machines, and that Matthew was very careful to say nothing his grandmother would have disapproved of.

'I'd better have a look at his car,' Jester said last of all, after he had taken off his white overall, marked 'Visitor', and put it with the others going to the laundry, together with the dreaded hat. There was a big bin next to the door from the office area into the production area, with a notice above it saying *Put Your Used Overall Here.*

The car was locked of course, but Matthew, who had carefully taken off his own overall and hat and hung them on his peg before going outside the building and was now revealed in sky-blue sweater and scarlet cord trousers, told him all about it. Its age, the name of its paint, its engine capacity and the remarkable fitments within were carefully detailed to an impressed Jester. The inside looked quite empty, although there might be some possessions inside the glove compartment. The boot was locked.

'But I'm going to have a Ferrari,' was Matthew's parting remark, as he stood on the step and waved the visitor off in the clean but worn police car.

James Jester went back to the station to write up his report.

'Very well done,' Bob congratulated him on the report later. 'Clear and careful.'

He was silent then and James wondered if after all he had done something wrong, omitted something. All the teasing had made him a little insecure.

'Have you any personal commitments for the next couple of days?' asked Bob.

'No, sir.'

'Just as well, because I want you to go down to Hampshire.'

'Hampshire, sir?'

Mr Smart will ring the Hampshire force and make the arrangements. You are to go to Pierre Fontaine's house and search it thoroughly. Then to his bank. Check his credit cards. What will you be looking for? Come on, now, lad, you ought to know.'

'Unusual withdrawals of money, or unusual deposits. Latest date of use of accounts, and the place used. In the house . . .' he hesitated, then went on more confidently, 'Evidence of what kind of man he is, his interests, as well as the numbers of his bank account and credit card accounts, which I should get from his financial statements – otherwise I can't check those.'

'Right. Also names and addresses of relatives and friends – telephone book or address book. While you're down there you could check those people by asking them when they last saw the man, whether his mood was as usual, whether they know of any reason for him to go away unexpectedly. Family illness over in Belgium, for example. Anything which does not go according to the normal pattern of his life.'

'Yes.'

'Get ready tonight and go first thing in the morning. Spend as long as you need, but it will probably be in the region of a couple of days. Meanwhile I want constant reports. Ring in, and fax the written ones on. The local police should have a fax machine – if they haven't, there are usually ones the public can use in libraries, or shops who do office services. Any questions? You know how to record your expenses and claim your reimbursements? Mr Smart can put you right on that.'

'Understood, sir.'

'There's one thing I noticed in your report.'

'Sir?'

'You say the hook behind his door was empty. Yet he would normally have hung his jacket there, do you think?'

'I did check that, sir. Miss – or Mrs – Hannah told me –'

'It's Miss, Jester. Apparently it is common knowledge in York that old Matthew Benn wanted a grandson to carry on the line and Miss Hannah obliged without the preliminary of marriage.'

'Oh. I didn't know that, sir. Well, I asked her where he usually hung his coat. She showed me the pegs inside the door of the seminar and board room area. There is a small lobby, only a yard wide but big enough for a row of pegs, to save hanging them in the offices. His was empty. She said that the morning before he had hung his suit jacket there when he put on his overall and white hat. The jacket is not there. She thought he must have put the overall in the laundry box, although regular staff normally use them for a week, she and her mother do.'

'Check. Before you do anything else, ring Benn's and ask them to check that laundry box and any washing that went to the laundry from midday yesterday, to see if they can find that overall. Was it marked in any way to identify it?'

'Oh yes. They had had it embroidered specially for him with his name over the pocket, where they all have them. It said Pierre.'

'Check. How many days has he been at the factory wearing overalls?'

'Three, sir.'

'Presumably they had more than one marked for him.'

'Yes. Miss Hannah told me. Three. One on, one clean and one in the wash, she said.'

'And they do the laundry every day?'

'Yes. It has a twenty-four hour turn-round, so that there are always clean overalls available.'

'Go on then, get on with it!'

Afternoon tea was being served in Benn's canteen. The tea-ladies had done their rounds. Officially they were still on duty, but they customarily spent the last ten minutes of their working day having a cup of tea themselves with the other three catering workers, the women who did most of the preparation of lunch and any other meals required. The buzz of gossip rose satisfactorily over the table.

'Elfie told me,' said Betty, her pixie-like face saucy under her mop of bleached hair, 'when I served her tea at half-past ten. There were two telephone calls to the police station this morning, first Hannah and then Faith. All about that foreigner, that Belgian.'

'He's gone missing, we all know that,' said Sue, brushing a crumb from its resting place on her bosom.

'They want the police to look for him. It was nice, that stuff he made. I had a bit yesterday.'

'Everybody had some.'

'I liked it. I hope we decide to make it.'

'We won't if he's gone.'

'Why not?'

'Well . . . it's his recipe, isn't it?'

'They can still make it, can't they?'

'Anyway, what's happened to him?' asked Vi, looking up from rummaging in the depths of her handbag.

'Nobody knows. He's gone off without telling no one.'

'We've had the police round,' said Betty again, importantly. 'I had to give one of them a coffee this morning, he was in plain clothes, a detective. Ever so young he was.'

'You know what they say about when the police start looking young.'

'We had uniform ones before then,' put in Sue. 'I was looking out of the window and saw the jam sandwich arrive. About half-past nine.'

'Well, I hope they find him,' said Betty. 'What do you think, Polly?'

'What?'

'You in a dream or something?'

'Sorry. You don't have to pick me up like that, Bet. I was miles away.'

'Love's young dream,' said Vi.

'I'm in a fix,' said Polly.

'Oh Lord, here we go again. He loves me, he loves me not. Which of them is it that's causing trouble this time? Can't you make your mind up and spare us all this?'

'Be quiet, Sue,' said Vi. 'Let the girl tell us about it.'

'I love Bri, you know that,' said Polly diffidently. 'We've been talking about getting married.'

'Not before time,' said Sue.

'You shut up, Sue. But I went out with Kev before then, you know that as well, and he wants me back again. He gave me a lift home on Tuesday.'

'What did you accept a lift for? Of all the daft pillocks!'

'I wish you'd shut up, Sue. It were pouring with rain and cold and going dark. Where's the harm?'

'Plenty, judging by the look on your face.'

'Well, he wants me to go back to him, that's all there is to it. He's promising me the earth.'

'Promises, promises?'

'Promises are like pie-crusts, made to be broken,' said Vi.

'I'm that miserable, Vi.'

'Look, I'll tell you what I'll do for you. I'll lend you my lucky hare's foot. Now I can't say fairer than that, can I? It'll bring you luck, love. And if you like I'll get my friend to tell you your fortune.'

'Thanks, Vi.'

Violet fished in her enormous handbag and drew out first the Lincoln Imp, then a Cornish Piskie and then the hare's foot, which was mounted in silver. She handed it over. Polly held it thoughtfully, then put it in her own handbag. 'Perhaps it really will bring me luck,' she said. Vi returned the Lincoln Imp and the Piskie to their home, to await further opportunities of usefulness.

5

After the mysterious disappearance of Pierre Fontaine and the exciting presence of the police car, there were two days when in

Benn's confectionery factory the matter seemed to be at a standstill. Pierre's door remained locked and he did not reappear, send a message, telephone, or write a letter. The large batch of Recipe 179 he had made stood unused in the locked room.

To most of the work-force other things were far more interesting, like television programmes and what was for tea, the state of the weather which had never been known to be so drab and cold and wet, and who was going out with whom.

It was on 6 January that the first snow of the year fell, and it did the job thoroughly. The children of the city woke to the white transforming beauty of the snow and dashed out to make snowballs as soon as they were able. By Monday the roofs of the town were wearing thick white hats and the traffic was having difficulties. Early that morning the gritting lorries were out in the darkness, the big automatics doing the major trunk roads and the minor roads having to wait for the manual gritting lorries, the ones with men on the back throwing shovelfuls of salty grit to left and right alternately as they moved slowly along the city streets. The change in the weather was exhilarating rather than anything else after the long dark days of wetness and cold. Now even in the night-time there seemed to be a pale glow and the air felt dry and crisp so that cold was more bearable.

As usual the Benn women were having an argument over the breakfast table. Matthew had not yet appeared, but noises over-head in one of the bathrooms signalled his possible arrival before too long.

'We might as well give up the whole idea,' said Faith, not without satisfaction.

'Of course not.' Hannah sounded tart, and she felt it.

'What if he doesn't come back?'

'We've signed an agreement. We can proceed with the test marketing. There's plenty to do. Devising a name and presentation. Organizing the research. Analysing the results. We can't launch a new countline navigating by the seat of our pants.'

'I wish your language was not so crude, Hannah.'

'Wasn't it one of Father's sayings? You didn't object then.'

Faith sighed in a martyred way. She left a good many remarks unspoken, but as most of them had been spoken so often before they hung in the air between the two women. One of the unspoken remarks was that they did not know the exact constituents or proportions or anything else relevant about Recipe 179, so there was no way they could proceed with trials. Pierre Fontaine had brought some things – probably condensed flavourings – with him.

All the same, progress was being made with the enquiries into Pierre's disappearance. Down in Hampshire James Jester had been making careful investigations, and his reports were being studied by the York police. He had received permission to go to Brussels and contact Pierre Fontaine's family.

'Dave? Busy?'

'Coming right away, boss.'

'This disappearance from Benn's is beginning to seem serious,' Bob Southwell said when Dave arrived in his office.

Dave Smart looked large, although not as large as a house, and imperturbable, though not as imperturbable as a rock. His face tended to be red and his hair was crisp, black, and inclined to wave. He was a little ponderous, but it was thick strong muscle which made him so. Bob found him invaluable. There was no one better to bounce ideas off than Dave Smart; no one better at bringing down to earth the wild theories Bob occasionally allowed to take flight from his active brain. There had only been one case where Dave had lost his cool, when his calm had broken up like ice floes in spring, and that had been when he had come across the body of that girl by the river early one Sunday morning in October a few months back – the girl all in black except for her red suspenders.

Bob looked preoccupied and sat silently for a while.

'You said the disappearance was beginning to look serious, boss?' prompted Dave when he thought the silence had gone on for long enough.

'Have a look at this report of Jester's. He faxed it through late on Saturday. Today he'll be in Belgium, not that I think that trip will be helpful one way or the other but we might as well clear up the possibilities as we go along. We should get a phone call from him late this afternoon and a written report tomorrow, faxed or delivered in person if he comes back quickly.'

'Has he come across anything suspicious?'

'Not really. That's the problem. Read it for yourself, it won't take long.'

Dave took the report and settled himself down in a hard office chair to read it while Bob went over to the window and looked down into Clifford Street. The rush of traffic far below came up to him as a faint – completely bearable – hum because the windows had had secondary glazing put in at considerable expense and with constant complaint from the financial people. Bob had explained that he could not concentrate with traffic noise and his wasted time was costing the department more than the cost of the extra glazing. There would also be a saving in his use of heat. After pointing out that it would take fifteen years to recoup the cost from fuel saved, the department had reluctantly agreed. It had been a great relief to Bob. The room was warmer, quieter and draught free. The financial department was not so happy because now he was campaigning for secondary glazing to be fitted throughout the building.

Below, the bicycles, cars, vans, trucks and buses went their way through bottle-necks and obstructions and jay-walking pedestrians. Beneath their wheels the spotless white of the snow was turning into brown slush in the gutters, but the centre of the highway was quite free of snow. Many of the people walking had put on their wellingtons or sheepskin boots. Those in fashion footwear were picking their way along like fastidious poultry.

'He writes a good report,' commented Dave.

'Yes. He's been working mainly with Rollo, hasn't he?'

'That's right. I haven't seen his recent written work.'

'Clear and complete.'

'It surely is.'

Dave went on reading the report.

'I see what you mean,' he said at last, putting it down.

'Sixty, rich, lived alone, not married, never been married.'

'He's not bound to be queer,' Dave protested. 'He might have a low sex drive, or not have found the right woman.'

'The suspicion's there, though, isn't it? We've got to bear it in mind. Possibilities of blackmail or undue influence. All kinds of nasty things coming out of the woodwork.'

'This job is giving you a dirty mind,' Dave protested. 'A nice middle-aged man, devoted to his golf and his dog, all his chores taken care of by a nice friendly housekeeper – she's a widow so might be very friendly – a man to do the thick end of the gardening, why should he tie himself up with a wife? Perhaps he had a few mistresses. If he felt the need of that kind of thing. Not everybody does, you know. Perhaps he had an unrequited passion.'

'Lifetime platonic devotion to true love married to someone else? That sounds too Edwardian to be true. He was born in 1930, mate, not 1890.'

Dave handed back the report. 'You seem to be overlooking the central fact, boss, if you don't mind me saying so.'

'Which is?'

'That there is such a thing as industrial espionage, that he had concocted a formula which was believed to be a winner, that he vanished from the centre of a locked and guarded chocolate factory.'

'Which doesn't rule out the possible relevance of his private life.'

'What are you going to do?'

'I feel that we ought to treat Fontaine's disappearance as a possible crime. OK, we haven't a body. At present. But they have a way of turning up, if dead, or ransom notes appearing for them, if alive.'

'Yes.'

'So I'm going to talk about it to the super and ask to be Senior Investigating Officer and get cracking straight away.'

Dave sat up straight, wondering if he was going to be involved.

Bob clapped him on the shoulder. 'Right, Dave. I'll be going out to the factory myself in a few minutes, tell Benn's that for me, will you? See you later. On your way out could you ask that girl why the hell I haven't had my coffee yet?'

At coffee time the news of the imminent arrival of a top detective spread round the factory. Hannah was proud of her security; it had never occurred to her that she ought to have tested the character and reliability of her switchboard girl. A few psychological tests, or a handwriting test, might have shown up Elfrida's inability to keep a secret; even a family historian might have been useful, for they could have pointed out that Elfie was related to half the factory, and what harm could there be, thought Elfie, in spreading what there was to spread among the family?

'I'm really sorry they've finished the egg line today,' said Polly as the tea-ladies were cleaning up their trolleys. 'It's interesting. The girls take a pride in the eggs.' She paused to tuck up a strand of her long hair which had escaped from the orange mob-cap.

'I should think we all take a pride,' said Vi. 'Everyone's proud of Benn's and the stuff we make.'

'Well, yes, but the eggs are different, aren't they? There are so many different designs and the work is interesting. You can't say a production line is very thrilling as a rule.' This was Betty, dashing briskly through her work as she usually did.

'I don't know. They seem to enjoy being on the lines. There's a lot of talking and laughing.'

'I tried once,' said Polly. 'It was all right at first when we were training, but once they had the line going full speed I'd had it.'

'Couldn't keep up?' teased Sue.

'I could keep up all right but the thing made me dizzy and faint and sick and after a bit I started getting migraines. The speed doesn't bother most of them or they couldn't do it. I feel funny in the back seats of cars as well.'

'Oh, we're back to Bri and Kev again,' laughed Betty.

When he first arrived at Benn's, Bob Southwell had driven past the clock tower and the grove of trees where early one morning in the previous week Hannah had heard the birds sing. Bob had driven into the delivery yard after satisfying the man on the gate that he was on official business. Then he sat for a couple of minutes in the car watching what was going on, before a man in overalls came up to the driver's window and said, 'Can I help you, mate?'

Bob had then driven round to the other side of the factory and in at the more imposing entrance with its rose garden, had again been stopped by a barrier and a security man, and had parked as instructed in the small area reserved for visitors. All this time Bob Southwell had been appraising the place from the point of view of the missing person enquiry.

As he walked to the front door, which led into the office and executive area, he noticed a Rolls Royce parked on the left, next to a Mercedes 190E. Presumably the Rolls was the car of the missing man.

He had duly noted the abundant tropical plants in the foyer and the carpeted floor in the office corridor. The carpet went as far as the door of the General Office, which closed the vista ahead. Opening off this corridor on the left was a door leading to seminar and board rooms, and he had peeped into each of these. The tiny lobby leading to them had a row of coat hooks, some in use, and a loo. Next were the doors to the directors' offices, one on either side of their secretaries' work area.

He had knocked on the door and been admitted by Faith's secretary, Ann, who after summoning her employer was now sitting at her own desk and quietly working on a computer. Ann, in her forties he guessed, had probably been at Benn's for the whole of her working life.

Faith Benn appeared and asked Bob to come into her office. She was in her sixties without doubt, judging by her out-of-date hair-do, struck him as an intelligent, alert woman, upper middle class in upbringing, undoubtedly well educated. He knew without having to discover the fact that she would be reasonably knowledgeable about gardens and old furniture and paintings and music and architecture and cooking and all the things which were needed by a woman with a large house to run and a position to keep up.

The view from the window, like that from the secretaries' window, was of the rose garden under its smooth layer of snow. Only the delicate tracks of birds' feet marked the calm perfection of the snow's surface.

Bob Southwell was impressed by the sense of solidity and permanence. The light oak furniture was likely to have been designed for the room when the building was put up, some time in the 1930s.

On Bob's behalf, Dave had earlier made a request for the names of employees who had left in the past year, and now Paul Change, the Personnel Officer, arrived with a piece of paper in his hand. He looked tense and nervous, with an almost hunted expression. He passed the sheet of paper to Faith who, after looking at it carefully, passed it to Bob. She came round to stand beside him.

'I take it you wanted names because you feel someone in the factory might be implicated,' she said, 'but why ask for those who have left?'

'We usually look into the possibilities of grudge bearing,' he answered, 'and people who think they have suffered unfair dismissal are strong suspects there. You have kindly already given us a list of present employees,' and he indicated the office directory which James Jester had acquired, and which was in the front of the file Bob had brought with him.

'As I thought,' said Faith, looking over his shoulder, 'three retirements in the past year. Two of the people had been with us forty years, so their photographs went up in the corridor.'

'I saw a row of photographs,' said Bob.

'Yes. Everyone no matter what job they do is photographed if they've been with us forty years and the portraits line the corridors. The earliest are down here, but as time went on we ran out of space so the newer ones are on the equivalent corridor upstairs and we are going to have to start hanging them in the canteen soon. Although nowadays not so many people stay with the same employer for a lifetime, which is what it amounts to, so they are not increasing in number as fast as they once did.'

'It's a nice idea. Who are the others on the list?'

'Those two at the top are the forty-year ones. I should think we could rule them out, don't you?'

'Probably.'

'The next retired after twenty years. He'd started off with one of the bigger confectionery firms in the city. He seemed very satisfied, and will be getting two pensions – one from them and one from us – so he shouldn't have lost out financially. We've heard from him since he retired and he seems to be enjoying himself.'

'Then there are ten other names,' said Bob.

'I'm surprised there are so many.' Faith gazed at them. 'Some of them I don't even remember. Perhaps, Paul, you could fill the inspector in on those later.'

'Yes,' said Paul, as earnestly as if his life depended on it.

'One or two were my girls. Yvonne Clark – she left when she got married. They had the usual traditional rousing send-off for her.'

'Traditional?'

'Dressed her up, you know.'

'I don't think I do know,' said Bob.

'I don't get much production out of them when someone leaves to get married. They knock off at twelve – my girls, this is, you understand, Inspector, my daughter wouldn't allow such shenanigans on her Benn's Bars production line and anyway they're all men – and they go for a slap-up lunch somewhere and come back very late and slightly merry and spend an hour dressing the poor girl up until she looks like a Morris dancer or worse, all paper streamers and funny hat and notices pinned on her, then usually she has to be collected by a friend or member of her family because she couldn't travel home like that, loaded down with presents and flowers.'

Bob reflected that although she sounded deprecating, Faith Benn was obviously delighted by this strange traditional practice.

'I'll leave Paul to tell you about the others,' she concluded.

'Would you like a coffee?' asked Paul.

'Had one earlier, thanks. I won't bother now.'

'Then . . .'

'Use the seminar room, Paul.' Faith saw his dilemma.

Seated in the seminar room the two men went through the remaining names on the list. They had all had valid reasons for leaving, no one had been sacked, there had been no known unpleasantness between any of them and their immediate bosses, their workmates, or the management.

'Hmm,' said Bob at last. 'Thank you, Paul.' He reflected that it was very handy everyone having their name embroidered on their chest, although he himself liked to know surnames. This egalitarian matiness was all very well but Christian names alone were confusing. It helped if you had the extra individuality of the surname.

'Any time,' said Paul.

'As I stated when I first arrived,' Bob said when he was back with Faith and Paul had departed, 'this visit is about Pierre Fontaine. After considering the matter at the station, we have decided to look further into his disappearance.'

'Good idea. We are very concerned. I at the strange behaviour of an old friend – we've known him many, many years, Inspector, I believe he was one of the guests at my wedding, on my husband's side of the church – he was Matthew's friend. My daughter, although she has known Pierre all her life, is probably more concerned about his recipe. Her hopes for the future were built on it. I hesitate to say *are* built on it.'

'While I'm here, may I have a look at his workplace?'

'You will have to put on a coat and hat. Our rules about that are absolutely rigid. When one is dealing with food, there is nothing more important than hygiene.'

'I don't mind at all.'

Faith put on her own overall and mob-cap and Ann found one marked 'visitor' for Bob, and a white hat. To his surprise, to reach the labs and Pierre's workplace they had to go past the large hall where Faith's work-force of girls were carrying out various tasks. The last section was that occupied by the Easter egg production line, now standing idle. It was not until they had passed the open archways leading into the various areas that they reached the stairs to the upper floor.

There the doors were marked 'Design Studio', 'Works Manager', and 'Research and Development'.

'Personnel and Sales Managers are downstairs as part of the General Office,' explained Faith, 'and Dispatch was moved to the new storage building when it was opened. Sally Binson really needs to be over there.' She went in at the door marked 'Research and Development', nodded and spoke briefly to the people she passed and then turned to Bob. 'I forgot to ask if you'd brought the key. It was taken away by PC Clark, and then, I gather, passed on to the young detective who came.'

'I have it,' said Bob.

He had already absorbed Jester's good description of the room, so he looked round without surprise at the trays of Recipe 179 and the gleaming cupboards, but behind him Faith gasped.

'Someone's been in here.'

'How can you tell?' asked Bob.

'But they must have been. The trays have been moved. The floor has been polished. The papers on the table have been straightened. The cleaners have been in here.'

It was obvious that there must be another key, that didn't need saying. Faith's forehead showed her growing anger. If Bob had doubted that she could be an autocrat he doubted it no longer.

'I'll come back,' she said and hurled away from him and through the research laboratory and down the stairs.

Left alone he looked round. If there had been evidence in this room of what had happened to its owner, much of that evidence must have been destroyed by the thorough cleaning that had been carried out. He wondered about that cleaning. True, the whole place was spotless. But cleaners, in his experience, were not so devoted to duty that they would seek out the key of a locked door. They would sigh gratefully and be glad not to have the room to do.

Faith returned, driving the caretaker before her. The poor man looked terrified. Bob Southwell was not surprised. He wouldn't have wanted to face Faith when she was in a temper.

'I told them they'd better clean it,' the man said. 'We couldn't get in when Mr Fontaine was working here, but I had a look and it didn't seem as if there was anything to spoil as long as they were careful not to make a dust. I thought when he came back we wouldn't be able to do it again so we'd better take advantage. He was that ratty if he was disturbed while he was working or if anyone moved his pans and that.'

'You gave them your master key? Didn't it occur to you that if the police lock a door they do it for a purpose?' asked Bob, but there didn't seem to be any point in rowing with the man over it now. The damage was done. The poor bloke had no doubt meant well and he would be terrified at the probable consequences of his action, from Faith Benn. There was of course the possibility . . . 'Did anyone suggest to you that the room should be cleaned?'

'No, sir. I'm responsible for general cleaning of the offices and labs. The workshops and storage is organized separately. I tell my cleaners what needs to be done and this is the first time there's been any complaint.'

Efficient in a limited way but lacking in intelligence, thought Bob. Well, it couldn't be helped.

He and Faith went back silently to her office, leaving Pierre Fontaine's last known place of existence locked once more.

'Oh, Hannah,' Faith called in her clear cultured voice, 'I was going to offer the inspector lunch. Time's getting on.'

As Hannah Benn came into view, Bob Southwell thought she looked very pleasant indeed. He had seen Lena Lindgren in passing, through Hannah's open office door, but her shining blonde beauty had done nothing for him. Hannah, however, was a different matter. Her short dark hair reminded him of his wife Linda's. Funny how one goes for the same type, he thought. Hannah was about Linda's height, too, although she did not look as athletic as Linda, who was always on the go in house or garden. Hannah was gathering a little softness around her figure, but Bob found he did not object to that. He looked down into her eyes which were dark grey or blue, it was hard to tell which, and found himself reacting to her as if they had some chemical affinity. Watch it, Bob, he thought.

'Do join us for lunch,' she said, and her voice was low and pleasing, not the eldritch screech she had been known to use on occasions.

'Another time, perhaps,' he replied, deciding it would be as well to leave her presence immediately. First impressions didn't always last. Probably the next time they met he would be prepared and she wouldn't have this effect on him. As he tried to think of something else to say to her, Bob gathered up his papers. 'I was surprised at the number of top management in proportion to labour,' he remarked. 'Have you more chiefs than Indians?'

'My department is labour intensive,' Faith answered, 'but Hannah's certainly needs very few Indians, unless you count the sales and invoice staff, travellers and back-up. The introduction of automatic machinery has made a tremendous difference to this industry. We used to employ five hundred people, now it is down to three hundred, yet our production goes up each year.'

'Did you have to sack a great many at any point?'

'No. You're back to that again. No, natural wastage, as they call it these days, took care of the decrease. It didn't happen all at once. Often it was more a matter of not recruiting new staff for a while, until numbers had stabilized at a lower level.'

'Other enquiries are being made about Pierre Fontaine,' Bob said. 'We will have the results soon. Then I'll be in touch again.' He was anxious to get away.

Before he left the factory he asked Paul Change for a separate list of the people who had joined the work-force during the past twelve months.

It was unusual for Bob Southwell to go home in the middle of the day, but he did just that. Linda was in the garden hanging out a lineful of washing.

'Will it dry?' asked Bob, standing and watching her.

'Frost is very good for whites, didn't you know that?' reproved Linda. 'Besides, it always amuses me to see the shirts all stiff so that I have to take them in sideways through the door and fold the sheets as though they were made of cardboard. The children think it's funny, too.'

'I'm above such childish things,' countered Bob.

'I hope you aren't wanting any lunch.'

'Yes, please.'

'An omelette do you?'

'Fine. I thought I'd like to get home for half an hour.'

Linda looked at him shrewdly. Now what had upset him? A particularly bloody scene of violence? Some cruelty to a child?

'What's wrong?' she asked as she turned the cheese and herb omelette on to a plate and added a slice of bread and butter. 'I'm getting a lot of firm glances, aren't I? Have I been breaking any regulations?'

Linda was wearing one of Bob's old sweaters over one of his old shirts, an ancient pair of jeans, rather battered trainers, and no make-up.

'You look smashing,' Bob said fervently.

'Better than who else?' asked Linda, who knew her Bob.

'Better than everybody.'

'That doesn't answer my question. Where have you been this morning?'

'Benn's factory. Do you know Hannah Benn reminded me of you?'

'Really? So that's why all the glances. Do I measure up?'

'No,' replied Bob. 'She was far better dressed and had make-up on and her hair was beautifully cut.'

'You'd better get me the name of her hairdresser if I've got to compete,' Linda said thoughtfully. She sat across the table from him and watched him eat his omelette. 'There,' she said as he finished it. 'You've touched home base, feel better now?'

'Much.' Before dashing off again Bob folded her in his arms and kissed her with long, emotion-charged kisses. 'There's no one to touch you,' he told her.

'Get me the name of that hairdresser,' she shouted after him.

6

James Jester arrived back in York late the following night from Belgium, so that he was able to be present at the briefing Bob Southwell held the following morning, Wednesday, 9 January. Gathered in the room were a dozen men, detectives and uniformed branch.

Bob felt strangely hesitant as he rose to take the meeting. 'This is an unusual enquiry,' he said. 'We have no body, so it cannot be a murder case . . . Yet . . . Instead we have the disappearance of a man under suspicious circumstances. Obviously, at any moment he may turn up alive and well, in which case we have been wasting our time. My feeling is, however, that foul play has taken place and that this man is very likely dead. Unfortunately – because we don't know whether or not he is dead – time has been lost which, as you know, we cannot afford to lose in cases of murder. Evidence has probably been destroyed, whether purposely or not.

'I am going to give you an outline of the man and the circumstances and will then set up an incident room. We will give it all we've got and we need to come up with something to resolve this one way or the other. If it comes to a dead end, then it does, but I want our best work on this.'

He turned to the display board on which was a plan of the ground and first floors of Benn's factory.

'You all know Benn's. I need not go into the history of the firm – which parallels the growth of Rowntree's, Terry's and Craven's in this city. Benn's had remained smaller than any of these, producing specialist confectionery in small quantities, until a few years ago when they developed the Benn's Bars which have been so successful. They are now in a bigger league due to their mass market success and are intending to develop a new mass production sweetmeat. Hence the presence in York of Pierre Fontaine, the missing man, who was staying with the Benn family and travelling each day to the factory where he had his own work area and was producing trial batches of the new product.

'Fontaine is a personal friend of the Benn family. He is an outstanding inventor of new recipes, having produced the formulae – or recipes as they call them – for Benn's Bars and for the Fontaine Special Selection. He is a Belgian naturalized in Great Britain, and as well as inventing the sweets he also invested in them at the development stage when large amounts of capital were needed, which is partly why he has become a rich man. He was well-heeled to start with.

'Fontaine vanished during the second half of 4 January from his work area in the factory and has not been seen since. His car is still there, but we will be arranging to have it taken away for examination. During, the last few days DC Jester has been investigating his background. Your report, please, James.'

Ignoring whispers from his neighbours of 'Did you take your magnifying glass?' and 'Where's your hat?' Jester moved to the front. It was the first time he had had to do anything like this, but he'd got it all written down so he kept telling himself there was no need to panic.

'I went to Fontaine's home in Hampshire and contacted the local force and Fontaine's housekeeper. They gave me access and assistance. On the surface all appeared to be normal. Fontaine lives in a large detached house built in the 1930s in brick with a lot of white-painted woodwork and a garden of about two acres. He grows roses and part of the grounds consists of a copse of mature trees. There are other mature trees in the grounds and the garden adjoins the golf course. When at home he spends his mornings experimenting in a special kitchen with his recipes, and his afternoons playing golf or walking his dog or tending his garden, although the heavy work is done by a gardener.'

James gulped and took a drink of water before going on.

'I hope you are all taking notes as usual,' Bob Southwell put in, and the atmosphere became even more taut and concentrated.

'He has a few friends with whom he plays bridge, and I interviewed them. He also has gardening friends, but they do not seem to have known him as well as his bridge friends. He is well known in the nearby shopping centre. His actual relatives are in Belgium and he goes over for a holiday with them at least once a year, sometimes more often. He leads what I believe is called a blameless existence.'

I bet, thought some of the audience.

'I contacted people in the address book which was by his telephone, and did not come up with any leads there. Nothing out of the ordinary appeared from the evidence of friends or neighbours or staff. He was known to be away for some weeks, and people wishing to contact him did so through his housekeeper, who seems a thoroughly genuine sort. She is also looking after the dog. In view of the possibility of blackmail which DCI Southwell thought might be present in this case, I looked carefully for evidence of his sexual activities, but found nothing except one magazine under his mattress, which I brought back with me. It is a normal heterosexual magazine with some emphasis on bondage.'

There was a stirring among the audience and a few smiles.

'After finding the numbers of his various bank accounts and Visa and Access cards and his solicitor's address, I investigated his financial affairs. He is a very rich man and keeps well within his income. He withdrew money before coming north on New Year's Day but has not withdrawn any since, nor has he used his Access or Visa cards. The cash he withdrew was a couple of hundred pounds, which one would think for a man of his type would be normal small change. Although like most rich people he is careful with his funds, he is not a skinflint as many of them are.'

'You notice the significance of this evidence, gentlemen,' said

Bob Southwell. 'Fontaine does not seem to have been gay or extravagant and the lack of withdrawals of money or use of plastic or, as far as we know at present, of cheques, seems to indicate that he was not being blackmailed and, I would say, shows that he did not vanish of his own free will. Unless he has carefully prepared a second identity, which is possible I suppose, he has lived for a number of days without the use of any money except the cash he had on him. This could indicate that he is dead and that the murderer has not taken advantage of the plastic – we have no way of tracing the two hundred pounds, which would be more than ample for any of *us*, I would have thought, for that length of time. He was not paying for his board and lodging and hardly using the car, so on the face of it he would need very little money.'

'I asked everyone he dealt with – bank, solicitor, local trades-people – to let us know at once if any trace of him turns up,' continued Jester. 'The solicitor thought it was too soon to arrange to have the accounts stopped.'

'Yes, it is,' went on Bob. 'In fact at the moment the financial evidence is inconclusive. We will have to wait and keep an eye on that side of it. Please resume your report, Jester.'

'On the instructions of DCI Southwell, I then proceeded to Belgium,' went on James. 'Fontaine still has an elderly mother in a nursing home and two brothers who carry on the family business, which is making chocolates. Their firm has been taken over by a large international conglomerate, but they are both directors and still very much involved although they are older than Fontaine – he is sixty – and they are both talking about retirement. Both are married, one marriage is childless and the other brother has two children, both married themselves and with small offspring. I met the whole family. They were charming and friendly and very much concerned to hear that Fontaine is missing. He spent Christmas with them and had seemed just as usual. The whole family seem to be as prosperous as he was himself. I enquired about poor relations, in case anyone thought they had been done out of all this prosperity. The other cousins and so on they do have, which are not many, seem to be comfortable if not rich and to be leading satisfactory lives. I could have investigated all those people but having done those nearest to him and made contact with the Belgian police, Mr Southwell thought I had better come back.'

'Thank you, Jester.'

James went and sat down again. The mood of the gathering

had changed and all present were becoming intrigued by the case. Some felt a tinge of envy at James Jester's opportunity but would not deny that he had presented his report well.

'The investigation of relatives was superficial at this stage,' said Bob, 'but does not seem of primary importance. Like the money angle, we must keep an eye on the family. The Belgian police are willing to do that for us, in that they will let us know if anything unusual occurs. The family have been asked to remain available in case foul play is discovered. The possibility of their involvement cannot be ruled out at this stage, but neither can industrial espionage. I hardly think the family would harm their brother for that reason, and no other reason for animosity has become apparent. The opposite in fact; they seem a happy and united family. Although Pierre cut himself off by living in Britain, he seems to have evolved recipes for the family firm and for other firms as well as for Benn's. A rival firm could have wished to prevent Benn's expanding into the mass market, or may have wished to obtain the new recipe for themselves. In either case an agent trying to influence Fontaine may have overstepped the mark. There has been no ransom demand. Any questions or remarks?'

Suddenly everyone had lost the desire to talk.

'Right. The incident room will be set up in Benn's factory. I suggested yesterday to Mrs Faith Benn that the seminar room would be suitable.'

Bob turned again to the plan on the display board, and pointed out the position of the seminar room. 'This, while within the factory, is near the front door and, if coming to the incident room only, you need not put on special clothing. If you move into the work areas themselves it is essential to put on the overalls and hats provided and I don't want a lot of levity about the hats. None of you would like to get a hair in your chocolate. Wear the hats, and tuck your hair in all round. We will go along there now and set up, then I want everyone in the factory interviewed. As they work shifts one team will go round to the houses of those who are off shift, so that the preliminary questioning can be done today. The policy book proper will start as soon as we are operational at Benn's. Jester's preliminary work and mine will be entered up, also a report of this meeting, then we carry on the book once we're on the air from Benn's. Records will be kept manually, because this is still a missing persons case.'

Bob went on to arrange for copying and circulation throughout local police forces of Pierre Fontaine's photograph; he was already on the list of persons missing from home. Experts from the Hampshire police force had tentatively identified his probable fingerprints from personal possessions such as his tooth brush and copies of these prints were available. His doctor had been able to supply blood type and a physical description which was rather more accurate and detailed than Faith and Hannah Benn's had been. His dentist had supplied dental records. All these batches of information had been coming through by degrees since the previous Saturday.

'We know everything about him but where he is,' sighed Bob, then remembered that we never know everything about another person, however close to them we are. He supposed there were areas of Linda's mind and heart that he himself didn't know anything about, although she was pretty good at reading his thoughts. She had guessed immediately that he had been stirred by Hannah Benn. He *would* ask for the name of Hannah's hairdresser – he didn't think she would mind, and Linda didn't spend enough money on herself.

Matthew Benn had been very indignant on Tuesday night when he knew that a real live top detective had been at the factory while he himself had been idly playing with Orlando. He could play with Orlando any old time. It was not until his grandmother told him that even more detectives would be at the factory the next day, and, it was expected, for several days to come, that he stopped looking sulky and became his normal self again. On Wednesday morning he could hardly wait to get there and was down for breakfast before anyone else.

Hannah cooked breakfast herself. It was something she enjoyed doing, and Mrs Goodwin, who cooked the evening meal, appreciated a later start in the morning to balance her late finish. Her husband was up and about early as a rule. When the family had departed and he had welcomed the daily cleaning lady, he could retreat upstairs to the flat and enjoy tea and toast with his wife, who by then was ready to face the day.

Tea and toast would not have done for Hannah, who thought breakfast the best meal there was. She insisted Matthew also had a well-balanced meal, but if her mother chose to eat only toast there was not much she could do about it. This Wednesday morning

Hannah was serving grilled bacon with stewed calves' kidneys and bread browned under the bacon in the grill pan, and it was delicious. Matthew was already sitting waiting as she finished cooking and ate his helping so quickly that she had to look to be sure that she had actually served it. The plate shone as if it had not been used. Well, he was growing.

Matthew slid off the stool and ran upstairs for his parka and then back in the kitchen to put on his wellington boots which stood by the back door. 'I'm ready,' he announced.

'They aren't going to want a little boy around,' said his grandmother. 'You would be much better staying here and playing with Orlando again. The snow is still lovely and crisp. If I were a little boy I would rather be playing in the garden than spending the day inside.'

'Grandma's probably right,' said his mother.

Matthew said nothing, but a stubborn look came on his face. Grandma knew that look. She had spent her married life noticing it on her husband's face and once Hannah was born she had also seen it on Hannah's. She knew that she might as well give up the struggle at that point, but she was stubborn herself.

'Do stay, Matthew,' she said.

'Mother,if he's a nuisance to the investigating officers I'll bring him home,' promised Hannah. 'You must see how exciting it is for a boy his age.'

Both Hannah and Faith found themselves rushing round – Matthew's silent waiting was so unusual that it was unnerving – and they were at the factory by the time Bob Southwell, in the York police station, was beginning his briefing.

'We don't want everything broadcast round the place,' his mother warned Matthew sternly, as they walked into Benn's. 'People will be bound to know that the police are checking on Pierre's disappearance, but that's all. Understand?'

Matthew nodded. 'Cross my heart and hope to die,' he said.

'Where on earth did you get that expression?'

'Orlando says it.'

It was a long wait for Matthew until the police vans arrived full of equipment. If he flattened himself against the wall of the foyer between the Swiss cheese plant and the rubber plant he could watch them without getting in the way or being a nuisance. Matthew had never before flinched from being a nuisance but he did so now.

'Hello,' Bob Southwell said to him in a friendly way.

'Hello,' said Matthew.

'Want to come and help?' Bob asked. This, he knew, was Hannah's child. His own son was a year or two older.

Matthew was in paradise. He helped carry things and helped plug things in. He ran obediently from here to there bringing things. He held things. He held his breath when things were tested, and was allowed to put earphones on and help test them. He went importantly to Hannah to ask about the commissariat arrangements and told Betty how many extra cups of coffee would be wanted. Life was real, life was earnest for Matthew that day.

Bob soon settled quietly at a desk and went on writing busily in the policy book. Dave Smart, who had organized the questionnaire, handed out copies to the men who were going to do the internal staff investigation.

James Jester was delighted that he had been appointed Exhibits Officer, although so far he had nothing much in the way of exhibits, only Fontaine's address book and the magazine from under his bed. Then he remembered. He had another exhibit, the contents of the wastepaper basket from Pierre Fontaine's work area. He had bagged it up and taken it back to the police station and put it in his desk. He made a manual record and put it in the file. More exhibits would appear in due course; meantime he did whatever jobs came his way. He and Matthew struck up a friendship – they had something in common; their attitude to life. In spare minutes Matthew told James all over again the details of Pierre Fontaine's car, which was still standing outside, covered in snow. Just looking at it through the window of the seminar room made both Matthew and James long to scoop the snow off the top and make snowballs of it.

Hannah made arrangements that the police officers could eat a midday meal in the canteen and a table was set aside for their use. She saw nothing of Bob, apart from the first greeting, nor of Matthew, but after the police lunch, which Matthew took with them, she looked up in the middle of dictating a letter to Lena and through the window saw her son and that young red-headed detective pelting one another with snowballs and laughing as if the world was the best of all possible places and they the happiest creatures in it.

'He behaves very young, that detective,' remarked Lena.

'He does, doesn't he? It is rather nice to see it.'

The snow game had been going on for twenty minutes before the arrival of Bob Southwell stopped play. He sent Matthew inside, then said to Jester, 'I thought I told you to organize the removal and examination of that car?'

'The low-loader was not available this morning, sir,' said the embarrassed Jester. 'I'm expecting it at two o'clock.'

Although Matthew hung about the seminar room all day, once the system equipment was up and running no one had time to spare for him. During the afternoon even Bob and James did nothing more than ruffle his hair or tell him to 'Mind where you're walking, kiddo,' or 'Don't touch that plug, Matthew.' It didn't matter, he was fascinated. Bob seemed never to have a minute. Someone was always coming in to report and be given fresh instructions, and in between Bob scrutinized the completed questionnaires or wrote in the policy book. A girl classified the information coming in and entered it up on file cards. It seemed to Matthew that the whole of York police force was trying to find Pierre Fontaine.

'Debriefing at five thirty, everybody,' Bob had said at lunch time. When it was five thirty and the policemen had gathered he put Matthew out of the seminar room. 'See you in the morning,' he said, comfortingly but dismissively.

'Right.' Bob looked round the room crowded with large policemen and slightly smaller policewomen. They looked tired, but interested. It was always good at the beginning of an enquiry. It was when you were weeks into an apparently fruitless investigation that the problem arose of motivation, when all the hard work led nowhere.

'This is a firm owned and run by a family trust,' he went on. 'The members of the family actively running it are now Mrs Faith Benn and Miss Hannah Benn, ably assisted by Miss Benn's son, Matthew Benn. I understand there are some distant relatives with voting rights in the firm, and there has been some profit sharing which has resulted in some of the managers having a say in affairs, but the overwhelming majority of the work and the power and the voting rights are in the hands of the two women, including the proxy votes of the small boy. Mrs Benn has the larger share of votes but because Miss Benn is her son's representative as well as having her own rights, she holds the balance of power. Hence a good deal of family friction lately as to whether or not to install a new production line of specially designed machinery to

78

make Recipe 179, which you have no doubt picked up among the gossip in the course of the day. Are all your reports in? Rundown on progress, Dave, please.'

'We have carried out a preliminary interview of all employees of the firm including managerial staff,' said Dave. 'The only exceptions are some of the artic and lorry drivers, who are away on long journeys and who we will catch over the next day or two, and a few of the cleaners. The object of the exercise was to discover who had seen Fontaine last Thursday after one o'clock. In addition we asked where they were during the relevant afternoon and what they were doing. This should help us plot out the distribution of the staff round the factory at various times during those hours. We will then be able to cross-check the stated movements of any one person with others said to be in the vicinity.'

'Good. How many drivers not interviewed?'

'Three, sir. Some early-morning cleaners were out or did not answer the door when we visited their homes. We should catch them when they come to work in the morning and the drivers sometime tomorrow.' Dave sat down again.

'We have looked for any sign of forcible entry anywhere in the factory which would give access to Fontaine's work area,' said another detective, 'and could find no trace of any such thing.'

'We have a sighting of Fontaine later than one o'clock,' said Sergeant Diamond. 'The tea-lady, Sue, who deals with most of the first floor, served him with a cup of tea at three o'clock.'

'Good. Progress. Note that, will you, Jenny?' said Bob to PC Jenny Wren.

'Noted, sir.'

'But as her evidence is at present uncorroborated, he will remain interested in all times after one.'

'She went back for his cup at quarter past three,' added Diamond.

'We'll say three to be on the safe side, Sergeant. No one reported seeing him after that?'

'Not so far,' said Dave.

'No one shouted out "Goodnight" to him as they knocked off at five thirty?'

'Doesn't seem so, sir. I gather he was a bit ratty if disturbed and they thought he was finishing off a batch of Recipe 179 so no one spoke to him then.'

'Why did they think that?'

'Saw his light on after they put their own off. The staff turn all lights off as they vacate the building.'

'So when he finished making his batch and came to out of his state of concentration, he would be a lighted oasis in a pitch-dark building?'

'Sir.'

Bob looked at his watch. 'Five forty-five. Dave, pop upstairs and switch on the light in Fontaine's work area. Here's the key. Has everyone gone but us, the Benn's Bars production line and the night security man?'

'Yes, sir.'

'When Dave comes back – Jenny, run out and tell security what we're doing or he'll be ringing the police station – we will fan out all over the building both inside and outside. You've all got your copy of the building plan with you? Good. We will spend a few minutes discovering where the light from his windows and doors can be seen, and getting the feel of the place at this time of night. Reconstruction if you like. Have you all got torches? Use them as little as you can. Use your brains. This is the factory at the time when Fontaine was last known to be alive. See if moving round can give you any ideas which might be helpful.'

Dave reappeared at the door. 'Light's on, boss.'

Jenny also reappeared. 'I've told the security man, boss.'

Bob went through his team and told each of them which part of the factory they were to inspect, inside or out. 'Use your torches as little as possible. I will be turning this light off as soon as you are all ready.'

Those who were going outside hastily finished putting on their outdoor clothes.

'Back here in ten minutes,' said Bob.

It was exciting and eerie moving quietly round the factory in the darkness, only flashing torchlight when absolutely needed. The team lost touch with one another; the turning of a corner or moving through a door was enough. Outside, the paleness of the snow itself helped the dark figures moving across it, no longer respecting its whiteness and purity. Inside, as eyes became accustomed to the darkness, they found that the snowshine, together with the distant street lighting and the faint pricking illumination of the stars, made the rectangles of the windows visible. Here and there curses were heard as someone banged their shin on a wastepaper basket or the angle of a piece of machinery.

At the end of the old building where the new range of single-storey sheds housed the Benn's Bars production line the brilliant illumination within spilled upward through the rows of roof lights, and the watchers on the floor above could look through to glimpse working machines and men. At one side of the works yard was the brand new warehouse building called TC1. The large rolling doors which led into it from the yard were locked and it was not possible to gain access from the factory itself, as the two security doors leading from the packaging area were locked.

Within the main block, they took sightings from the vantage points of kitchen, canteen, offices, labs, and production areas, colliding as they did so with cold steel or soft cardboard, touching papers or handbasins or chairs, the mysterious objects which had their place in that darkened building.

Outside they went the rounds completely; then out to the roads, on all sides; then criss-crossing the yard and grounds and parking areas, until their trouser legs were wet with melting snow.

Once back in the seminar room at the end of ten minutes which had seemed more like hours, everyone wrote down what they had seen of Fontaine's light, and where they had seen it, and any other points of interest or observations. Everyone was very quiet. It had been a strange end to a busy day. Then without further discussion they went home; the superintendent had not authorized much general overtime on the enquiry. Only Jenny Wren, Bob Southwell and the indexer, Sandra Powell, who had just arrived, remained in the seminar room, Jenny plotting her diagrams of where the staff had been, Bob carefully reading through all the questionnaires again, and Sandra settling down to her night's work.

The night-watchman had enjoyed the break in routine. He was far more awake than usual. It was quite half an hour before he gave a sigh and settled down again to reading his magazine.

Bob put down his papers at last, and sat looking towards the window. The reflection of the lights inside made it impossible for him to see anything of that cold outside world. The factory was a world in itself, he thought. It was a hierarchical world with everyone in their order and degrees. No matter how often the staff called the Benn women 'Faith' and 'Hannah' the realities of power were still in place, the managers still commanded the overlookers, the overlookers' every change of mood still seemed to be of life and death significance to the work-force. In spite of that it was, he imagined, a good firm to work for. The paternal – no, maternal

– benevolence must give a feeling of security. The value placed on individuals of whatever rank, evinced by the rows of photographs of people who had worked there for forty years, must make for happiness in the workplace. He did not think he was putting it too strongly. As he had read the reports from his men, as he had himself moved round the factory, he had had the vivid impression that this was a community who enjoyed being together and working as a team (or many little teams) to produce something they were proud of. Many people within the organization had their own small domains, their own familiar places, their own areas of responsibility and pride, their own mates whom they would greet with pleasure every morning.

Yet someone may well have carried out in this very building a murderous or in some other way criminal attack, or kidnapping.

He was sickened by the idea; that where something good had been created and was working, doing no harm as far as he could see to anyone, this should happen.

Bob decided to go home and forget all about Benn's for a few hours if he possibly could. Often forgetting a problem was the best way to progress towards enlightenment.

'Come on, Jenny,' he said. 'We'll go. Are you seeing Dave tonight?'

'I'm washing my hair,' Jenny answered.

'Really?'

'Well, yes, really. You see, Dave and I are going to the Barbican Centre tomorrow night so I want to look good. But in fact he did say he might pop round later this evening for half an hour.'

'He might catch you with your hair in curlers,' smiled Bob.

'I don't use them.'

'What's on tomorrow?'

'It's an evening called *Hiawatha*, by the York Children's Company.'

'Very good, I've heard. Well, I hope you enjoy it. That's if no dead body turns up,' Bob ended, rather caustically. 'If it does, believe me there'll be no evening out for any of us.'

'I hope it doesn't turn up then.' Jenny allowed herself to be a little pert, as they were off duty.

'I don't know.' Bob sighed aloud. 'If it did turn up, at least we'd know where we were with the case. Goodnight, Sandra. Keep the door locked. You have the radio and telephone if you need to contact anyone.'

Sandra was a sensible woman in her thirties who liked night work because then her husband could look after the children. She liked the quiet of the night hours, too, and the feeling of responsibility for all the records and equipment. She smiled and returned their goodnight.

They passed the security man as they left the building.

'Goodnight, Stan.'

'Night, sir! Night, miss!'

'Do you need a lift, Jenny?'

'No thanks, sir. I brought my car this morning.'

As they reversed out of the entrance the two sets of headlights briefly illuminated the whole length of the building.

7

It was Thursday, the 11th of January.

Hannah Benn and Bob Southwell were sitting in the board room, the incident room being noisy and busy at this time in the morning on the second day of full investigation.

Superintendent Birch had made every policeman the force could spare available to Bob to carry out a thorough search of the factory for Pierre Fontaine's body, or any obvious traces of it. In the end a hundred men had descended on the place, been garbed in white coats and hats and gone about the task.

The work-force, Hannah thought, would have noticed Pierre without fail had he still been about, accidentally injured, perhaps, or trapped in a cupboard or storeroom. Bob, however, was not prepared to believe anything but the personal testimony of his men.

Hannah was hoping that they would not be hindering production or upsetting the staff.

'Miss Benn, I want you to tell me about last Wednesday, everything you can remember,' said Bob. 'It was Monsieur Fontaine's last normal day. You have already given us a great deal of information, I know, and your full co-operation, but I hope you will be good enough to do this.'

'Of course. How long are those men of yours going to be, Mr Southwell? I hope no one is upset. I really ought to be out there soothing people.'

'Didn't you talk to the shop stewards earlier this morning? I thought it was all agreed.'

'Well, yes, I did, but they might be upset all the same. You have no idea how difficult it was to find a hundred overalls and hats at such short notice. The laundry is going to have to work overtime tonight.'

'I'm sure our men will be very tactful.'

Hannah sighed. 'I suppose . . . Ought I to start by telling you about Tuesday night?'

'If you like.'

'Pierre's first day at the factory. It was the 2nd of Jan, the day we restarted after the Christmas break. During the afternoon he'd made a small quantity of Recipe 179 – enough to fill three biscuit tins. When we got home in the evening he cut some of it up into small bite-size pieces and set them out on little china plates with lace doileys and put them on the coffee tables in the sitting-room. I came into the room about half-past seven and he asked if Matthew had settled down all right . . .'

Hannah went on giving her account of the evening as she reran the events through her excellent memory. She had nodded in answer to Pierre's enquiry, and gone to the drinks cupboard, looking at him questioningly.

'My usual, dear,' he had said. 'Whisky and soda. I'm very set in my ways, you know.'

Pouring the drink, Hannah had smiled and the smile crept into her voice. 'Not in all things, are you?'

'Not in my work,' he had agreed, taking the glass from her hand.

'A small sherry, dear,' said her mother.

Hannah had poured herself a dry Martini and put in ice cubes and lemon. On their own the two women would probably have eaten dinner in the oak-panelled breakfast room, with the thick deep green ripple-velvet curtains pulled close, shutting out the gloom of winter. In Pierre's honour they ate instead in the enormous dining-room, in which the entire work-force of Benn's could have been accommodated at a cocktail party or buffet lunch. The brocade curtains were lined and interlined and the very thick ancient central heating pipes were roaring hot, and a log fire was sending flames up the chimney and sparks on to the rug, but

Hannah had still given a shiver as she walked over to join the others. Mrs Goodwin came in with the wine bottles. She had not needed to use any of the spare mahogany leaves for the table, and the smallest of the white damask cloths had proved amply big enough.

For the next hour and a half no one had mentioned countlines. They had plenty of other gossip to keep them going: the previous evening's dinner party, the changes Pierre had noticed at Benn's, Hannah's promising new temporary secretary, and Matthew's little friend Orlando. It was not until after soup, fish, casserole of beef, and bread and butter pudding that they had settled down round the graciousness of the peaceful sitting-room fire with their coffee and Pierre had handed the little platters of sweetmeats to them.

Faith had been the first to taste. 'You couldn't afford to do this for mass production,' was her comment.

'Very nice,' had been Hannah's remark, as she had savoured the flavour very slowly. 'I wonder how Matthew will react. I'll give him a piece at breakfast.'

'He's already had some,' Pierre had confessed. 'If you remember, he was with me while I was making it.'

'And?'

'He wanted more.'

'Good sign. Mmmm. Not in the least cloying – rather surprising with some of the ingredients you asked for. Mother's right, Pierre. This tastes expensive. Price is all-important in countlines, as you know. A penny makes all the difference.'

Pierre had looked smug. 'You will be amazed when you see the costings.'

Just before they went up to bed Faith had said to her daughter, 'Did you mention a phone call from Brandt's, today?'

'I didn't mention it, no,' Hannah had replied.

'Funny. I thought you did.'

'Nothing's secret in our office,' Hannah had spoken heatedly. 'I hope security's a bit tighter on Recipe 179. Your secretary took the call from switchboard as mine was at lunch. Then I suppose Ann told you.'

'That must have been it.' Faith had been quite unblushing.

'Yes, Max Brandt rang. He's coming to England and wants to see us. He asked me to dine with him.'

The two older people had looked speculatively at Hannah.

'It isn't the first time.' She had countered their gaze.

'Do I scent a take-over bid in the wind?' Pierre had asked.

'Is he suggesting a merger?' Faith had said simultaneously.

Hannah had paused before answering. Max Brandt, coming to England, taking her out to dinner – the idea was making her heart thump, yet she was convinced that she didn't even like the man. 'Purely business,' she had said at last. 'And if he thinks he's getting Benn's he's another think coming.'

Hannah had skimmed over this part of the narrative as she told it to the rather attractive policeman, Bob Southwell. She felt he needed to be completely in the picture – to see how normal things had been – and as Max Brandt was undoubtedly going to crop up in conversation and probably in person he had to be brought in some time. She went on to relate the events of the following morning, Wednesday, 3rd January.

'After only one day it already seemed like routine to load up the car with Matthew and Pierre as well as Mother,' she said. 'Although I was looking forward to Matthew starting school again. At least I'd managed to leave his bicycle at home. We arrived a few minutes after the office workers. I would rather arrive at half-past seven myself, but that's how it was. It was still quite dark, even so. I remember asking Pierre if he was making another batch of Recipe 179 and he said he was going to make double the previous day's quantity. The remainder of the first batch had been put in the salad compartment of our fridge. Mrs Goodwin, our housekeeper, was very complimentary about it when she had some.'

'Did he make the new batch?' asked Bob.

'Yes. He made enough for all the factory employees to taste. I remember he said he was going to start the rounds with Sally Binson, head of Dispatch, whom he remembered from when he was here before. Five years ago, when he and my father developed Benn's Bars, Pierre spent weeks around the factory. He seems to have grown friendly with her then. He called her "such a pretty lady" but I would say handsome, myself. She has one of those smooth, firm faces and solid shapely hands. But you will be meeting her. Anyway . . . Pierre made enough during the morning, and we have a woman in the sample department who is in charge of the mechanics of these tastings, she went round the place with him, getting people to fill in forms with their reactions to the product.'

'Is that by any chance the lady in a mob-cap and print gown, very Laura Ashley, in that charming reproduction Victorian sweet shop you have in the foyer?' asked Bob.

'Yes, that's her, Mrs White; it is part of her job. I'm so pleased that you like the little shop. It is Mother's hobby-horse. She saved the square sweet bottles from an old retail outlet. The shop takes to pieces like a stage set and it is in great demand for fairs and carnivals and other public events, and Mother makes small batches of old-fashioned sweets and pastilles for sale. Mrs White really enjoys going with it and serving quarters of sweetmeats in paper pokes. Unfortunately the project is too labour-intensive to look well on the balance sheet, but it is good advertisement.'

'Did the tastings round the factory take Monsieur Fontaine all the afternoon on Wednesday?'

'I believe so. Mrs White will tell you.'

'Perhaps I had better speak to her now. Will you be available later to complete this . . .'

'I expect to be in my office all day unless I'm called away anywhere.'

Mrs White was delighted to tell all she knew. 'I helped get the samples ready,' she said. 'We have test pieces all the same size and I'm used to doing it. We set off about two o'clock, well, a few minutes to because the Benn's Bars change shift at two o'clock. We caught two shifts that way, one going off and one coming on. Then Mr Fontaine insisted we go over to TC1, to Dispatch. He wanted Miss Binson to taste first, I think he likes her. They knew each other when he was here before.'

'Anything in it?' asked Bob Southwell.

'Oh, I'm sure there isn't. Only a bit of favouritism, you know how it is.'

'Then you went round the rest of the factory?'

'Yes. Apart from taking TC1 out of order, we did the round I usually do. The small production lines are switched off for a few minutes while they taste. The office staff, though, come to me in the shop instead of me going to them. We have tastings quite often, you know. Someone's always coming up with an idea. One or two of the men spend a lot of time at home trying to invent sweets.'

'Aren't they jealous of Monsieur Fontaine, coming in at the top like that?'

'Oh, I don't think so. They invent their recipes like trying to win the pools, you know. There's always the chance you might scoop the lot. But Mr Fontaine – he's proved himself already, hasn't he? It stands to reason that he'll get preference.'

'What kind of questions do you ask them?'

'I've brought you one of the forms.' Mrs White produced it. 'Multi-choice, you see. They only have to tick the boxes. They fill them in ever so quickly – used to doing it.'

Bob asked if Hannah could spare him a few more minutes of her time.

'I know how Fontaine spent his afternoon,' he told her. 'Now I'd like you to tell me how he spent his evening.'

'Well, after dinner that night – there's nothing to tell you about that – we sat round talking about the trials so far of 179. We all felt they'd gone very well. The employees, of course, don't know that this may be a new countline . . .'

(I bet they do, thought Bob.)

'. . . so they judged 179 solely on taste, texture, aftertaste and so on.'

'I've got one of the forms.'

'Then my mother said we'd never get the price down far enough for mass production, and that we'd be better letting her have it to make a new one of her range of products. Then Pierre challenged the whole basis we were working on – which took the wind out of our sails.'

'How?'

'He said, "Why not make an expensive bar? Benn's Bars beat anything on the market in their price range, so why have another cheap bar? Why not have a luxury bar at a quite astonishing price for super quality?" I remember his words exactly, they were so surprising.'

'How did you both respond?'

'Neither of us said anything for a while, then I said, "With very elegant packaging," and Pierre said, "Slightly padded, perhaps. Carrying the Fontaine name into the market-place." Then Mother said, "The name of the bar would have to be carefully thought about and audience-researched, but your name would be on the product as well, of course, Pierre."'

Hannah paused, then went on, 'So I said, "We'll have to choose a suitable town for the market research and make a sufficient quantity. It is going to take weeks, months, like last time." Though to be honest I didn't have much to do with developing Benn's Bars, Father did that. Matthew was only an infant when it was going on and I was preoccupied with him. Pierre said in a quite hard tone, "Are you going to take up your option on further development?" and Mother said, "No" and I said, "Yes" and Pierre said, "What is it to be?"'

'So Fontaine was in on this family row,' said Bob Southwell.

'I'm afraid he was. He seems – seemed – oh dear – he was part of the family, or at least it felt like that.'

'I see.'

'I'm afraid I reminded my mother that I control Matthew's shares and that the scales are weighted against her if it comes to a showdown. She could summon up all the aged relatives who have voting rights but she still couldn't win. It wasn't very nice of me to say that, especially in front of Pierre. So Mother got up to leave the room in a huff. I realized I'd been rotten. So I reached out my hand to her and said . . .'

Hannah couldn't think why she was telling Bob all this. 'Look, it's terribly confidential,' she said.

'Don't worry. I will keep this to myself. What happened next? It's probably not important, but it might be.'

'I appealed to her . . . I said, "Let's pull together." I stretched out my hand. My poor mother was shaking. She's a proud woman, Chief Inspector. Then she told Pierre that she was sorry he had witnessed family discord under our roof. After a bit she said to me that she knew I was right, I had the whip hand, so she agreed to further development of 179. I went over to her and put my head on her shoulder, and Pierre went out of the room. I told Mother how I hated to cross her, that I was only thinking of Matthew and his future and the future of Benn's. Pierre came back with the agreement – we hadn't been going to sign it until after the first market trials, but he was very insistent. I think after the quarrel he wanted to tie us up so that progress was not threatened. After all, he could easily sell the recipe to someone else, as he kept reminding us. We called the Goodwins and they were witnesses of the signatures, mine and Pierre's and Mother's. That's all that were needed.'

'Didn't you have any solicitors there?' asked Bob in surprise.

'Oh, they'd already done their part of it. Every clause had been argued over, it was all agreed. We had intended to wait to sign until preliminary tests and marketing trials were over. As I said, signing was really earlier than we'd intended, but Pierre was pushing us and we could see his point. If we spent weeks on trials and then through family disagreement didn't take up our option, he would have wasted a lot of time and time is money. We'd already done a preliminary tasting. The next thing is to use spare capacity on the Benn's Bar line to make up batches as nearly approximating as we can to the finished article – the machines are different, actually. Then public market tests. By signing earlier in the process we were committing ourselves finally, that's what we were doing.'

'So you all signed.'

'Yes. Mother and I on behalf of Benn's. We signed there in the sitting-room on the semicircular walnut card table that was brought into the family by my great-grandmother on her marriage in 1870. I can't think why I'm telling you that. Except that it seemed incongruous and yet traditional – we are overloaded with tradition. Everything is what someone did before or what someone started in the year dot.'

'Did you sign with a quill pen?' asked Bob quizzically.

Hannah laughed. 'I am getting heavy, aren't I? No, with Pierre's gold-nibbed fountain pen. Very grand. I wish I knew where it is now. Incidentally I sorted out the business of the overalls for you.'

'Overalls?'

'The question was what happened to Pierre's overalls.'

'Oh, DC Jester asked. I remember.'

'We supplied him with three, embroidered with his name. One was found to be clean and one to be in the wash. It is back from the laundry now. The third he put on clean on Thursday morning and it is nowhere to be found. He must have changed each day. Mother and I don't get dirty so ours last a week as a rule.'

'Right, thanks. Many thanks.'

'Coffee's ready, I think.'

They went through into the incident room.

As soon as Bob was back on the job he called Dave Smart and James Jester to him. 'The clothes Fontaine was wearing,' he said. 'We know now that during Thursday morning he worked in his shirt-sleeves under his overall, because the secretary, Ann, saw his jacket hanging in the lobby here. During the afternoon it wasn't here any longer, but Fontaine was in his workroom until after three p.m. according to the tea-lady, and the Research and Development bods in the laboratory next door heard his voice raised in Gallic swear words as late as four-thirty, according to the latest information. No one saw him come out of his work area after that. It only has one door, and several people were in the lab immediately outside it. It could be assumed that had he come out they would have noticed, but what we want in fact; what we want is evidence. When they went at five thirty and turned their light off, his was still on. They assumed that he was there, working. The testimony such as it is points to the probability that he was wearing both his jacket and his overall. Presumably during anything messy like cooking, where the jacket would have been a constraint and might have become marked, he did not wear it, but when he was doing paperwork or a clean job he appreciated the warmth and perhaps needed things from the pockets. These may have included a gold-nibbed fountain pen.'

'So he went missing wearing an overall?' Dave Smart said. 'And without his car?'

'Yes.'

'He's still here, surely?'

'You've been back at the station all morning, haven't you, Dave? So you don't know what's been happening here. The super sent us a hundred men, no less, and they've searched the factory. No luck. No body, not even a trace.'

'I would have thought, with all those store places . . .'

'Most of them are in regular use, don't forget. It's not easy to hide a dead body. There's the smell apart from anything else. If he'd been buried in the rosebeds the disturbance would have been obvious. Anyway the ground is as hard as iron. There the thing is – we've carried out a search ourselves, the result is negative. I'm glad we did it, though.'

'Could he have been taken away in a lorry?' asked Jester.

'Possible, I suppose. In fact I'm beginning to think it is the most probable solution. It is too bad that the cleaners went into his workplace.'

'It's lucky I bagged the contents of the wastepaper basket first,' said Jester.

'What, James? You did what?'

'It's in my report, sir.'

Bob scuffled among the papers on his desk in an agitated manner. 'Yes,' he said. 'Here it is. How one can miss things among all this detail. Good work, James. Where is it now?'

'Exhibit JJ1, sir. The others are his address book and the magazine from under his mattress.'

'Send JJ1 to Wetherby at once, for forensic examination. Probably no use at all,' 'Bob's face dropped, 'but one never knows.'

'No point in getting scene of crime officers now, to a place like this,' remarked Dave.

'Not really. Three hundred workpeople trampling about and regular cleaning means traces are going to be destroyed long ago, I would have thought. Obvious blood would have been noticed and reported by somebody, I am sure. No body and no blood and no smell. What could scene of crime officers do? Time – think how much time it would take – and time is money . . . They could go over his work area, even though it's been cleaned . . . blood could still be found even after washing and cleaning procedures. We'll see what happens in the next day or two.'

'I've been investigating cleaning procedures,' said Dave.

'Yes?'

'On the big production line the operatives clean the machines down at the end of every afternoon shift and the factory cleaners go over the floor every morning. Then on Sunday mornings they have a big strip down, clean and general overhaul of the line.'

'I thought they were like the Windmill, never stopped,' said Bob.

'They stop for weekly cleaning. Then the other work areas and laboratories are cleaned every day, so are the offices, but there are some places which aren't done as often, such as the mélangeur where the chocolate itself is actually made, and the nut room and essence room. The men who work in the mélangeur go in clean but come out impregnated with chocolate, you can smell it on them. It's rough work and messy with the chocolate dust. Specially good chocolate is mixed or beaten, whatever they do, for three days continuously so that's why the cleaners don't get in so often. The men themselves do what's necessary in between. The storeplace – TC1 – is only swept round every few days because it doesn't get dusty, it is a controlled environment and everything's sealed. The other production lines don't work at weekends unless demand is exceptional, so they are stripped down and cleaned by the maintenance men on Sunday mornings when they have finished the big line. They are given a daily clean every afternoon, before the women finish the afternoon shift.'

Later that day Hannah told Bob Southwell about Thursday morning. 'When I went to open the garage doors he appeared, key in hand, ready to back out the Rolls. "It's a pleasure to take you down with us," I said. He said I mustn't spoil him and that he was quite used to driving on the wrong side of the road. He often said that, it was one of his little jokes. He'd lived in England for twenty years at least. Then he went on to say that he intended to make a third, yet bigger, batch of Recipe 179. We plan to have a tasting trial at certain selected retail stores, inviting members of the public to try it. Then there are tests to do on storage and keeping qualities. I told him he needn't work himself to death. Oh dear.'

'We all say inappropriate things all the time,' comforted Bob.

'Well . . . He said I mustn't forget that 179 was his baby and that he wouldn't be happy until he saw the new production line rolling, saw the product in the shops, and saw people buying it as a special treat for themselves and their children. I said I couldn't thank him enough for giving us the chance of it. He said he knew it was safe with me, as long as I didn't let Brandt's get their hands on it, and I said he needn't worry. That's actually all I said to him that day. We had lunch at separate times, he was with my mother then. I only made some remark as I passed them when they came into the canteen.'

She thought for a minute, gazing blankly over Bob's shoulder and out of the window at the now trampled snow.

'I never spoke to him again,' she finished quietly.

Ann, Faith Benn's secretary, sat opposite Bob Southwell in the board room. 'I've told your sergeant everything,' she said.

'I think your interview was with Detective Inspector Smart,' Bob had often found that top secretaries – or secretaries to top people, which wasn't at all the same thing – got a bit above themselves and needed deflating occasionally.

'Oh well, detective inspector, then,' replied Ann, flouncing a little.

'I have the record of your interview with the detective inspector,' went on Bob, 'and only wish to add to it, if we may. I am going over the events of last Thursday, anything at all you can remember about the day might be useful, even if the usefulness is not apparent to you.'

'I can't think of anything new except silly little things.'

'Tell me those.'

She thought for a minute. 'I remember talking to our temp – the Swedish girl – in the morning.'

'Go on.'

'But really, it was only about grass!'

'Yes?'

'She said she couldn't understand how everything was so green outside. This was before Hannah arrived in the morning, we were standing talking. The leaves, she said, the grass, all green. What leaves? I said. Then I realized she meant the hollies but they looked black to me, and the grass was brown and dead-looking. So she said that in her country everything would be covered with snow and very cold. She couldn't get over the greenness. I said it was cold here already. I hate frosty nights and damp dark days with sleety rain – if that is New Year weather you can keep it. I was tired of her going on about how green everything was, but her desk was clear, she'd nothing to do until Hannah came so I couldn't put an end to the conversation that way. So I asked her if she'd tried Recipe 179, and she said it was very good. Then the bosses arrived so talking was over. We switched our computers on and the junior from General Office came in with a query. Bruce Swallow and the Personnel Officer both arrived wanting to discuss the Easter eggs. Bruce was on about the designs like he always is and Paul wanted to talk about a bit of trouble they are having. The overlooker had complained to him. One of the girls on the line doesn't like one of the other girls and she keeps putting her chocolates in the wrong places so the other girl hasn't got the right places to put hers in and she gets upset about it. Hannah and Faith went with them into the seminar room, that left Lena with nothing to do, so little Matthew Benn offered to take her round the factory. He's good at that, he often takes people when he's not at school.'

'Did she ask him to take her?'

'No. He's taken a fancy to her and he'd tidied up her pins and got the fluff out of the bottom of the pin tray, the day before. Then on the Thursday he was going to do her paperclips – they get themselves tangled up in a right mess – but when his mother vanished he knew she'd be free so he said would she like to see chocolates being made and off they went.'

Ann really did not have anything material to add. Bob thought he'd try Lena.

'Do sit down, Lena,' he said.

'It is pronounced Lay-na,' she answered. 'Lay-na.'

'Sorry, Lay-na. How do you like working at Benn's?'

'It is a clean place,' said Lena, 'cleaner than most places in England. It is clean like Sweden and I like all the white overalls and hats and all the democracy with everyone's Christian name on their pocket.'

'You're from Sweden?'

'Yes, but one of my grandfathers was from York.'

'Tell me about last Thursday,' he said.

'Nothing happened last Thursday.'

'I thought you were taken round the factory by young Matthew Benn?'

'That is right. It was on Thursday that Matthew took me round the factory.'

'Tell me about it.'

'He took me to the Victorian sweet shop and I think he would have liked to stay there but I did not think it was very interesting so we went to the Benn's Bars and I thought that was very interesting. Then we walked through the packing area and to the new storage building and looked from the balcony.'

'Yes, I've stood on that balcony too,' said Bob.

'There are three people with computers and they control all those machines. One person is telling the machines where to put the packages and two people are telling them which package to get from the storage racks. Matthew was very good because I was interested but he was not very. So we went up to the top of this building and saw the nut room and the gum room and all the other rooms where produce is cleaned and stored, and saw the hoist which takes goods up to that floor from the yard where they are delivered. We went past the door of the mélangeur but Matthew said I would not like it because it was hot and rough and dusty and he knew I would not like that. We saw where they make boiled sweets and Victorian lines for the shop, that is only a little place because they are only small quantities. Then we saw where they make the Fontaine Selection and the other expensive chocolates and I tasted some. Matthew showed me where the very beautiful wrappings are and the little room where they make the special wrappings if people order boxes of chocolates for a special occasion, for presentation.'

Bob nodded.

He had already decided that he was going to surprise his wife Linda by ordering a specially packaged box of chocolates for her next birthday. They were certainly very attractive and he doubted if any factory in England would go on producing them much longer. Take advantage of anything while it is still here, was becoming Bob's motto. Firms went out of production or were taken over so rapidly these days, shops which opened with a great flourish soon found they could not stand up to the high business rates, old-fashioned products which had proved their worth over more years than he had lived were dispensed with as firms were asset-stripped or streamlined. He could see that before many years were over Benn's would be costing out the production of those special boxes and deciding they were too expensive, and one more small delight would have vanished from the earth. Take advantage while it is there. Use it or lose it. Lose it whether you use it or not.

'That was all we did,' Lena said. 'Then we came back to the office and I worked for Hannah until it was time to go home.'

'Did you have lunch in the canteen?'

'Yes. A nice girl in the General Office asked me to have lunch with her.'

Lena had waved at the tea-ladies when she went into the canteen, but she had not gone over to sit with them on that Thursday. She did not bother to tell Bob Southwell anything about her friendship with them. They had not minded her defection. 'Found her own kind, eh,' Betty had said, without malice, nodding her blonde head. 'You can't expect her always to sit with us,' Vi had responded. 'She's got more in common with them.'

Bob Southwell was not made privy to any of that. He asked Lena about her social life, was she making friends in England, where was she living, and so on, in a kindly way. She said she sometimes asked her friends back to her flat for coffee, and sometimes went out with other girls or men. He thought it all sounded rather innocent and quite in order, and felt satisfied about her welfare. Today she was wearing a sweater knitted in a Scandinavian design and he remembered a family friend, Julia Bransby, who was in textiles and thought that she would be interested to see it.

'Thank you, Lena,' he said aloud.

*   *   *

It was that evening in the pub that Bri, one of the drivers of heavy goods vehicles for Benn's, was talking to his friend Len, another driver. The pub was full and so noisy that it was as private a place to talk in as anywhere.

'What's up?' Len had asked him.

'It's that bloody Kev. He's been sniffing round Polly again. I'm that mad with her. She let out that he'd given her a lift home last week, when I was away.'

'What she let him for?'

'It was pouring down, she said. She walks home, you know. It's not that far. Hardly worth catching a bus and a bit of fresh air does her good, she says. He'd been swanking again. Some big flash car went past them and he says, "I'm getting one of those," he says. "I'm going to trade this one in," he says. Fat chance he's got.'

'He's bad news,' said Len. 'Inadequate, that's what he is.'

'I'll have to remember that word, Len. I'll tell Polly. You're dead right. He never was any good. Never had any friends much at school. Nobody ever liked him.'

'Polly used to like him all right.'

'Well, they went together for a bit. I don't know that she was that keen on him. Sorry for him more than anything.'

'If he throws his money about . . .'

'Polly's not that kind. She wouldn't go with anyone just because they threw their money about. But you're right about him. She had a brooch on her lapel, one I bought her last time I was on the Edinburgh run. A thistle with two leaves. Not expensive but it was pretty. "Is that the sort of tat Bri gives you?" he'd said. "I'll get you something fit to wear, a bit better than that."'

'She didn't take any notice though, did she?' asked Len.

'She hasn't worn it since.' Bri sounded depressed.

Len dipped his moustache into his beer. He was glad he and Betty had come to an understanding. She was a right nice little armful was Betty. He was sick of not being settled. It would be good to have a little wife, not to have to bother any more chasing wenches. Mind, she was a bossy boots. But he didn't mind. Gazing into his beer, Len decided he liked a little bossy boots. It didn't bother him. He felt sorry for Bri.

'You want to dot him one,' he said.

'It's being away that does it,' said Bri. 'When I'm away on a long run how do I know what she's doing? How do I know it was only a lift home he gave her?'

8

The following morning Polly's trolley started squeaking. She did her first rounds, putting up with it and hoping it would go away, but by the time she was back in the canteen cleaning up, she could stand the irritation no longer.

'In trouble, Polly?' asked Kev, looming up beside her.

'Oh! Jack needn't have sent *you*,' she greeted him.

'It's no trouble,' he leered at her.

'If Jack had sent an oil can I could have done it myself.'

'Always so warm and welcoming,' Kev said, getting down on his knees and squinting underneath the trolley.

'If you're going to upend it,' she snapped, 'at least let me get it cleared first.'

'Rather upend you,' he said.

'I'll have you up before the works council for sexual harassment if you talk like that.'

'Oh, go on, Polly, you like it.' Kev gave the wheels of the trolley a squirt of oil. 'There, try that, see if it's any better.'

Polly rolled the trolley to and fro. The squeak was still there but fainter. Kev operated the oil can again.

'Try that.'

This time the squeak was definitely less.

'It takes time for the oil to work through, run it to and fro for a bit. Here, let me.'

He took the handles from her and worked the trolley briskly. It was by now almost completely quiet.

'It's a rotten thing anyway,' she said. 'It's like those supermarket trolleys that only go crabwise. It tires me out pushing this thing.'

'Well, wheels going crabwise is too difficult for us maintenance men. What you want on that is one of the fitters. They get paid extra for being able to sort out stuff like that. Crabwise is not in my brief, lovey.'

'I'm not your lovey.'

'Who sez? Tell you what, I got that car I was telling you about.'

'You didn't, did you, Kev? I thought you were only swanking.'

'Take you out in it tonight if you like. We'll go somewhere and have a slap-up dinner. Bottle of wine, anything you like. Call for you at seven o'clock, shall I? Bri's away, isn't he, so you needn't be afraid of him.'

'I'm not afraid of Bri. He's a good bloke, Bri is.'

'Come on, Polly. You know you're dying to see the car. Seven o'clock do you?'

'Well . . .' said Polly.

Kev ran his finger gently up her forearm.

'Hey, you stop that. You know what I said about sexual harassment.'

'We could try a bit of sexual harassment tonight if you like.'

'I don't like.'

Kev whistled softly under his breath. 'Anyway, touching your arm isn't harassment.'

'Get on with you, I've work to do if you haven't.'

'Seven o'clock then,' said Kev.

She did not reply.

Among the people Bob Southwell interviewed were all the heads of department. He had no doubt that the key to the whole mystery probably lay elsewhere – in the knowledge of one of the cleaners, perhaps, or the young post room lad who went from department to department with internal mail, but protocol and dignity could not be left out of the question, and among three hundred employees he had to be selective. He saw the top brass one after the other and noted down his reactions and observations.

Sally Binson impressed him at once with her immense calm. He looked at the monumental young woman as she sat opposite to him, her hands clasped on the edge of the table, and knew that a sculptor would have liked her as a model. She was solid and shapely, about five feet seven, her dark hair drawn from the face and fastened somehow at the back. He knew now why Hannah had mentioned Sally's hands; they looked capable as well as beautiful and they were usually in view, folded together.

Bob asked this enigmatic lady to explain her job to him, and she did – at length. He realized that she was intensely proud of her position at Benn's; she had risen from being an assistant in the post room when she first left school to being head of TC1, with its computer-controlled dancing cranes loading and unloading the enormous frameworks in the warehouse, putting produce into store and taking the pallets out again when wanted and moving them to the vehicle loading bay. She was also dealing efficiently with the stream of transport taking finished goods away from the factory.

Bob looked down at his notes. 'You are not married, Miss Binson?' he queried. 'Do you live alone?'

'Quite alone.'

'Do you enjoy that?'

'I like my own company,' she said.

This phrase always intrigued Bob; as if the speaker could split herself in two, providing a doppelganger companion. He sensed a certain unease in her at this point, and went on probing.

'A small house?' he asked. 'Have you bought your own, or was it your parents'?'

'My parents still live in their house. I bought my own ages ago.'

'My wife and I are thinking of moving,' Bob said mendaciously. 'What kind of house is yours?'

Her eyes lit up, though there was a sudden wariness in her. 'I moved a year ago. This is my fifth house of my own, actually. I started with a street house when I was in my teens and I've been trading up ever since when the opportunity was right. Last year I found another bargain. It is a big detached,' she said with a light of enthusiasm on her face which bordered on the fanatic.

Bob wondered. Granted, she might have spent every spare hour doing up these houses and selling at a profit, but to rise from a street house to a *large* detached was going it a bit, he felt, even if she was good at finding bargains. He looked again at her beautiful hands. Those hands, he felt sure, had not wielded saw or sandpaper. They were too perfect, too well manicured. Capable hands intended to be looked at. He was puzzled.

'You enjoy plenty of space?' he asked.

'I like my privacy,' she said, and the beautifully shaped lips closed firmly on one another as if determined not to let anything out.

Bob made some smiling remark and closed the interview on a friendly note.

After a minute's thought he sent for James Jester. 'A bit of something for you, James,' he said. 'I know Exhibits aren't keeping you fully occupied at present. Go to the reference library and look up the electoral register for the last ten years or so. Find out this lady's addresses over that period. You should have time before lunch.'

Bob went back to considering the list of the work-force. Managers – sales and marketing, engineering, research and development, recruitment and personnel, dispatch. Departmental managers, overlookers, secretaries, clerks, wages clerks, receptionist cum telephonist. Nurses. Workers – storerooms and preparation, mixing, baking, chocolate, moulding and enrobing, creaming, packaging. Weighbridge man, gate and security, drivers. Cooks, tea-ladies, canteen staff, cleaners. Analytical and quality control. Research engineers, maintenance, fitters. Salesmen and marketing assistants. Studio designer.

He ticked off those he had just interviewed and wondered which of the rest ought to take up his time and attention.

It was almost noon on Friday when the detective superintendent appeared in the incident room at Benn's factory.

'This is an unexpected pleasure,' said Bob.

'I don't know about pleasure. I think you're going to have to stop this enquiry, Bob.'

Bob looked up, appalled at this. Three days of hard work had been put in by a large team and he was beginning to feel that they were getting somewhere. The super saw his disappointment. 'Well . . . tell me what you really think now, about the case. Pierre Fontaine hasn't been found, I know that. You had a hundred men here all yesterday morning without locating him.'

'Yes; thank you very much for that assistance, sir. It was a great help. As you know, a negative result is often as useful as a positive result in an enquiry. I've just heard, too, that an examination of his Rolls Royce has yielded nothing. Fontaine certainly hasn't turned up, dead or alive, and I have come to the conclusion that he left the factory, willingly or unwillingly, in a lorry or van or a container vehicle, during the evening or night after he was last seen.'

He had discovered that arrangements were made for pick-ups and deliveries of goods out of normal hours; it was only the intervention of the Christmas and New Year holidays that had caused the problem with the Turkish driver and his load of nuts.

'So if he was shipped out there's nothing else you can do here.'

Bob was silent. Then at last he said, 'Has something else turned up?'

'There is other work in the department, yes. You know I was giving you your head, following your instincts on this case. But I told you at the beginning that time would be severely limited if results were not obtained pretty quickly. What is happening about the formula – what did you call it . . . ?'

'Recipe 179, sir. What's happening is that the Benn family have decided to try to recover the recipe from the sample already made up. I gather this is a difficult thing to do, but not impossible. They know what they ordered in for his use, but he did bring certain flavourings and so on with him. Finding out the exact proportions and method of preparation will take some time and be a very tricky operation. Miss Hannah Benn has commissioned an outside firm of analysts to do the job.'

'She must trust them?'

'They wouldn't be in business long if their clients couldn't trust them.'

'True. So by the time he reappears Pierre Fontaine may be superfluous.'

'They are going to have to spend a lot of time and trouble, and that means money, recovering the recipe and preparing batches again to make sure it's the same as the first lot. Then they have to find out how well it keeps, if it deteriorates in storage by crystallizing or candying or anything, though Fontaine should have checked all that.'

The super walked around the incident room, humming to himself. Jenny Wren behind her computer tried to be invisible. She was sure Bob didn't want her overhearing this.

'Look, sorry, Bob, but I mean it. Pack up here tomorrow. Tell the Benn family you'll be keeping a watching brief and that you'll be in touch. There's nothing else we can do. You haven't got anything to follow up. We can't do a nationwide hunt for the man, it's not on. If he was a young girl or a small child it would be different.'

'If you say so, sir.'

'The work won't be wasted if the slightest lead appears. You can start again at once and all the basic investigation will have been done already.'

'I don't feel as if we'd even started,' Bob replied.

*   *   *

The Personnel Officer had collared Hannah again.

'As soon as the Easter eggs go out we'll start to have complaints from the public,' he began. Part of his job was dealing with complaints.

'I hope we won't.'

'About the packaging. They will say we use too much packaging and use up too much of the world's natural resources.'

'Bruce,' Hannah turned to the head of the Design Studio, 'this year, did you put into operation what I asked you?'

'What was that, Miss Hannah?'

'I asked you to use recycled paper and cardboard wherever possible in the egg boxes and cartons.'

'Oh yes, we did that.'

'Then what's the problem? Paul, issue some statements to the press – nearer the time of course, but you can get them ready now while it's on your mind. Say that although the egg itself is only touched by the newest of materials, as much as possible of the packing is made of recycled. Say in addition that all our office stationery and the outer cartons are also made of recycled, as well as all our loo paper in this building and all the paper towels. No, perhaps you'd better not mention loo paper in the same breath as Easter eggs. You can slip that in some other time when you're talking about how green we are. Say we are constantly on the look-out for ways to save more energy and create less pollution. Ask the overlooker on maintenance – yes, Jack – to see me and I'll ask him how the energy saving is going. Yes. I'll have a progress report both from him and from the works engineer. What's the use of sending them on special courses, I ask myself, if it is not reflected in results? The reports had better be with me by the end of next week.'

'Yes, Hannah.'

'Look. New idea. Posters throughout the factory. We'll bring in a bonus scheme for everyone who consistently comes to work on a bicycle. Extend the bike sheds. Improve security on them. Move them perhaps to where the watchman can keep an eye out. Work on the details for me, Paul, there's a good chap. And publicize it,' Hannah threw over her shoulder as she walked away. 'Tell the press. Tell York Radio. Some publicity photographs of me and Mother and Matthew arriving on bicycles, but not until the snow's gone. Jolly scarves flying as we glide along. Draft scheme to the next meeting for discussion.'

'I wish I hadn't mentioned the public's complaints about the amount of packaging,' said Paul.

Matthew had been turned out of the police incident room early in the morning and his mother, grandmother and both their secretaries were busy. So, remembering his new computer, he then did the rounds of the General Office, standing at everyone's shoulder in turn and asking them what they were doing on their PCs, and why, and what happened if they did it differently. At last the Sales Manager's secretary had asked him politely to go and play somewhere else.

He couldn't think of anywhere else with computers until he remembered the packaging area near TC1, and he could not get there without passing through some of the areas his mother had forbidden as dangerous and out of bounds. Strictly speaking, Matthew knew that even the packaging area wasn't really on. It was the place where the pallets were finished and placed on the moving track called the ski run, which took them into the warehouse itself. There were many powered trolleys moving the packages and pallets and these his mother would consider a potential danger. He overcame this problem by asking one of the clerks from the General Office to take him there and put him in the charge of the new young man, Mark Smith, who had been recruited to manage the input computer.

'You can enter the new consignments, if you are very careful and do exactly what I tell you,' said Mark.

Matthew was elated, so pleased he couldn't speak. He stood between Mark's knees and was told which buttons to press. Mark was working down a long list of packed products which, under his computer control, moved past his cabin on the ski run. Once in TC1 the cranes had to put them away on the shelves in exactly the right place so that at the touch of a button they could be found again and brought out. Mark had been growing bored with sitting there on his own entering them. It made a nice change for him to be instructing Matthew, and if his boss, Sally Binson, came into the little control cabin, he had the perfect alibi – how could he refuse to instruct one of the owners in the use of the firm's equipment?

They worked together happily until midday, when Matthew

decided he had had enough of computers. If life was going to be as boring as this he wished that he had stayed at home and played with Orlando.

'Why don't you draw?' asked Mark. 'I used to spend hours when I was a boy drawing aeroplanes.'

'I've nothing to draw on,' complained badly-done-by Matthew.

'You can have some old computer paper. Look, that pile over there is waiting to be collected for recycling. You can have some of that and draw on it and then put it back afterwards.'

'I suppose I could.' Matthew sounded anything but enthusiastic.

'Of course you could. Do some drawings and then bring them and let me see them, this afternoon.'

'Oh, all right, then,' said Matthew.

Mark fished around in the pile of paper for some which was suitable and gave it to him.

Matthew remembered that the police would be taking their lunch break and if he was quick he could join them.

'Please will you take me to the canteen?' he asked Mark. 'I'm supposed to be under the supervision of an adult if I'm in dangerous areas of the factory.' Mark agreed to escort him and for a couple of minutes stopped the progress of the ski run.

'What have you got there?' asked James Jester as Matthew, breathless, climbed on to the chair beside him.

'Paper. I'm going to draw an aeroplane for you, James.'

It was not a good sort of day, not like the day when James and Matthew had snowballed each other. It was a day of low cloud when the temperature had gone up enough to make the snow damp and unpleasant instead of crisp and clean. It was a day to be got through somehow, rather than enjoyed, the kind when one longs for a hint of spring. James replied quietly, without his usual brightness.

'That will be good. As I won't be seeing you any more I can take the drawing home and hang it up in my bedroom to remember you by.'

'Why won't you be seeing me any more?'

'This is our last full day here. We're packing up in the morning and you won't be in.'

'Why are you going? You haven't found Monsieur Fontaine?'

'No, we haven't. But there is other work in our department and we have to go and do it.'

Matthew had chosen fish and chips for his dinner and he stared down at his plate silently, trying to fight the tears which had come into his eyes. He was going to lose all the excitement of his friends the detectives. He was not going to see James Jester any more. At that moment his new friendship with Mark Smith in packaging seemed dull in comparison.

'What's the matter?' asked James, misinterpreting his silence. 'Don't you want me to take the drawing home?'

'Of course I do,' answered Matthew gloomily. 'Utterly brilliant.'

When Vi, the eldest of the tea-ladies, arrived in the canteen for her lunch she only had to take one look at Polly to see that there was something wrong. 'What's up, Poll?' she asked, taking her large handbag from the end of the trolley where she always perched it and plonking it on the table. 'Lost a sixpence and found a tanner?'

'Nothing like that,' said Polly.

'Boyfriend trouble again?' put in Sue.

'Go on then, tell,' said Vi.

'Oh, it's like this, isn't it, Kev's making a dead set at me and you know, we went together for a long time.'

'You mean –' Vi struck a histrionic pose – 'it is not all over between you?'

'Well, no, it isn't. I can't resist him when he looks at me like he does, as if I was the only girl in the world, Princess Di or someone. But Bri's a far better bloke as a long term proposition.'

'Just boring?' asked Vi.

'Not really, no. He isn't boring. But he is away a lot and, there it is, Vi, when he's away I'm darn lonely and Kev offers to take me out and . . .'

'If you can't stand a bit of loneliness it isn't fair to a chap who's a long distance heavy goods vehicle driver,' put in Betty, who looked very disapproving, and was without her usual saucy smile. She never felt tempted when Len was away. There was too much to think about, planning what kind of house they'd have and what she wanted in it.

'You'll have to make your mind up sooner or later,' said Sue.

'Oh, I don't know.' Vi pursed her lips. 'You're only young once. May as well enjoy yourself. The more the merrier.'

'She'll get herself into trouble.' Sue sounded more disapproving than ever.

'I won't, you know, I'm on the pill,' exploded Polly.

'All right, don't tell everyone in the building. That wasn't what Sue meant, Polly. Look, you need more than your fair share of luck at present. Give me back that hare's foot and take – let me see . . .' Vi drew out of her bag a black cat with vivid green eyes.

'Oooh, that's really sinister-looking,' Betty remarked, picking it up.

'You leave that alone, Bet. My property is not for other people to handle unless they are given leave.' Vi snatched up the cat.

'You needn't be so touchy, Vi. What else have you got in there?' asked Sue, leaning over in the hope of having a look.

Vi drew out a St Christopher. 'Have this instead of the hare's foot, Poll. I always think he's more powerful. He will protect you on your journey through life. And if he doesn't sort you out there's one or two other charms you could try that I happen to carry round with me.'

'Oh, you *are* superstitous, Vi,' remonstrated Sue. 'And you're as bad, Polly. It's all nonsense. That bag of yours weighs a ton, Vi, with all the charms you've got in it.'

'I've got to decide which of them I really want,' Polly said dreamily, fingering the St Christopher.

'You mean the hare's foot or that medallion?'

'No, Kev or Bri, you stupid.'

'I've finished,' said Sue, getting up from the table. 'I'm going for a cup of tea. Shall I bring you all one while I'm at it?'

James Jester presented himself to Bob Southwell with a list of Sally Binson's addresses for the last ten years.

'Now go and look at the houses,' instructed Bob, 'and estimate how her capital investment has grown from first to last. Get an idea of her financial situation. Check on her salary level from Wages Group – make that part of a general enquiry or it will draw too much attention. It is my opinion she has some other income from somewhere. Or else she's head over heels in debt. She could be pilfering on a grand scale – computer control is beyond the ken of most people in this establishment, I should think. I don't know why I'm asking you to do this. There's something, I know that. Something not quite right. And in the situation we've got here anything not quite right may be significant.'

It was a task which might well have taken over a day, but Jester was keen. After putting in a general enquiry to Wages Group about salary levels, he asked around the city as quickly as he could, and arrived back towards the end of the afternoon.

'Miss Sally Binson you asked me to check on, sir,' he said.

'Yes? Interesting?'

'I think so. There's definitely something. She's on a good salary and she gets a bonus, but her house is worth a lot, it's on Stockton Lane, that's a snobby road and the prices reflect it. I noticed that one room had internal blinds closed very thoroughly. Perhaps she's keeping this Pierre Fontaine prisoner there.' James Jester's face wore a hopeful expression.

'Anything else significant?'

'I have spoken to a few people who have been her neighbours at various times. She has the reputation of being very houseproud.'

'So I would have thought.'

'She lives alone but has a lot of visitors.'

'She didn't strike me as being very sociable,' remarked Bob.

'Mostly men,' finished James.

'She is an attractive lady, although not my cup of tea. Well, we'll remember this. Make a report, James.'

That night at seven o'clock promptly Kev, the maintenance man, called round for Polly, the tall tea-lady with the dark hair which, now no longer confined in an orange mob-cap, was streaming on to her shoulders. She had prepared herself for an evening out, and looked so glamorous that her employers would hardly have recognized her.

'That's my girl,' said Kev.

'Look, because I'm coming out with you tonight doesn't mean anything,' she snapped.

For once he was wise enough not to reply. He waited while she locked the door and then ushered her into the car.

'Where are we going?'

'The Tree House, I thought.'

'Great.' Polly could not help glowing with anticipation. She had been convinced that she loved Bri, but he never took her out like this. He never opened the car door and waited politely for her to be seated before going round to the driver's side and getting in himself. Bri hopped in first and then sometimes he remembered to unlock the passenger door for her and sometimes he didn't and she had to knock on the window, standing there in the freezing cold and wet. Polly did not recall at that moment that it had not been Kev's habit, either, to be so polite and caring, in the months during which they had practically lived together. All she was thinking of was the pleasure of being cosseted and admired and taken out in the way a lady ought to be treated by the men in her life. She knew that she was looking particularly good. Even if Bri heard about the outing – and they might well see someone who knew them both during the course of the evening – she didn't care. It wouldn't hurt to let him know there was a bit of opposition, he wasn't on to a walkover, not by any manner of means. He might lose her, back to Kev, if he didn't look out.

After the long luxurious evening they went back to Kev's place. He had a small flat in a converted terrace house. He had left all ready; clean, tidy, soft music at the touch of a switch, glasses and a bottle on the low coffee table. He switched on the two low-level lamps and the room looked reasonably romantic. It did not take long to get Polly into bed.

Afterwards they lay and looked at the ceiling and Kev had a cigarette. It was a while before Polly said, 'I could do with a cup of tea, Kev.'

'I'll make you one, my love.' He obediently got out of bed. 'You lie there like a queen.'

'No, I think I'll put some more music on.'

'You know where it is.' He waved with a generous hand in the direction of the rows of cassettes, which were on the same set of shelves as his books.

She went naked to the shelves and ran her finger thoughtfully along the row. In the tiny kitchenette she could hear Kev putting water into the kettle and whistling as he took cups and saucers out of the cupboard. Polly took out first one cassette and then another. She decided on one, started it going on the machine, and went to put back the cassette she had taken out of the player. There was something lying at the back of that row which stopped her fitting it in properly. She pulled out a bunch of newspaper cuttings fastened together with a paperclip and riffled through them, scanning the sense very quickly. Then she slipped them back, carefully, so that they went down behind the row of tapes slightly to the right of the one she had been replacing.

As she turned away from the shelves Kev put his head round the door from the kitchenette.

'Biscuit?' he said.

'No thanks.'

He turned away but in a moment reappeared. 'You all right? Your voice sounded a bit funny.'

'I feel tired,' she said.

'We'll both sleep in in the morning,' he said. 'Good job it's Saturday.'

When Kev came back into the living-cum-bedroom Polly was dressed.

'What you got dressed for?' he asked, pouring the tea.

'I think you'd better take me home, Kev.'

'What for?'

'I've got a bit of a headache.'

'Good job you didn't have one earlier.'

'Tummy ache as well.'

'It can't be anything you ate, we both had the same and I'm all right.'

'No, of course it isn't anything I ate. I think I've drunk a bit too much, that's all. I'd be happier in my own bed, you know what I'm like when I'm not very well.'

'I'll run you home when you've had your tea, but I must say, I'm disappointed. I'd hoped we would have the night together.'

'Not this time.'

'You do sound off it, Polly.'

'Yeah. Well, I've drunk my tea now. Let's be going.'

On the short drive to Polly's minute house she did not speak and Kev's cheerful remarks were ignored. She gave him a very cool kiss on parting. Women! he thought. You give them a good time and then they turn sad on you. He shrugged his shoulders and whistled softly to himself. At that moment no warning bells sounded in his head. He had regained Polly from his rival, all was well with Kev's world. There was no accounting for the strange behaviour of females.

Bob Southwell's evening had been very different. He had gone home straight after the debriefing at five o'clock, leaving Dave

Smart to close down the incident room and install Sandra Powell in charge for the night. Once home and fed, he rang his friend Tom Churchyard who lived next door.

'Tom? Good to hear you. We didn't get our usual night out this week.'

'You were busy, weren't you? We spoke about it, don't you remember? We said we'd leave it. Linda told me afterwards that you didn't get in until nearly midnight.'

'I feel like a drink now. Are you doing anything?'

Tom did not reply for a minute. He looked round his sitting room. The slow-combustion stove was glowing comfortably, he himself was wearing old sloppy clothes and his slippers and on his hi-fi system Beethoven's Ninth Symphony was moving through its opening section. The curtains were closed against the cold night. The last thing he felt like doing was changing and going out.

'No, I'm not doing anything special,' he said to Bob Southwell. 'Great idea. I could do with a drink and a natter. Give me five minutes to change. If you're seen with me looking like I do now everyone will think you've just run in a most suspicious character.'

'Five minutes, suspicious character,' said Bob and put down the phone.

'Oh, Daddy!' complained his daughter Susan.

'You've not been home all week at our bedtime. I was going to ask you to read me a story.'

'Tomorrow,' he said as he kissed her. 'I promise.'

'I wanted to show you the picture I did at school,' struck in his son Paul.

'Show me quickly, Paul, I'm meeting Tom in five minutes.'

'Boozing again,' remarked Linda.

She wasn't really going to oppose his going because these regular nights out with Tom from next door had been her own idea in the first place. It had been when she was so worried about Bob overstretching himself – never being off duty and relaxed. She had asked Tom then if he would help by giving Bob a bit of normal male social life. Tom had thought of playing chess once a week, but she'd vetoed that and suggested the pub. Much better. Chess involved thinking and Bob did too much of that as it was.

'Come with us,' was Bob's response.

'And what about the kids?'

'We'll be all right, Mum. I'll look after Susan.'

'I don't think I will, Bob. My hair needs washing.'

'Oh, I got the name of that hairdresser for you.'

'You didn't! I never thought you'd ask her.'

Bob passed over a slip of paper. 'Treat yourself for your birthday and we'll go out somewhere special.' he suggested. 'I'll ask Tom if he'll baby-sit.' Then, taking advantage of the furore about not being babies and not needing sitters any more, he slipped out of the house.

'How's it going, or shouldn't I ask?' said Tom when they were in their local and comfortably established at a corner table.

'You shouldn't ask is right. It isn't going. Three days' all-out round-the-clock staff-intensive work and the super walks in and says, "I want you all back in the station on Monday morning, put this on ice."'

'That's how it goes,' said Tom, who was an engineer for British Telecom. 'It's the same for us. I remember when we spent a year planning a big major investment programme and were on the point of letting the contracts, and there was a general election, a change of government, and sorry lads, scrap the investment programme, there isn't going to be any capital available. All that work down the drain. Of course, that was before we went private. I'd only just joined.'

Bob leaned back and gazed round at the other inmates of the pub. It wasn't a grand place, which was why they liked it. They felt at home and comfortable. It had been done up years before in the way pubs were at that time – panelling and delf racks in what looked like dark oak; dark oak furniture with a good bit of turning, and flowery cretonnes covering the upholstery. Brass ashtrays on the tables and pretty bits of pottery round the delf rack. Prints of hunting and racing scenes, dark maroon velvet curtains and hardly any women to be seen. One blonde creature leaned up against the bar and a couple of stolid old ladies sat in one corner, but mostly the clientele were men, playing dominoes or talking. From the next room came the thwack of darts and a louder hubbub of voices. The only food the landlady did was sandwiches, and not many kinds of those.

'Thank God I'm away from the smell of chocolate,' said Bob.

'Has it been a murder case?'

'You shouldn't ask, but yes, it is a murder case. A damned nasty murder in my opinion. But no body, Tom, no body.'

9

The next day was Saturday and in the early morning the detectives were in the middle of clearing up and closing down their incident room at Benn's factory when Hannah Benn walked in at the door.

'Mr Southwell,' she said, 'I think you ought to see this immediately.' She held a letter out to him. 'It arrived this morning. I don't know if it has fingerprints on it. Unfortunately Mother and I both handled it before we thought about those.'

Bob took it carefully and opened it. In appearance it was commonplace; the kind of paper and envelope which is sold in most post offices and general stationers throughout the country. At once he saw the reason for Hannah's concern. It was a ransom note, demanding that a certain sum of money in used bank notes be left in a certain litter bin at a certain time. He drew in an immense, deep breath.

'At last,' he said. 'A breakthrough. I can't understand why they've been so long.'

'You thought he'd been kidnapped?'

'I thought he'd been murdered, but no body has been found and they aren't the easiest of things to hide. Among the other alternatives kidnapping seemed the most likely. He could have been taken out of the factory on the Thursday night or early on the Friday morning, in a van or artic.'

'Wouldn't the security man have known about any such van? He opens the yard gates when there is an out-of-hours collection or delivery.'

'That's one of the problems in sorting this thing out. Your man Stan was on duty – he seems to have been on night and day over the first days of the New Year – and he says there was nothing scheduled for that evening but the record sheet does show a collection.'

'Stan and Bert were having to cover as best they could while two of their colleagues were off sick.' Hannah looked worried as she explained. 'Harry only had flu but George is likely to be off for weeks; I'll have to get someone else on the rota. Probably we ought to have a larger security staff anyway.'

'I would advise it,' said Bob drily. 'Meanwhile the damage is done.'

'What action are we to take?'

'It is possible that you may have to pay this. The whole of the police force will be mobilized if necessary now we have something to go on but a bait might be needed. We would keep surveillance and follow the person who collects it, hoping to apprehend the whole gang and rescue Fontaine. If we succeed in that then you would almost certainly get the money back. If we fail . . . then they should release Fontaine and he may give us information which would lead us to them. How did you get this? You wouldn't normally be in at work today and the demand is for the money this afternoon – that's very short notice.'

'It was delivered by hand at home,' she replied. 'Presumably early, before the normal postal delivery. Our gardener cum handyman picked it up with the other post and put everything on the hall table as usual. It looks like a perfectly normal letter from outside and he didn't notice anything different, though of course there's no stamp or postmark.'

'Did he see anyone come to the house?'

'No, he says not.'

'We'll send someone out to question him.'

'It's awful, isn't it?' said Hannah. 'We feel as if we're living in a bad dream. These sort of things don't happen in real life.'

'Unfortunately life sometimes imitates art.' Bob was looking at her kindly. He had managed to conquer that first instant attraction but Hannah remained to him one of the most desirable women he knew.

'Well, I feel as if I was living in a cross between a detective novel and a thriller, if you can call those art,' sighed Hannah, 'and I don't like it one little bit. The excitements of normal business life are enough for me. Will you stay on here now this has happened?'

'I don't think so. We can work just as well from the station on a kidnapping case. We have a room there we can use for the files and computers, kept for that kind of purpose. We'll stay in close touch, don't worry.' After a moment's hesitation, he added, 'It might be as well not to ring us from here.'

'What do you mean?'

'Only that we will have to suspect everyone of involvement until it is proved otherwise and switchboards are dicey things for security.'

'In Benn's I think that's nonsense.' Hannah sounded indignant but she agreed to ring from other places, like home.

When Hannah had gone Bob had time to look at the letter objectively. He called the others round the desk, and, stopping whatever they were doing, they crowded up, looking over one another's shoulders, agog to view the first ransom demand note most of them had ever seen. Bob read out the message for those who could only see it wrong way up.

'A bit chancy, isn't it, leaving things in litter bins?' remarked Dave Smart. 'You would have thought there were better pick-up points.'

'Does anything strike you about this note, Dave?'

Dave pondered. 'Not very professional,' he said at last.

'Ye-e-es.'

'Come on,' Bob said after a pause. 'This has got to go to Wetherby in the hope that forensic science can enlighten us in some way. Copy the message, will you, Jenny, and have a few run off, we'll need them. Back to work, everybody. The sooner we're in the station the better. I have the feeling that the super will want to take this case over as soon as he hears about this note.'

'He hasn't been so active lately, though, has he, boss? Not since his heart attack.'

'You wouldn't be active either if you'd had what he had.'

'I did hear that he's going to retire.'

'Everyone knows Joe is going to retire,' Bob said. 'He might have left on health grounds before now if he hadn't been so near retirement age anyway. It made sense to stay on if he could for the last little bit.'

'Then we'll get a new super,' remarked Dave. The remark hung in the air unanswered. Bob Southwell only pressed his lips together and didn't say anything. Getting a new detective superintendent was a tricky thing. Who would be applying, who would be chosen, what changes they would introduce, what the feel, the whole conduct of the department would be like under someone else . . . It would be enough to keep the office and canteen gossip fuelled for weeks. Of course Bob knew what they were all dying to ask him, 'Will you be applying, boss?' and that wasn't a question he was prepared to answer at the moment.

'Come on,' he said again. 'We're investigating a crime, remember? Kidnapping is a serious crime and the hostage might well die if we handle it badly. Such things have been known. Get moving. All I said was that Superintendent Birch might want to take over. Does it have to start you off speculating like a lot of old women?'

Hannah Benn was very grateful to Bob Southwell and his team for the help and support they gave her during what became an extremely fraught Saturday.

Fortunately Faith took charge of the loving task which Hannah usually performed – the task of packing Matthew's things and making sure that he had everything he needed, and resisting his demands to take everything he thought he wanted. As an occupation it was bitter-sweet and in one way Hannah was glad to be spared it, but in another way it was precious to her. She liked to satisfy herself about everything appertaining to Matthew and those hours in his bedroom packing his school trunk, with the slightly squabbling intimacy between them, seemed the only way she had of ensuring that some of her mother-love went with him to protect him during the weeks away.

As her mother was doing Matthew's packing, Hannah was able with a free mind to co-operate with the police. It was not easy to obtain a large amount of money in cash at short notice at a weekend but at last they had managed it, and packed it in the manner specified.

Strangely enough the kidnappers had not demanded that there should be no police involvement, which Hannah had assumed, from what she had read from time to time about such cases, would be a standard requirement.

'They must know we're already involved,' Bob Southwell said to her. 'So there was no point in asking that.'

'They still could have done.' She looked puzzled.

'Yes. But don't forget we were actually on your premises when the demand was delivered.'

'They could still have said that if you were involved they would kill him.'

'They might be very over-confident, believing that they have the whip hand and that nothing we can do will catch them. Don't forget, they say that if they are intercepted when making the collection or followed afterwards he will suffer for it.'

'You are sure you'll get them?' Hannah felt very nervous and almost trembly at that moment. She had enough nerve for anything in her normal life but this contact with crime was different. She could not help picturing Pierre tied up and ill-treated.

'We can't be sure we'll get them, only that we'll do our best.'

In the dusk, at four o'clock that afternoon, Lena Lindgren was walking along Stonegate. Some of the brightly illuminated shop windows were still full of festive offerings but most of the shops were well into their January sales. Other windows were dark, where hopeful traders had been knocked out of business by the sixfold increases in their overheads due to the Uniform Business Rate.

Lena dawdled, looking into first one and then another window. Her mass of blonde hair was down, flowing free in the winter air.

A tall man overtook her lingering steps and tapped her on the shoulder.

'Max!' she cried out softly. 'You startled me.'

'We must talk.'

'I am here.'

'Where shall we go?'

Without further discussion Lena led the way to Coffee Yard which opened off Stonegate a few yards further on. At the entrance a notice advertised Thomas Gent's Coffee House. They walked along Coffee Yard to a door on the left and stepped inside, into another century – the rather bare room was straight out of an engraving of a Georgian coffee house. The floor was sanded and the furnishings were sparse; several wigs and three-cornered hats hung on pegs and a notice asked them to leave their swords with Reception. Fat white candles, the only illumination, burned on each of the tables. The serving-girls were in period dress. The only jarring note was the modern appearance of the customers.

Max looked round. All the tables were for six or eight people. 'This is not suitable,' he said.

'We will go down the stairs.'

Below, in the cellar, it was very dark. Windowless, it was lit only by the individual candles, but the tables were small and intimate and there were no other customers. They settled themselves in a corner, both facing the door so that they had instant warning

117

of anyone's approach. A serving-girl came in, swishing her long skirts, her face modest under a white lawn cap, playing her role. They ordered tea and Lena chose a cake called a 'wig', with an apricot in the middle, while Max had parkin, which he was assured was a traditional Yorkshire dish.

When the serving-girl had brought their order and departed again, they could talk. Their common language was English, so that was what they had been using, and went on using.

'It was not wise of you to tap me on the shoulder in public like that,' said Lena.

'Nobody noticed,' he said.

'Please. If I am to be any use to you in this project I must not be known to be in any way connected.'

'I know that. All right, it was a mistake. There is no harm done. Please do not go on about it. We may not have much time.'

She was silent.

'We are pleased so far,' he said, 'but what has happened to Pierre Fontaine?'

'I do not know. The English police have been trying to find him. They have given up and are going away.'

'He was approached, you know,' Max Brandt said thoughtfully. 'Approached by . . .' and he named one of the biggest names in the international chocolate industry. 'He refused to sell them the recipe. I think they have a contract out on him. They are determined that if they do not get it no one else will.'

'Surely they would not behave like that? That is Mafia talk.'

'I heard on good authority that at one of their board meetings they were discussing how to get rid of him if he did not agree to their offer.'

'I wonder why he did not agree? There would have been more money in it for him than by selling to Benn's.'

'Because he is a maverick, did you not know that? He likes working alone, he likes making his own decisions, he likes Benn's. Why do you think we are so keen to take them over? His best work has been done for them.'

'And there is the Single Market to think about.'

'Of course.'

'I can see why you want Benn's. It will fit in well with your other operations.'

'That is right. What about the recipe? That is part of the attraction of the deal at the moment.'

'They have brought in analysts to recover it. It does not seem to have been written down.'

'I see.'

'When it has been worked out again and is there on paper I will be able to get it for you.'

'If they agree to a take-over drastic action will not be necessary,' said Max thoughtfully.

'Theft, you mean.'

'Unlawful obtainment. No, it would not then be necessary. I am seeing Hannah Benn tonight, taking her out to dinner.'

'The soft approach?'

'If she will play ball.'

Lena fiddled thoughtfully with her cup and plate, cutting small pieces off her cake and eating them.

'What do you think?' said Max, tired of waiting for her comments.

'I was thinking about . . .' She in turn named the world-dominating company who had apparently been prepared to take Pierre Fontaine's life if they could not get his recipe. 'I did not realize they were quite so unscrupulous.'

'Oh yes they are. Where money is concerned, Lena, there are no scruples.'

'I know that. I am willing to take risks. But murder! And murder for a recipe.'

Max shrugged his shoulders. 'It has been done before, I think you will find. Murder is often done for very little. A few pounds, a moment's anger, a slight jealousy. How much more likely for a successful money-making idea. You will remember the leader of the peasant people of the tropical rain forest who did not wish their trees to be cut down and replaced by cattle ranches for hamburgers.'

'That was different,' said Lena with conviction.

'The man stabbed with a poisoned umbrella on a bridge in London.'

'That was politics.'

'The head of an Italian bank who was found hanging under a London bridge by his neck.'

'That was finance.'

'One Mr Bull who invented a super-gun.'

'That was the Middle East.'

'And this is only industrial espionage? Can you separate these things?'

They did not talk much more. Max consumed his parkin hastily and left. Lena sat on for a quarter of an hour, exactly timed by her watch, before leaving herself.

The plans the police team laid during that Saturday and the actions they took to catch the kidnappers were not successful.

The drop in a litter bin in a busy pedestrianized street seemed almost childish in its obviousness and it was hard to believe that anything could go wrong with the police surveillance. A man was stationed in a window above a shop opposite to the bin and several more were in the street loitering about, when the drop was to be made.

York was crowded that afternoon with shoppers from all over the county visiting for the sales, which were in full swing in all the large shops and most of the small ones. January used in the old days in York to be a quiet month, like all the winter months, a time when the eternal city could be itself and not on show, a time when it could put its feet up and the population could enjoy the old feeling of being little more than a village, where people knew each other and knew that their grandparents had known each other, and you could be sure of meeting certain groups of folk foregathering at set times in accustomed places.

Those times had, most decisively, gone.

Now even in such months as October the Minster would be as crowded as if it were a market, so that you could hardly move in the throng and to pray peacefully there you had to go into the Zouche chapel. Now it was only in the few days between Christmas and New Year that you could count on any of the old quietness at all. By this Saturday the occupying army was back in force and the streets were bright with the visitors, the new lifeblood of the city.

In the early winter darkness of this January day the crowds were still there when the weather changed and turned nasty. Everyone decided at the same time that they ought to go home, and a mass exodus of tourists, day visitors and the York people themselves began, snarling up the place generally.

The figure which picked up the money escaped the pursuers in the buzz of traffic and the bitter fine sleet which was now slicing down on to the city. The freezing sleet, half snow, half rain-wrapped ice, made the pavements like skating rinks underfoot and blew into the eyes of the pursuers. The figure in close fitting black leather and black Kiwi motor-cycle helmet slid down one of the alleyways, into a yard, over several walls and through several more yards as well as over a few low roofs of outbuildings, discarded the helmet, put on a light anorak from the shopping basket of a bicycle which was waiting there, put the parcel of money in the shopping basket in place of the anorak, jumped on to the saddle, merged with the traffic and eluded them.

As soon as it was obvious what had happened Bob Southwell went round to Oaklands, the Benn house. He arrived just as Hannah was giving Matthew his tea in the breakfast room. Faith was there too, sitting in a low chair by the Cornish slate fireplace with its bolection moulding and its merry little fire burning at hearth level. She was sipping her evening sherry and talking to her daughter and grandson.

Matthew had nearly finished, so Bob waited until Hannah had taken him upstairs and put him in the bath with instructions not to splash too much.

Then Bob went through an unpleasant quarter of an hour, admitting that the kidnapper had got away with the money.

'I don't see that you need blame yourselves,' Faith said at last. 'We all know what York is like. Anywhere within the walls to someone who really knows the place would offer many opportunities to elude you. It would be exactly like trying to catch Brer Rabbit. You remember how he said, "Do anything to me, Brer Fox, but *please* don't throw me into that briar patch," and then after Brer Fox had thrown him in, he cried out that he had been "Born and bred in a briar patch, Brer Fox!" I'm sure your kidnapper must be a York man, born and bred in this briar patch.'

'What happens now?' asked Hannah.

'Presumably they release Pierre Fontaine. We must pin our hopes on that.'

'You did promise us that none of this would get into the papers?'

'The press have agreed to an embargo on this for the moment.'

Hannah sighed and went over to the square bay window, parted the curtains a little and looked out. It was a favourite action of hers.

Now the colder air, which had been trapped behind the velvet curtains, and the blackness of the night, together allowing her only an impression of the garden she loved so well, calmed her and brought her teeming emotions a little back towards normality.

'I'm going out later,' she said. 'You will keep us in touch with events? I don't feel I can cancel. Mother will be here if you ring, or if Pierre is brought here. We can tell Mr Goodwin to patrol the grounds in case he is dumped, tied up, or something like that. One hears of such things.'

'We are on full alert. The whole of the force is on the look-out for Monsieur Fontaine and his kidnappers.'

'Well, I hope you're exaggerating,' Faith put in with a touch of humour. 'There must be all kinds of other law-breaking going on.'

'Of course, to that extent.' Bob smiled back at her. 'Everyone on duty is going about their normal tasks but bearing Monsieur Fontaine in mind, and in addition a good many personnel are working overtime purely on this case.'

Bob left the Benn family worried but calm. There was nothing whatever they could do at this point to help him.

That evening two women from Benn's factory were preparing themselves for a night out.

Hannah Benn was dressing in a simple timeless dress of dark jersey which fell in sculptured lines to mid-calf, ornamenting it with a pendant on a gold chain, which her father had given her for her twenty-first birthday. It had been designed and made by a famous craftsman in gold and precious stones and was the only one of its pattern in the world. She touched her eyelids lightly with gleaming gold shadow and her lips with soft red flecked with gold and put on her evening sandals with the gilt straps. She touched her neck and ears and wrists with a perfume which cost a king's ransom per ounce.

'Goodnight, darling,' she said to Matthew and pressed her cheek to his. He was too sleepy to reply. 'Goodnight, Mother, don't wait up,' she said to Faith.

'Mind, no concessions,' said Faith. 'Not of any kind,' she added, her eyes sweeping over her daughter.

'No concessions,' said Hannah, wondering to what extent she would be able to stick to that resolve.

Polly the tea-lady was also going out – with Bri, the long-distance lorry driver, and their friends Len and Betty. She had bathed and washed her hair and spoken sharply to Kev, the maintenance man, when he rang her, slamming down the phone. She tried to shake her mind free of him as she brushed her shining hair and sprayed scent over her body. She and Bri were going to one of the pubs by the river and it was a cold night, although the sleet had long since stopped. She looked in her wardrobe and chose what she had known she would wear anyway, clean dark trousers and an informal top, dark and loose and sparkly with some kind of lurex thread in the fabric. It fell in soft folds round her neck almost like a cowl collar and the armholes were deep. She added elaborate long ear-rings and white openwork sandals with high heels. On top she wore her sheepskin jacket and spent time skewering on to the lapel the brooch Bri had given her with the thistle and two leaves.

She looked round her little home before leaving it. Upstairs there was the bedroom and bathroom and downstairs there was the living-room and the kitchen. There was a little yard at the back and nothing at all at the front because it was one of the houses at the end of a terrace just off Hull Road, and its front door opened directly on to the pavement. The whole tiny dwelling had only cost a third of the price of the pendant which Hannah Benn was wearing round her neck.

A car horn sounded outside.

Bri sat waiting for her. When after locking the house she ran over and tapped on the window he remembered the car door was locked and leaned over to open it. She wondered as she climbed into the car whether to mention that it would have been considerate to have the door already open, but she knew what Bri would say – 'You're always whingeing on.' She didn't think she was always whingeing. With a spasm of longing she remembered the way Kev had held the door of his new car open for her and made sure that she was ensconced and comfortable before closing it and going round to his own side. Then she remembered Kev's little bundle of newspaper cuttings, and she turned to Bri with a kiss.

They went to a pub on the river bank and met their friends. In the ladies' powder room Betty said, 'I'm glad you're seeing sense, Polly,' but Polly only replied with a smile. They went back into the pub to join the others and formed a group at one end of the bar. It was all pleasantly noisy without any air of aggression, there were no yobs or self-styled hard men among the customers. A group of Benn's assembly line girls came in, joined them for half an hour, and went out again. A couple of electricians from another firm who had been at school with Bri came in and had a gossip before progressing to the next pub on their planned route.

At last Len suggested eating and they moved to a table in another part of the pub for chicken in a basket.

They broke up at a respectable hour and Bri took Polly home and they went to bed. She clung to him and kissed him with unusual fervour as they made love, and was sorry when he got up in the small hours and set off back home to his parents' house.

That left her to her thoughts, and Polly did not want to think.

Hannah Benn knew that she would have to spend her evening acting a part. She could not forget Pierre Fontaine's situation for an instant, she could not forget that, while she was socializing with Max Brandt, Pierre might be recovered from his kidnappers. But, she reasoned with herself, what alternative had she to going out and acting as though nothing untoward was happening? Certainly the last thing she wanted was for Max to get wind of it all. She had had a long discussion with her mother and they had agreed. The evening was to take place as planned and Faith would hold the fort at Oaklands.

Max had called for Hannah Benn at eight o'clock, and she insisted that he came in and had a few words with her mother.

'We will be meeting on Monday,' he had said to Faith, with a courteous bow over her hand as he touched it with his lips. 'Business discussions. We can be even more helpful to one another. I have various plans to put before you.'

Brandt's were already acting for Benn's as distributors of Benn's Bars in their own country, and old Matthew Benn had become an agent for Brandt's main product, in the UK. The partnership, if a working arrangement could be called that, was mutually beneficial.

But Brandt's were a much bigger concern than Benn's and were aggressively expanding their share of the world market. Faith felt a chill of fear as she watched Max go off with her daughter. She hoped that Hannah was not going to be placed in a vulnerable emotional position. Not for the first time, she wondered; who was the father of her grandchild Matthew? Matthew was fair and was going to be tall and there was no doubt that Max Brandt was tall and fair. It was a matter which Hannah had kept secret and her parents had respected that, but Faith knew that her husband Matthew had also suspected Max. Hannah and Max had both been at the same international confectionery conference in Pasadena when Matthew had been conceived, that much they knew.

Max was taking Hannah to dine at Murtwick Hall. He paid off the taxi and joined her in the warmth of the entrance.

'You should have been here a week ago, Max,' she said to him. 'I came with a few friends at Christmas time and there was a most magnificent Christmas tree, it stretched up the stairwell here. I don't know how they manoeuvred such a colossus inside and into position. It was really delightful.'

'I wish I could have seen it with you,' he said with a warm glance as he took her wrap and handed it to a waiter.

'Drinks before dinner, sir?' asked the man.

Even without the Christmas tree the building was exceedingly pleasant. There was period furniture which looked as if it had always been in place and big log fires. They could have been dining with friends; the illusion was there, if it had not been for the necessary serving staff and the fact that they were a party of two. They sat in one of the rooms, sipped their drinks, and studied the menu.

Hannah was acutely conscious of Max. Since her father died her life had been so devoted to the firm and to her mother and her son that an evening out on her own was very rare, and an evening out alone with a handsome man even rarer. Before Matthew was born it had been very different. Then various eligible men of her own status had constantly asked her out and she had been wined and dined all over England, Scotland and Wales, frequently a guest at house parties and one of the crowd on skiing holidays. She had jetted all over the world as representative of Benn's, makers of fine and exclusive chocolates.

She reflected how different her life had become, by her own conscious choice. Her own choice not to marry, her own choice to have a child, her own choice of the father. She thought of him now, briefly, and wished he were opposite her instead of Max Brandt.

Max was difficult for her to deal with. She had become used to command; he took charge. She had sublimated her sex urge; Max breathed out powerful male sexuality in every movement. When he stood close to her and she realized how much he towered above her and caught the vibrations of him and the faint scent of him she trembled. As a physical animal he was one of the most attractive she had ever known and although they had met fairly frequently over the years she had been part of Benn's, they had not seen one another during the twelve months since her father's death. During that year her thoughts had been channelled exclusively to keeping the firm on its successful course. Now she could not help it if her emotions leaped from their prison and took charge of her, turning her bones to water when Max touched her, softening her mouth until it looked like a flower and expanding the pupils of her eyes into dark pools without her knowledge. It was simple sexuality unmixed with love; she did not like Max Brandt. Hannah looked ahead to the social evening before them to be quickly followed by a day of negotiations over the renewal of their firms' trading contracts, and shuddered. How was she going to manage?

'Are you cold?' asked Max solicitously.

'A goose walked over my grave, that's all,' Hannah said, and went on to choose what she would like to eat from the enticing menu.

Max looked at her through narrowed eyes. He knew his effect on women and he knew what effect he intended to have on Hannah. This was business and in business there are no scruples.

10

On Sunday Max Brandt had friends in the North Riding to visit, for which Hannah and Faith were grateful as otherwise they would have felt obliged to offer him hospitality at Oaklands. They had enough to occupy them without him. Every hour seemed like a week as they waited for news of Pierre Fontaine.

Hannah had to drive Matthew back to his boarding school for the start of term, and in addition she had to liaise with the police. Fortunately she had been able to avoid the subject of Pierre when she was out with Max, and as far as she was aware the disappearance was still a complete secret except in the factory, where everybody knew by now, particularly after that search by a hundred policemen; and the police force knew too, of course. The ransom demand was a deeper secret; only a few members of the police force knew of that.

On Monday Max arrived at Benn's factory for the formal talks with the main trustees, Faith and Hannah. Max intended to aim at global marketing. Hannah could not help it; she was excited by the spread of his plans. Faith looked increasingly worried as the day went by. He politely refused their invitation to lunch in the canteen and whisked them both off to an expensive restaurant. When during the early afternoon Lena was in the office with them, no one would have guessed that he had ever seen the girl before.

He left at a quarter to three with their promises of future co-operation, but the details remained to be worked out.

'He didn't say anything about an offer to buy us up or take us over,' Faith said thoughtfully.

'Because I told him it would be no use.'

Today Hannah had dark circles under her eyes and Faith had noted them without asking for an explanation. Had she asked, Hannah was ready with an answer. Matthew had gone back to school and she hated parting with him; any mother had a right to circles under the eyes when her only child has begun a new term at boarding school.

'Did he mention it while you were out on Saturday, then?'

'Yes. I told him there was no possibility of us selling out to anyone. Of course I put it tactfully and said if ever such an eventuality should arise, he would have first refusal.'

'I didn't like the whole atmosphere he brought with him,' Faith remarked. 'Of course he is a delightful man. But big business – business on a global scale, words which he used so often – we are not equipped for that, Hannah. Not ruthless enough, not single-minded enough. Nor do I want to be, personally.'

'I found him unsettling, too. You aren't alone in that. The association has been good for us, though, tradewise.'

'Yes, I agree, as far as the Benn's Bars go, but we do as much for Brandt's in return.'

The normal work of Monday for the two directors had not even begun; their post was still lying unopened.

It was Faith, this time, who opened the letter from the kidnappers . . .

'I'm taking you home, Mother.'

'Don't be silly, dear, I am quite all right.'

'You don't look all right. It will only take me five minutes to run you home.'

'I'm all right, I tell you!' Faith sat up straight and patted her hair.

'I'll have to take that to DCI Southwell. Lena, have you a plastic folder or envelope? Thank you.'

'Are you going now?'

'No, I'm not leaving you. This will wait.'

Hannah put the letter in its folder under her slim leather handbag on the desk. She did wonder whether to ring the police station and have someone come to collect it, but Bob Southwell had asked her not to ring from Benn's. She would take her mother home and ring from there.

Ann came in; there was a journalist in Reception asking to see a spokesman for the firm. Who did they wish to deal with him?

'A journalist?' Faith sounded worried. 'What does he want? What is it about?'

'I'll go and find out, Mrs Faith,' and Ann disappeared again.

No one said anything while she was gone.

'He says there is a rumour in York that we are going to be taken over by Brandt's,' she announced when she came back, 'and he would like to know if it is true or not.'

'However do these rumours get about!' exclaimed Faith.

'We'd better see him ourselves,' said Hannah. 'In the seminar room, Ann.' It meant a delay in getting to the police station but it couldn't be helped.

Faith was positively shaking, Hannah saw with concern as they went through into the other room. The journalist did not notice their agitation. He saw only two self-possessed and very important women, waiting impassively for his questions.

'No, there is no question of a take-over,' Hannah said. 'We are a very happy and forward-moving firm and although we co-operate with Brandt's to a limited extent in marketing, that is as far as the arrangement extends.'

'If you want to know more about us,' Faith put in, 'you are welcome to move among the work-force and ask them whether or not we are a happy and caring organization. You can ask them anything you like. Benn's have nothing to hide. I suggest that you meet them in the canteen; if you go round to the outside door into it you will not need to put on an overall and hat. There will be some people there now having their afternoon break. I'm afraid we are too busy at present to allow you to tour the factory, but you will find out all you want to from the staff, I am quite sure.'

The journalist looked surprised at this *carte blanche*, but not more surprised than Hannah felt. When they were alone again she asked her mother, 'Was that wise?'

'We stand or fall by our people,' Faith said. 'We have stood by them in their problems and times of trouble and treated them like our own family. If they cannot stand by us now, they are not what I thought them.'

As expected, the journalist reappeared in about a quarter of an hour. He looked faintly dazed.

'What did you ask them?' enquired the curious Hannah.

'If they wanted to be taken over, if they thought it would be better for them – better working conditions, prospects of advancement and so on.'

'And?'

'You have a very loyal work-force, Mrs Benn. They were very indignant at the idea, and said they knew you wouldn't sell.'

'Nor would we.' Faith lifted her head proudly.

'They were very happy working here, they said. As a matter of fact there is a happy atmosphere, I can sense it myself.'

When the journalist had gone Hannah insisted on taking Faith home at once, and Faith had to admit that she was developing one of her rare headaches. There was more to it, of course, Hannah was sure, but home and bed seemed the best immediate remedy.

Once at home Hannah was dismayed to see her mother crumple into an armchair and burst into tears. She had only seen her cry a few times in her life, and could not understand it now. She paced about the sitting-room for a minute, then went to her mother's chair and knelt on one knee on the floor beside her.

'What's the matter?' she said gently. 'What's all this about?'

'Oh, Hannah . . .' Her mother could hardly speak for sobs. 'Everything's going wrong. Everything. I never thought when your father died that within a year we'd come to such a pass as this.'

'What's worrying you most?'

'Everything. Pierre disappearing. These horrible ransom demands. The last two days when we've been expecting him back. The police established in the building and asking all sorts of questions. Journalists wanting to know if we're going to be taken over.

Max Brandt trying to pull us into his organization. You and Pierre wanting a new countline and all the expense and worry. I can't take it any more. There isn't any pleasure in running the firm with all this to contend with.'

Hannah sat silently for a while with her hand on her mother's arm. There seemed to be little she could say, because everything Faith had said was true. All these things had happened or were happening. Suddenly, as if Faith's misery had been transmitted through their touch, she too felt low and depressed. Her contact with Max and having to fend off his advances when her body was screaming for loving congress with a human male had left her shaken and vulnerable and wondering whether, as St Paul said, it was better to marry than to burn. The last thing she wanted was an unrelated male in their Benn dynasty, threatening Matthew's pre-eminence, but . . . was it good for him to have no father figure? Was it good for herself to have no mate? The dangers surrounding their little ship of state seemed as huge and forbidding as the rocks and whirlpool of Scylla and Charybdis had seemed to Odysseus, and her self-confidence deserted her. She bent her head towards her mother and tears came to her eyes too.

It was a while before either of them recovered a little. Then Hannah took her mother upstairs and ventured to treat her like a child, helping her to undress, bringing her a drink of hot milk fortified with a drop of brandy, and at last even tucking her up under the fleecy pure wool blankets and the billowy old-fashioned eiderdown. With a last light kiss on the cheek and the gentle words 'Rest now,' Hannah left her and went to warn Mrs Goodwin not to disturb her mother, and not to bother with the usual evening meal but to cook something light when required. Then she went to the police station.

'Another ransom letter,' Hannah was saying to Bob Southwell, passing him the plastic folder. 'It upset my mother a great deal when we opened it this afternoon. That is why I wasn't in touch with you then. I came as soon as I could.'

'Let me see now . . .' Bob took the letter out and unfolded it with great care. He gazed at it thoughtfully.

'We can't go on like this.' Bob could not miss the note of strain in Hannah's voice. 'It isn't only the money, though obviously no business can carry unproductive expenditure of this kind. It is the worry of it. We can't stop thinking about it, night or day, wondering what dreadful kind of conditions Pierre has had to endure, wondering if he will really be given back to us when they have got as much money as they can squeeze out of us.'

Bob Southwell had already told Hannah that the superintendent was officially in charge of the case, but as DS Birch was out just then she had been shown up to Bob's office.

'Surely they'll release Pierre now?' Hannah cried out. 'I thought when they'd got the money he'd be free and it would all be over . . .'

'In the first letter the kidnappers wanted money left, now they're demanding more,' Bob said. 'Then they promise, again, to release him.'

'I don't like it. We might find Pierre dead or dreadfully hurt.'

'We've got all the normal procedures in motion,' Bob said. 'At present we can only do that. You have been a long time bringing this letter, Miss Benn, if it arrived at your factory this morning.'

'It was only opened an hour and a half ago,' she said indignantly, and explained the events which had caused the various delays.

'I suppose it can't be helped.'

'You cannot imagine what a strain the last days have been, ever since the first letter on Saturday. We've been expecting to hear something every hour about Pierre, either from you or from him turning up. I feel devastated and it is much worse for my poor mother.'

'Of course. At least the kidnappers aren't in such a rush this time. They want this for Wednesday. Why the delay, I wonder? Today's Monday, although we've been on duty continuously more or less since Saturday morning and all days of the week begin to seem alike after a few days of that. In the next twenty-four hours we may catch them. I think we must now put out missing person messages on the local radio and ask people to search all their sheds and outhouses, or report anything suspicious that they've noticed in neighbouring houses or garages.'

'Whatever you think best.'

'I'm afraid the media will want all details. We won't be able to withhold his name. It will be the end of privacy.'

'That can't be helped. I'll go now.' Hannah rose.

'Back home?'

'No, Mr Southwell! I have a factory to run.'

* * *

131

It was already very late, past five o'clock, by the time Hannah was back in her office. With her mother's work to do as well as her own, she knew that she would be kept busy until late in the evening. She let Ann and Lena go at their usual time and stayed on alone. When she had almost finished what needed most to be done she remembered that she had left some progress reports she wanted to check in the Works Manager's office and she went along for them, turning lights on and off as she made the journey.

As she returned, she switched off the corridor light before reaching her own door and stood for a moment feeling the same eerie sensation which had visited Bob Southwell in the darkened building. She remembered how she had thought of the factory in the early morning of 2 January as a great beast, emitting those soft clouds of vaporous air. Now, inside the creature, she knew the heartbeat of the Bar production line was quietly functioning on the other side of the building as the rest lay in darkness, only the moonlight from the slenderest imaginable moon and the paleness of the remaining snow and the dim shining of the stars bringing light into the rooms and workshops.

Moved by she knew not what, she walked along the corridor past her own office. She was still clutching the progress reports as she walked towards the nearest lighted area, where human life promised contact with something other than her own thoughts. The night security man would be on duty.

As she came within sight of the light from his post she heard voices. She drew closer, then stopped; there was an argument going on. Both voices were male, and she recognized one as belonging to Stan the watchman. The other voice was high and light; a tenor of the upper register, but without volume enough to make a singer. It was a country voice with a soft accent which was an intonation more than a dialect and was hard to place. Hannah listened to it with pleasure and wondered who it was. A picture formed in her mind of a small man, slight, used to working on the land, middle-aged; there was the courtesy, the correctness, which she had come across in such people. Whoever it was was complaining bitterly about something. The country-voiced man had come to collect something on a certain night, by arrangement, and TC1 should have been open and somebody there to help him load up. It had all been arranged and TC1 had been dark and apparently deserted when he had rolled up to make the collection.

The night security man explained that it had nothing to do with him. The complainant had better grumble at those responsible, not at him.

Hannah felt at this point that she ought to intervene. This gentleman, whoever he was, was entitled to make his arranged collections.

At this point he said something which stopped her in her tracks.

'I didn't want to get anyone into trouble,' he said. 'That's why I told the police that I'd made the collection and everything was normal. You don't get me letting my mates down. But the coppers were on to me after that, suspecting me of all sorts. I'm not having it, I tell you, Stan. I was collecting that night to make an early start in the morning and avoid the worst of the traffic. Instead I had to come in at half-past seven, by which time, you will agree with me, Stan, I should have been over Shap. Winter weather you need to be on your toes and I like to miss the traffic if I can.'

Hannah walked forward into the doorway of the room and stood still in surprise. The small middle-aged country voice was coming from one of the biggest young men she had ever known. He was a mountain of a man. His fine dark hair was receding a little and he was perhaps about thirty; an enormous black moustache drooped and curved over his mouth. He wore a white T-shirt with nothing over it or under it although it was the depth of winter. The T-shirt was stretched to the utmost over a vast beer belly, a beer belly of monumental proportions under which the blue jeans struggled to meet up with the T-shirt. A battered jacket was slung over one shoulder. Hannah recognized him at once. How was it that she had never heard him speak before, never noticed that polite countryman's voice?

'When was this collection you couldn't make, Len?' she asked.

Len and the watchman both shot round and stared at her in amazement, and Len swallowed. His voice went higher and squeaky, but he could not refuse to answer.

'It was 4 January,' he said.

'And what has Stan to do with it?'

'The watchman knows about out-of-hours deliveries and collections, you know, miss.'

'You knew nothing about it, Stan?'

'No one said a word to me.'

133

'How was it Len couldn't contact you? You were here, I remember.'

'I must have been on my rounds, miss.'

'So what did you do, Len, when you couldn't get in?'

'Went home and came again next morning at half-past seven.'

'Why didn't you complain to Stan then about it?'

'We were working funny shifts over Christmas and New Year, Miss Hannah, because of Harry and George being off ill and me and Bert doing it all between us.'

'So you had gone off . . .'

'And Bert was here.'

'Why haven't you brought the matter up before, Len?'

'It's the first time I've got Stan on his own without everyone about, like, Miss Hannah.'

'So you were having a quiet word. But you have lied to the police, Len.'

'Couldn't let my mates down, miss.'

She looked at her watch. She knew that unless an emergency arose, the detectives tended to work normal day hours and by now they might have gone home, but the kidnap threat had created an emergency and they might still be there.

'I have to see Detective Chief Inspector Southwell. You had better come with me, Len. Pass me your phone, Stan.'

She dialled the police station and asked to see DCI Southwell on a matter of urgency.

'Not a word, either of you,' she cautioned. 'Not to anyone, do you hear? Not a word to wives or girlfriends or mates. If either of you breathes a word to anyone I'll have your guts for garters.'

'Yes, Hannah,' they said.

Bob Southwell looked at the big slob sitting opposite and could have hit him.

'You've wasted police time, you know,' he said fiercely. 'You've obstructed the police in the course of their duty. You've acted like a bloody fool.'

Len looked apologetic and woebegone, and mumbled something about not letting down his mates.

'At the best,' Bob went on, 'it was a clerical error – your collection not arranged for some reason. Apart from blame for carelessness, that would not rebound on anyone, certainly not any of your particular friends. Why the hell couldn't you have told us? At the worst . . .' He paused. 'At the worst, something was happening to Pierre Fontaine inside that factory which should not have been happening and if you had said something we might have got on to it straight away instead of wasting days, days!'

Len looked as if for two pins he would cry, and he gazed reproachfully at his great fists which were resting aimlessly on his knees.

'What could I do?' he said.

'If you couldn't find the security man, and everything was locked up instead of being ready for you with someone to assist in loading, you could have told the police or contacted Miss Benn at home.'

'I would have got Stan into trouble, I thought,' replied Len, 'and it didn't seem as if it was a job for the police or worth troubling Miss Hannah about.'

'What happened at New Year when that Turkish artic arrived?' Bob still sounded heated. 'There were both traffic police out in force and Miss Benn fetched out as well, weren't there? Or hadn't you heard about that incident?'

'I saw it, as I was on my way to the pub.'

'So why did you do nothing?'

'Well, it wasn't quite the same, was it?' Len was at last roused in his own defence. 'It was a nuisance to me but it didn't really involve anyone else. I could turn round and go home again and collect in the morning, but that foreign chap was stranded.'

'Why did you wait until last night to grumble to Stan about it?'

'I hadn't seen him, and I would have forgotten about it, only I'm making another evening collection tomorrow and I wanted to be sure it didn't happen again, so, as I was not far away, I thought, I'll call in and have it out with Stan. I'd already had a go at the dispatch blokes.'

'And what had they to say?'

Len shrugged. 'They said they'd been sent home at half-past five because there was nothing else for that night.'

'All right, Len. Now, I want you to make a statement, then you will have to sign it. It will take a while. Miss Benn is waiting in the outer office, would you tell her I'm free? I know she wants to see me on another matter. I will send someone out to you to take your statement in a minute. Have a coffee from the machine if you want to. Don't mention this to anyone, please. And next time, don't keep a problem like this to yourself. Tell the management.'

Bob leaned back in his chair and looked seriously at Hannah. 'I see the papers printed a rumour that Benn's are going to be taken over by Brandt's.'

'Pure nonsense.' Hannah was indignant. 'I hope you also saw our denial of any such thing. We have a reciprocal marketing arrangement with them, have had for some time. That's as far as it goes.'

'I'm glad. It is always good to see old family firms carrying on, in this day and age.'

'We're carrying on very nicely, thank you. Or we were . . .' Hannah's voice faltered, 'until all this . . . this . . . what with Pierre's disappearance and ransom notes and take-over rumours and . . . my mother's terribly upset,' she finished.

'And Matthew?'

'Well, he didn't really understand, and now he's gone back to school, thank goodness. I'm pleased he's out of it.'

'You realize that your driver has reopened a whole line of enquiry we thought was exhausted? Why was your dispatch department closed on the night of the fourth? What was happening?'

'Wouldn't we like to know,' said Hannah wearily. 'I thought I knew my own factory. I'm beginning to wonder if I know anything about it at all.'

It was Tuesday morning when Polly felt desperately in need of a talk with Vi, who was the person above all others to whom she turned in an emergency. They were both busy all day apart from meal breaks and it was not easy to get Vi on her own. The more she thought of unburdening herself the more Polly felt she needed to, but by degrees as the morning wore on she wondered whether it was wise to say anything, even to Vi. At last she decided not to mention the newspaper cuttings or her suspicions, but only to say that she had decided to make an absolutely final break with Kev and ask advice on how to do it.

'I shouldn't have thought you would have a problem,' said Vi when at last Polly managed to corner her. 'He's been going round looking as miserable as sin.'

'He's been asking me to go out and I've been refusing,' said Polly.

'I thought that must be it.'

'He thought he'd got me back, last Friday, you know, Vi, when I went out with him, and he can't understand it because he hasn't. He keeps asking me if it's something he's done.'

'And is it?'

'I'm just happier with Bri. Trying being with Kev again made me see how much I prefer Bri.'

'But he won't take no for an answer?'

'No, he won't. Look what he gave me this morning. I tried to refuse but he slipped it into my pocket while I was pouring tea and when I was free he had gone.'

She held out a small packet of white paper. Vi took it and could feel something hard and knobbly inside. When she unwrapped it, it turned out that the paper was written all over with messages of ardent love, and the thing enclosed was a brooch which looked very valuable – a large opal surrounded by small diamonds.

'It's not real of course,' Polly said nervously.

'If it isn't, it's a very good imitation,' said Vi.

'Oh, Vi, you don't think it's real? That would make it worse than ever.'

Vi wrapped up the brooch again. 'I think you had better pick a quarrel with him. Give him this back, yes, you had better not keep it in case it is stolen or something.'

'Stolen?'

'Well, he could have been offered it in a pub.'

'Yes, maybe.'

'He'll be hurt because you've given it him back anyway, and then you can go on to make a few insulting remarks, and have a blazing row with him if you can manage it, and that should be the end of it.'

'I won't know what to say.' Polly sounded nervous.

'Of course you will. There are two sure ways of insulting a man and getting him going, be rude about his driving, and if that fails, belittle his performance in bed. Tell him Bri's better in that vital aspect.'

'I don't want him picking a fight with Bri.'

'You'll have to risk that.'

'Oh well, if that's what you think.'

'If you want a break, that's how to do it.'

Polly thought she would leave it until after work – she didn't want any shenanigans at Benn's, she might lose her job if that happened and she had her mortgage to think about. She couldn't imagine Hannah and Faith being very sympathetic towards problems of the heart among their work-force. Perhaps Kev would try to intercept her going home, he often did that. She didn't actually want him in her house with her when she picked this quarrel, in case he lost his rag and went for her. For the same reason she didn't want to be in his flat. Even in the street she felt a little windy about it – nights were still dark soon after four; although the days were lengthening a minute or two at a time the progress towards light nights always seemed to take so long. Even in the street – she read accounts in the papers the whole time about people being attacked in crowded places and everybody standing round and not doing anything to help. She shivered. She didn't really want to take this extreme step; she wished she could tell Bri all about it and get him to tell Kev where he got off. But she couldn't bear to tell Bri – she'd have to tell him she'd been with Kev the Friday night before and he wouldn't like that. He might easily cast her off himself. There wasn't any help for it, she'd got to do it herself.

11

It started quite easily in the end.

Kev drew up beside Polly as she was walking home on Tuesday night and he opened the car door.

'I'm not taking this, Kev,' she said, and tossed the brooch in its paper wrapping on to the back seat of the car. 'And I'm not seeing you no more.'

He was silent as if stunned for a while. The car was stationary and she was standing on the pavement.

'What do you mean?' he said at last.

'What I say. I've finished with you, Kev. I'm going to tell Bri I'll marry him.'

She couldn't understand why the minutes spread out silently and why he did not appear to be reacting at all. The other homeward traffic rushed past them; one or two cars hooted because Kev had stopped in a very awkward spot for anyone to pass.

Then he said, 'All right, then.'

She couldn't believe it. 'You don't mind?' she said.

'Of course I mind. But I can't force you, can I? It's your choice.'

'Oh, it is good of you, Kev, to take it like this. I was afraid you'd be upset. I didn't want to hurt you.'

'No. Women always say that when they're cutting your heart out. "I didn't want to hurt you."'

'Oh, go on, it's not as bad as that. There's plenty of nice girls about. You'll soon forget me.'

'You're wrong.' He looked at her and his eyes seemed strange. 'There's no other girl for me but you, Polly.'

'Get along with you,' she said.

'No, I mean it.' His voice was still very quiet and calm.

For a little longer they looked at one another through the open door of the car. Then he said, still quiet and controlled, 'You may as well have a lift home, Polly. Don't worry. I won't touch you, and I won't ask to come in.'

'All right then,' she said.

As she fastened the door and her seat belt he sat immobile, then when she was ready he started the engine.

With a roar the car ripped into the line of traffic. On the dark road under the glare of the yellow sulphur lights visibility was strange and rather difficult, but Kev drove as if there was maximum daylight and as if the road was clean and dry and not still cumbered by slush and the last remnants of the snow. He overtook cars doing the regulation thirty as if they were standing still and drove in between the two lanes of traffic with barely an inch to spare on either side. He cornered so fast that his brakes screamed in protest and they almost went into an uncontrollable skid.

Before they had gone many yards Polly was clinging on to the fascia board with one hand and her seat belt with the other and her feet were digging into the carpet in front as if they could find a brake there.

'What the hell do you think you're doing?' she shrieked.

Above the din made by the protesting car he shrieked back at her, 'If I can't have you nobody will. I'm going to kill us both, what do you think I'm doing?'

'Oh, my God, Kev!' she cried out as they hit a patch of cobbled road which had never been tarmacked. At the end of the short stretch of vertical jack-knifes her stomach was rebelling, her head was going round and round and she was shaking with fright.

He drove, crashing through the gears like a maniac and, when she managed to look sideways she saw that his eyes seemed to be glowing red and maddened as she thought the eyes of a bull must look when it was about to charge. She was afraid that nothing could reach him – that he would not even hear, still less respond to any words of calm or of sense.

Her end might come at any moment but though a hundred times he could have crashed the car and taken them both to eternity, he avoided the final crunch, the tearing and ripping, the cascading effect of vehicles crashing into one another which must have been the result of a moment's misjudgement in the homeward rush of commuters.

Although she was already far past consecutive thought, it flashed across her mind that this might be punishment, that he might not intend to kill them both but only to scare her so thoroughly that she would never dare look at another man again, that she would be a petrified slave for life. That was before the next crazy stretch when she began to pray without words as Kev's car seemed to pounce on the car in front with a growl as though it would eat off the rear bumper, then passed it so closely that her face seemed to be within an inch of the horrified driver of the other car, then cut in so closely that if the other man had not stood on his brakes there would have been no hope for them in this world.

When a narrow channel opened up again between the two lines of cars moving in opposite directions Kev headed into it regardless of the non-existent clearance available on either side and put his foot down even harder on the accelerator. The air seemed to be full of vibration and noise and looking ahead Polly could not imagine that they would come out of the next few yards alive. When she saw the extra width of a heavy goods vehicle looming out into the few feet of space down which they were shooting she completely lost control of herself and without intending to or knowing what she was saying she screamed out, 'I know what you've done!

'I know what you've done!

'I know what you've done!'

Polly did not know what she was saying and certainly did not think that Kev would hear her or give any response except perhaps for the final *coup de grâce*, a head-on crash into the artic ahead, a slewing across both lines of traffic, a multiple pile-up, herself dragged dead and unrecognizable from burning wreckage.

'You what?' he said.

Unexpectedly he braked. The cars in the nearside lane, who had been skimmed by his brutish progress, were braking even harder. A space opened up. With a hair's breadth to spare Kev slid into it.

'You what?' he asked again.

'Oh God!' cried Polly and put her hands over her face.

He was silent for a while, driving as normally as anyone else around them. 'What did you say?' he asked again.

'I didn't say anything,' and the words came from Polly trembling and hesitant. She was too shattered to know what she had said or was saying.

'You said, "I know what you've done."'

'Did I? Well, I do know what you've done.'

'We've got to talk about this, Polly.'

'Talk!'

'Talk.'

'Talk! You just get me home safe, Kev, and then I never want to see you again and I mean that. You're not sane, you're not.'

He drove into a quiet side road and stopped the car.

'Now we'll sit here until you tell me what you mean.'

They sat there without speaking for several long minutes. Polly felt as though her heart was still thumping in her chest and she still felt horribly sick. Looking at her hands, she could see them trembling. She could not think properly and the nightmare images of the drive swam repeatedly before her eyes.

'Come on,' he said at last.

She had gathered her wits enough to be able to speak clearly. 'It was at your flat. There are some newspaper cuttings behind the tapes on the shelf. They are all about kidnapping and about ransom demands. I knew at once how you'd got the extra money you've been throwing about. We get to know everything in our place between us, me and Vi and Sue and Betty. I know there's been two demands for money. I know you, Kev. You're like that. I don't know if you kidnapped this bloke or not, but I'm damn sure you said you had and demanded money off them.'

'And why would I do a thing like that?'

'I don't know why. You've always thought you were different, you've always thought you could get away with anything. Well,

141

I don't want anything to do with it. I can't take it, Kev. I want an ordinary life with an ordinary bloke and you – you're not ordinary. I think you're twisted. You're dishonest. I can't live with that.'

Kev let out a long sigh. 'It isn't that you love him best, then? That he's better in bed, all that stuff?'

'I went with you first, didn't I? For a long time. If you had been more ordinary it would have worked out, you and me. There's ways I like you better. There, that's the truth and you can believe it or not as you like. You gave me a lovely night out last Friday. Then you behave like just now, as if you weren't right in the head.'

Polly had already undone her seat belt. Now she opened the car door and climbed out. She shut the door decisively. 'I don't want to see you no more, Kev,' were her last words and she turned and on shaking legs walked off into the strange patchy light and dark and half-light of the winter city.

'It was all for you,' Kev whispered to his folded fingers on the steering wheel. 'All for you, the lilies and the gold, the scent of wine and roses.'

On the Wednesday morning John Finch, head of Research and Development, was approached by his assistant who was in charge of routine testing of the products leaving the factory. Together they looked sadly down at an open box of Benn's Bars, split out of their wrappings by the assistant, which were showing a slight whitish bloom.

'It can't be sunshine, this weather,' John said. 'More likely to have been standing near a radiator. You'd think people working here would have more sense. They know the effect of heat. Yes, it must have been a radiator. We'll have to examine all that day's production, although it is likely to have been only the one pallet.'

'Shall I go and organize it?' asked the assistant.

'No, I'll go. You've a lot of work on and my desk is clear. Do me good to get out of the labs. What day was it?'

'The fourth of this month. The third working day after we started again after the break. I remember going down as usual for a random check, opening one of the pallets waiting to be shrink-wrapped, taking this box out and replacing it with one straight off production.'

'You mean this was produced in our first three days back?'

'They cleared all the waiting pallets before going off for Christmas and put them into the store. So this must have been produced on 2 or 3 January, unless it was from morning production on the fourth. I went down in the late afternoon on the Thursday, just before I went home. I'd finished what I was doing and you said, "Instead of lounging about go down and do a random sample check."'

'So I did, I remember. You get fidgety if you've nothing to do. I expect if it's from the first few days' production there's some excuse for it. It always seems to take a while to settle in again after the winter break. Even so you'd think they would be very conscious of where the radiators are. Any fault like this is so darned expensive. Check the bar code on the outer, that will tell us exactly which day and shift. Why is it you haven't examined it before today?'

'I put it in the cool store here to check when I had a spare minute.'

Taking a note with him of the bar code from the offending package, John Finch went down to the packing area near the entrance to TC1 and spoke to Mark Smith in his box of a check-in office next to the conveyor belt known as the ski run.

'I only book them in,' said Mark. 'They stop at my window as they run past me and I key in their bar code. I don't do the stock control or make the decisions about where they go in TC1. That's done by the office upstairs.'

He called up the record on his computer screen. 'Would you like a print-out?'

Armed with the print-out listing the warehoused production of 4 January, John Finch went to the computer office which controlled stock and the extraction of goods from TC1.

'It was mostly eggs and bars that day,' said Philip Camidge. 'I can give you a listing of production on the fourth.' He turned to his computer and, while he waited, looked at the listing John Finch had received from Mark. 'The pallet you're after isn't on this listing,' he said. 'But it is included in the day's production. Wait a minute.' He fiddled with the computer.

'We're well down on some stock lines,' he said as he was waiting for results to appear. 'The Fontaine Special Selection and the other fancy mixtures have sold well over Christmas and we're low on them, because the teams have been busy on the Easter eggs and so stock hasn't been replaced. It will be built up again now the egg line has closed down. At present TC1 is fairly empty. People eat more chocolate in winter, and we've a fortnight's lost production to make up. In summer things sometimes pile up a bit, but at the moment demand is brisk and the drivers have been filling up warehouses all over the country.'

'This was a pallet of bars.'

'Most of the pallets of bars have gone out already, we've been delivering like mad all week,' he was told. 'There's really only those you locked in, John.'

It was one of John Finch's tasks to designate a certain number of pallets to be 'locked in'. They were not to be sold, but stored until he gave the word. Other products were locked in if the time was not ripe for their sale – Easter eggs produced before Christmas were not sent out until after the Christmas selling peak was over, so they were locked in for a specified time. John Finch's locked-in pallets were purely for checks on faults and quality after certain specified periods of storage.

'Are you telling me that this pallet of bars has gone missing?' John Finch asked. 'Do you mean they've been stolen? I thought we had a foolproof, pilferproof system.'

'No system is proof against pilfering if people are determined enough,' Philip answered him. 'But I don't think they've been stolen, no. Most of the produced pallets I have listed for the fourth were warehoused and then sent out on delivery. There are three pallets left from that day's production apart from what you locked in. That was four pallets, so a total of seven. Why weren't they warehoused the same day, I ask myself?'

'And what do you answer yourself?' John Finch sounded both impatient and worried.

'Wait on. I think I know what might have happened. Yes. That's the answer for you.'

John Finch hated computers and gazed at the screen blankly, wondering what it was supposed to tell him.

'They were warehoused the following day,' explained Philip.

'Why?'

'Well, I expect they were the last to be packed on the fourth and by the time they were ready Mark had gone off duty, so they would be left standing on the ski run waiting for him to arrive next day. It must have been pretty late in the afternoon when your bloke went down and took his sample. There you are, simple as that.'

'And one of them, before going on the ski run, had been left next to a radiator for a while?'

144

'Must have been.'

'Let's hope it is only one of them and we've spotted it in time.'

'If it's one of the locked-in ones you're all right. There's no way you can check those that have already been sent out, but after all they hadn't been kept hanging about so they should be all right.'

'Can you arrange for them to be brought out of TC1 for me? We must examine them. The three before they're dispatched and my locked-in four.'

'When do you want them? Now?'

'Now. Before those three reach the shops. They might all have to be destroyed.'

'I'll do that for you. They should be out in about an hour.'

The three pallets due to be dispatched when required were in the most accessible racks in the warehouse, and they were produced first. By now John Finch had fetched his assistant down to help him and they had the pallets moved to a fairly quiet spot where they could work undisturbed.

Sally Binson walked past as they were breaking open the first pallet.

'Something wrong, John?' she asked.

'Bit of heat damage.'

'Were those due out? We need all the bars we can get at the moment.'

'Sorry and all that.'

'They'll be waste?'

'Afraid so.'

'How has it happened?'

'Parked near a radiator by the look of it. You might give your packing staff a lecture and tell them to take more care.'

'Strictly speaking, packing isn't under me.'

'I'm sure you've the authority to speak to them about it.'

'I'll do that.'

John Finch and his assistant examined every package contained in the pallets and only in one of them did they find any more traces of the harmless whitish bloom which develops in chocolate products subjected to heat.

'We needn't break open all the locked-in pallets, need we?' asked the assistant. 'They won't be going anywhere and they'll be opened in due course when we want to check their condition.'

'It won't be a proper test if they weren't in correct condition when stored.'

The assistant saw that there was no point in arguing.

The locked-in pallets were stored, as usual with locked-in stock, in the least-used part of TC1, farthest away from the control side, in the remote corner, in the top section of the storage racks. As the two from Research and Development waited, one of the fitters came to them.

'We've got an order down to bring you four locked-in pallets,' he said.

'Right. I'd like them here, please. We've been waiting a quarter of an hour.'

'You're lucky it isn't longer when you come in the middle of the morning.' The fitter was justly indignant. 'There's something funny about this.'

'Like what?'

'This order is for four pallets but on the rack there are five with that bar code. Now do you want all five or not?'

'If they've got the same bar code they are the same consignment, right?'

'Right.'

'Bring them all. Probably someone's keyed in the wrong number.'

'If you say so.'

In a few more minutes the five pallets arrived.

It was in the third to be opened that they discovered Pierre Fontaine's body.

The time had crept round to midday.

12

Kev had seemed moody all morning, so his workmates said afterwards. They none of them spoke to him much after discovering that he was biting everybody's head off.

'Row with Polly?' one bloke had asked him, and had back in return such a stream of abuse that the rest of maintenance had shrugged their collective shoulders and left him to it. At lunch time after eating his meal silently he had muttered something about the car not running right and gone out to try to adjust it. Usually he parked on the road, but to work on the car he ran it into the factory yard and into an unfrequented spot in a corner.

For a while he was noticed from time to time putting up the bonnet, peering inside, then sitting in the car, starting the engine, getting out again and watching the engine revolve, then switching it off and bending over it again, absorbed in his task.

It was twenty minutes later at the end of the maintenance men's lunch break that he was seen to be sitting motionless in the car as if asleep.

'Dropped off, dozy ha' porth,' said one of his mates. 'I bet it's a bit warmer in his car than in the factory, if he's had the engine running and the heater on.'

Together with the man he was talking to, he stood and looked over at the parked car in its unobtrusive corner.

After a few minutes they both had the same idea.

They turned to one another and said simultaneously, 'Do you think he's all right?' and with one accord began to run towards the car and Kev.

They were too late. Kev sat with eyes closed in the driving seat. His face was a queer pinkish colour they didn't like at all.

At first they banged on the window, when they found that the doors were locked.

'Fumes,' one of them exclaimed, but that was before they noticed the hosepipe which was leading from the exhaust. The engine was ticking over quietly by itself. It had killed its owner some minutes before.

There was a suicide note of a kind in the car but the words were not very explicit. *I made the ransom demands*, it said. *My life is over*, it said.

John Finch had sent his assistant to tell Faith and Hannah Benn of their discovery of the body in the box. Lena was at lunch but Ann showed the excited young man into Faith's office. It was the factory rule that anyone wishing to see the directors urgently was to be allowed to do so if at all possible.

'We think we've found a dead man,' he said, gasping from the speed with which he had run down the long corridors.

The Benn women looked at one another. The conclusion that it must be Pierre sprang into both their minds.

'The police,' Faith said instantly.

'They said not to ring through the switchboard.'

'What nonsense.'

'That's what Mr Southwell said. There's a call box on the corner.'

'Will it take money or is it one of those stupid card phones?' Faith asked.

'How should I know? Mother, have you any tenpences? Stay here,' Hannah added to the young man, then changed her mind. 'No, go back to John Finch and tell him to stay there on guard and tell no one.'

In her indoor clothes and light shoes Hannah ran as fast as she could to the telephone box. It seemed to take forever to reach it and she was not used to running, so that her breath was short and her ears ringing by the time she picked up the receiver.

Behind her the whole factory already knew that something very peculiar had been found in a pallet of Benn's Bars. The information could hardly have spread more quickly on a public address system, but afterwards no one could be found who would admit to mentioning it, to being told it, to passing it on, or would in any way take responsibility.

By the time DS Joseph Birch and DCI Bob Southwell arrived the suicide of Kev in the works yard was also common knowledge. Having driven in that way, the police officers were immediately involved. A great deal of hoo-ha was going on. In an effort to revive him his mates had lifted him out of the car and stretched him on the ground, and their fingerprints had been left all over the car doors and practically everything else.

Joe Birch used his personal portable telephone.

'Where's our back-up?' he asked the station. 'Aren't they supposed to be following us? We have two bodies now, and although one looks like a suicide we can take no chances. Coroner's officer, the lot. The scene of crime officers. At once. Pronto. This minute. Also Forensics and the police pathologist. Get them out here.'

'I expect they had to collect their stuff,' said Bob.

By the time the two detectives had left the car-park, walked through to the packing area, and were approaching the two men who were standing at the side of the half-open pallet, the experts they needed were driving as rapidly as they could through the city.

John Finch had sent his assistant for two cups of coffee with sugar. He remembered from somewhere that hot sweet drinks were what one took if severely shocked and the shock they had both sustained was pretty severe. He couldn't think of anything worse.

'I understand you reported finding a body?' Birch said to him.

'We assume it is, sir. We haven't uncovered it. As soon as I saw the foot and the hand I sent to tell the management.'

'And you haven't touched it since?'

'No. I did cover it up. It seemed best if no one else saw it until you were here, unless of course Mrs Faith or Miss Hannah had come along and asked to look.'

'They haven't?'

'No. I expect they took young Martin's word for it.'

'Miss Benn rang me,' Bob Southwell said, 'and I told her we would be here as soon as possible. I know the layout fairly well so we came straight along. Perhaps your assistant would tell them that we have arrived and will be in touch directly.'

The two detectives stood and looked at the general scene, the bustling trolleys transporting pallets a few yards away and the eight pallets fetched out for inspection by John Finch standing separately in this side area. Five of them had obviously been thoroughly examined. Their contents were all opened and after having been inspected had been heaped back roughly.

Most of the pallets concerned consisted of a number of packages or boxes of Benn's Bars, shrink-wrapped together to form a large cube. Two of them consisted of a large cardboard box with a lid. All the pallets were of a standard size which Bob guessed to be about four feet square, about sixty-four cubic feet. He couldn't relate to metric, although he was sure the measurement would actually be in metres or millimetres.

Coming down to brass tacks, the pallet they were concerned with was immediately in front of them, and was one of the large cardboard boxes. The shrink wrapping had been slit open all round with a knife and the top turned back so that the lid of the box could be lifted.

A few packages from the top layer had been removed and these lay on the floor beside the box. The packages removed from the side of the box had revealed the second row of packages which lay beneath them. It was one from the next row, towards the centre, which John Finch now lifted carefully once more.

The two detectives peered in. There, sure enough, was a neatly shod foot, and a hand just visible close to it.

They drew back. It would be best to wait for the arrival on the scene of crime officers, the police doctor, Forensics and the police pathologist before doing anything else. Standing a little aside, they talked quietly together while John Finch and his assistant drank their coffee.

'You can go back to your work,' Joe Birch told them then. 'Research and Development, did you say? We'll send someone along to take a statement from both of you during the course of the afternoon.'

'We may as well have lunch first,' said John Finch, 'although something like this takes your appetite away.'

'Keep quiet about it,' said Bob Southwell.

As soon as their staff arrived more could be done. The area was roped off, not to avoid the destruction of evidence because in this case that rule could hardly apply, but to separate the area of the investigation. The overseer in charge of packing came up.

'If it is a dead body,' he said, 'we don't want any foodstuffs coming through while it's here.'

'Quite right. We'll move it as soon as possible.'

'I'm closing down the department until you do,' said the overseer.

Soon the whole busy place was empty of men and pallets. Everything containing foodstuffs had been taken out at the end adjoining production.

'I want photographs of every stage of this,' said Joe Birch. 'Plenty of photographs, Michael. Every possible thing.'

As the photographer worked, recording every stage in the process, the doctor delicately removed the remaining boxes hiding the body. Everyone assumed it was that of Pierre Fontaine, and when they saw him properly their opinion was confirmed. He was a short man, slight in build, and was curled up in the foetal position. On every side he was surrounded by a wall of packages one layer thick. It must have been a work of art to pack him into so small a space, hemmed in by the foodstuff he himself had invented. He was fully dressed and rather dapper with his grey suit, grey socks, black lace-up shoes, and the white overall with his embroidered name, 'Pierre'.

'Barely any smell,' Bob said. 'It is really very odd. There is no sign of putrefaction and he's been in here – one would assume – for something approaching a fortnight. Perhaps that assumption is wrong and he's only been put there very recently, even yesterday.'

The police doctor looked up at them. 'He's definitely dead, anyway,' he said. 'But you need a specialist forensic pathologist on this one. It is outside my experience. You see, he's been stored, as it were. The details are up there.'

He waved towards a large notice-board, which read:

74 pallets long
18 pallets wide
11 pallets high
13 degrees C (55 F)
65% humidity

'He's been shrink-wrapped, too. Like a chicken or a joint of meat.'

'The specialists are on their way. He looks very peaceful, with his right hand tucked under his cheek,' Joe Birch remarked. 'As if death was sweet, and had come to him softly.'

'A very hygienic kind of death,' Bob Southwell added. 'No blood, no apparent bruising, no damage, virtually no smell. I think if he'd remained in there he would have quietly mummified long before anyone found him.'

'Would one of you like to identify him before we take him away?' Bob Southwell had been sent to ask Faith and Hannah Benn. 'There's the maintenance man too.'

'Isn't it supposed to be a relative?' asked Faith.

'For Monsieur Fontaine I would suggest that we could accept your evidence, certainly for now, although we will be sending a message to Belgium and asking one of his family to come over. It would be a pity to ask them to come and then be told that it was not Pierre Fontaine. My men are tracing the maintenance man's family at the moment. It seems he lived alone and wasn't married, but he may have parents living in the city.'

'Is it all wound up, then?' asked Faith. 'Did Kevin kidnap Pierre and then kill him and himself?'

'It is one possibility, but we must proceed with an open mind. It is dangerous to jump to conclusions.'

'I can't believe this,' said Hannah. 'What was the point?'

'The ransom money, I suppose.'

'In that case why didn't he cut and run?'

Bob shrugged his shoulders, and Faith Benn got up and said, 'I will identify Pierre.'

'Thank you. Then, as soon as we have the Coroner's permission, we'll take him away. The maintenance man too.'

'Until we have the forensic evidence we can't do anything,' Joe Birch said. 'I don't mean that literally, of course. There's all sorts we can do. But that's going to be the crux of the matter.'

'We've already sent men to go over Kevin Marrish's bed-sit with a fine-tooth comb,' Bob Southwell replied. 'He can't have hidden him there. It's tiny.'

'Bodies have been known to be shoved under baths, under floorboards, any old place. But the question really is, when did this man die, and where? One thing you may or may not have noticed.'

'What?'

'Hypostasis. When they lifted the body there was that purpleness underneath. Not much of his skin was visible but I saw it on the underside of the head, caused by the blood obeying the laws of gravity. The doctor agrees with me that on a first impression it looks as though Fontaine was put in that box immediately after death. He saw no secondary hypostasis.'

'The ransom notes made it sound as if he was alive.'

'Of course. No one pays ransom for a dead body. Not usually anyway.'

'One scenario is that this maintenance chap killed him, somewhere, packed him, got him stored, made ransom demands, then killed himself. Why should he kill himself?'

'We'll have to approach this the usual routine way, don't you think so, Bob? Means, motive, opportunity. It is lucky that you put that time in last week. We can already go a long way towards means and opportunity. If it was the lad Kevin, money was the motive. So we investigate the circumstances of his life. Debts? Expensive habits? *Routine*. That's what is going to get us somewhere.'

Almost immediately routine took them to Polly. Asking the rest of the maintenance men about Kev and his life inevitably, sooner or later, led to Polly. Apart from anything else, on the back seat of the car was the opal and diamond brooch still wrapped in a piece of thick white paper addressed to Polly using her full name on the outside and written all over inside with messages of love. Before very long Polly was sitting on one side of a table and Joe Birch and Bob Southwell were sitting on the other, waiting for her to tell them all she knew.

She told them about the long time which she had spent going out with Kev – practically living with him, though she tried to disguise that part of it. She told them that the affair had cooled, on her side at least, and she had begun to go out with Bri, the long-distance lorry driver who also worked for Benn's. It didn't take Bob Southwell long to connect up Polly and Bri with Betty and Len; Len whose supposed loyalty to his mates had made him tell lies and waste police time, Betty who, being Polly's workmate, had introduced her to Bri.

No, Polly had to admit, Kev hadn't liked her change of heart. No, he hadn't taken up with anyone else. She wished he had. He'd kept on at her, wanting her to go out with him, obsessively jealous of anyone and anything she had to do with.

Why had she changed towards him? they asked her. She shillied and shallied at that, because Kev had killed himself that day and she was in a state of shock although no one seemed to have much consideration for her feelings, and she had been brought up to think that one did not speak ill of the dead.

'Tell us about your relationship with Kevin during the last fortnight,' Joe Birch asked her gently at last. The look of sheer fright in her eyes made him add, 'Don't worry. We aren't going to tell your new boyfriend anything. As far as possible what you say will be completely confidential. If we need you to give evidence as to Kevin's state of mind we will give you due warning and only bring out as much as is absolutely necessary.'

'He wasn't sane,' she said then. 'He wasn't normal. Otherwise how could he do such a thing? That's why I was breaking it off with him, he wasn't normal, Kev wasn't.'

Moody, temperamental, irritable, unsociable was the picture they already had from the other maintenance men.

'Do you mean you believe that he kidnapped Monsieur Fontaine?' asked Bob Southwell.

'I don't know what to believe.' Polly looked down and fiddled with her fingers. She opened her handbag and rubbed the St Christopher. She felt that it was only due to the St Christopher that she had escaped alive from that awful car journey. 'It was those newspaper cuttings, you see.'

'What cuttings?'

'Those cuttings behind his cassettes on the shelf.'

Bob turned to the woman police constable who was sitting in the corner. 'Go and get a message to the boys who searched Marrish's bed-sit, will you, Sandra, and ask them if they found some cuttings behind his cassettes on a shelf. If not, will they go back and have another look.'

'He might have got rid of them last night after I told him I'd seen them,' Polly said.

'Tell us about last night.'

Then she told them about the nightmare journey, her accusation, and how she had walked away and left him with his head bent over the steering wheel. 'I had ever such a long way to walk home, too,' she finished.

'So he might have gone back to his bed-sit and destroyed the cuttings – yes, quite likely. You seem to have believed that he might have kidnapped someone and demanded ransom money?'

'Well, not that, exactly,' said Polly.

'What, then?'

'You see, we all knew that Mr Fontaine was missing and that the police were looking for him and couldn't find him.'

'Who do you mean by "we all"?' asked Joe Birch.

'Everyone at Benn's.' She looked surprised that he should need this elucidation. 'So if he was missing, someone like Kev with a twisted mind might have thought of writing a ransom note, mightn't they?'

'It wouldn't occur to many people,' said Bob.

'It's exactly the sort of thing that would occur to him.' She sounded bitter.

'Nothing made you conclude that he actually had kidnapped Monsieur Fontaine?'

'Well, no, but I suppose he could have.'

The newspaper cuttings had gone from behind the cassettes on the shelf, but they had Polly's word for it that they were all concerned with kidnapping, and specifically with ransom notes.

'Hmmm,' said Detective Superintendent Joe Birch, looking over at DCI Bob Southwell, who said 'Hmmm' in reply.

It was about then, when they were sitting revolving various

thoughts in their minds, that the Exhibits Officer, young James Jester, knocked and came into the office.

'Sorry to interrupt, sir, but a report on Exhibit JJ1 has come from Wetherby,' he said.

'Remind us, James.'

'The contents of Monsieur Fontaine's wastepaper basket, sir. I bagged them up at the beginning. We didn't say it was urgent and Wetherby have been very busy.'

'Better late than never. Have you brought the report?'

'It's the plastic carrier bag that is interesting, sir.'

Joe almost snatched the report out of James's hand.

'Plastic carrier bag!' He scanned the typewritten sheets quickly until he found it. 'Inside the bag were a few hairs? Hairs? What were they doing in a carrier bag? Human hairs? Grey? Insufficient to test for DNA? Possibly male as natural in colour, straight and short. How the heck did they get there? So after finding the hairs they looked at the carrier bag more closely? I bet they did . . . Saliva? There was saliva on the inside . . . the saliva and nasal secretions were on the inside . . . Good God, Bob, the poor bloke was suffocated in a plastic carrier bag.'

James Jester stood there. He had read the report and he realized the significance but somehow, hearing it put into words like that . . .

'Poor blighter,' said Bob. 'No wonder we couldn't find any traces of the crime in his work area, even now it's been gone over again with murder in mind. Of course it wouldn't leave any traces.'

'But can you imagine anyone murdering someone with a carrier bag and then leaving it casually in a wastepaper basket?'

'They probably didn't think of it as affording any evidence, and they would expect normal cleaning procedures to empty that WPB first thing in the morning about half six or seven o'clock.'

'The work area door was locked.'

'It is only a Yale,' Bob said thoughtfully. 'Whoever was carrying out his body to dispose of it might have let the door bang behind them without meaning to. They were probably in a hurry. The bag may have fallen off him, or they may have taken it off to see if he was still alive. Rather than leave it on the floor they perhaps put it in the wastepaper basket to deal with later. The place did have a very deliberate clean, didn't it? If James here hadn't been on the ball enough to take the contents of the wastepaper basket we would never have had this evidence. It is very likely that the criminal doesn't know we've got it. They most likely think that the bag went the way of all the rest of the rubbish from Benn's.'

James Jester decided that carrier bags would never seem quite the same to him again.

'Has it occurred to you, Bob,' said Joe Birch, 'that if Marrish was involved in this, he was not alone?'

'Not?'

'No. Granted as one of the maintenance men he had access to all parts of the factory and could hide the body, no problem, but while we were waiting for the scene of crime officers I was watching them operate the shrink-wrapping machine and two men seemed to be working together. We must check if one can do it alone. It would be awkward for one man to bring a body down here from the labs, too, and pack it into a pallet.'

'More than one of them, then,' Bob said thoughtfully.

'And if Marrish was guilty, to whatever degree, the other person is still at liberty.'

'Right.'

'We'd better go and have a word with the Benn family.'

'You will be pleased to hear that we found some at least of the ransom money in Marrish's flat,' Joe Birch told Hannah and Faith. 'It seems from our investigations that he used part of it to pay off a loan he had taken out to buy a car. He also bought an expensive brooch for his girlfriend, who was Polly, one of your tea-ladies. She told us that he gave it to her but she returned it. That is confirmed by one of the other tea-ladies in whom she confided – Vi, a short middle-aged lady in a woolly hat. Polly is going out with one of the drivers and had rejected her former lover. On Tuesday night she told him she never wanted to see him again because she knew what he'd done. On Wednesday, instead of collecting the fruits of his second demand, he killed himself.'

'She knew what he'd done?'

'She was leaping to conclusions on circumstantial evidence but his suicide and the note he left seem to confirm at least that he sent the letters.'

'What melodramatic lives our staff lead!' cried Hannah. 'I would never have believed it.'

'Polly is obviously the Helen of Troy kind.'

'She's a most ordinary girl,' put in Faith. 'Pleasant enough, but

I wouldn't have thought any man would have committed crimes and then killed himself for her.'

'Can we have the money back?' asked Hannah.

'It is evidence at present, but you will have it back eventually, also that part of it represented by the car, which will have to be sold, and the brooch, likewise.'

'You are sure Polly is not involved?'

'I'm sure she knew nothing of Fontaine apart from what was common knowledge round the factory, and she was very distressed by concluding that her former boyfriend might be involved.'

'Shouldn't she be suspended from work until this is all cleared up?'

'I don't think that's necessary, but a day or two's compassionate leave might be helpful to her.'

'I'll ask her,' said Faith.

'What is happening about your new recipe?' asked Bob.

'The analysts have promised us their report this week – any day now. Then we will have the ingredients and hopefully the proportions. What we won't have is the exact method. It might be difficult, very difficult, to reproduce the recipe exactly. We can only try. He told us it was not written down anywhere, but it is possible that he might have done so and put it in a safe-deposit.'

Now that Pierre Fontaine was known to be dead, all kinds of things could take place which were impossible before. The legal agreement about Recipe 179 was signed so that was not open to doubt, but Pierre's possible contribution to development costs was now out of the question – Benn's would have to find the whole investment alone. A brother flew over from Belgium to take charge of Pierre's estate and he visited York to carry out another identification of the body, which when released was to be taken to Belgium for interment in the family plot. Hannah and Faith found the brother pleasant and co-operative enough, but this stout paterfamilias was not their friend Pierre, in spite of some general resemblance.

Life proceeds in spite of death. Ann, Faith's secretary, had put in the advertisement for a new secretary for Hannah, and appeared one morning with a pile of applications.

'I really can't bother with that now,' Hannah said impatiently. 'Lena is perfectly all right. Whatever possessed you to advertise?'

'Shall I tell them the post is filled, Miss Hannah?'

'Tell them . . . tell them that selection has been postponed but their applications will be kept on file and that we will be in touch with them when the time arrives. I really can't think about it at the moment.'

In the same way in the police force the selection procedure for the next detective superintendent was in train. Joseph Birch had given in his notice before the moment when he decided to take over the Fontaine case and no postponement was either asked for or suggested. Everyone knew that his health was in such a state that he ought to retire at once if he was to have any hope of a few quiet and enjoyable years.

In a certain proportion of high-level posts it is police policy to open the competition to all forces, which gives more people a chance than would be the case if they were promoting within the local organization.

Bob Southwell was applying as a matter of course and he knew exactly what his opposition was from his own colleagues. Ever since being transferred to York on promotion he had been lucky in that Joseph Birch's long illness and consequent low level of energy had given Bob the opportunity to take command in a number of interesting cases and carry out work he might not otherwise have had the opportunity to do. He knew that if the competition was within the local force he stood an excellent chance of being promoted and nothing would please him more. But it was not within their own force. People from all over the country might decide that they wished to be a detective superintendent stationed in the pleasant city. Competition was open – very open. He did not feel secure of even a reasonable chance.

All this did not damage the relationship between Bob Southwell and Joseph Birch, and the relationship between Lena Lindgren and Hannah Benn also seemed a smooth one.

Benn's factory, though, was in a state of turmoil and excitement such as had never been known before. Among the twenty maintenance men one less did not make much difference to their work load, but among four tea-ladies Polly's protracted absence on compassionate leave made a very big difference indeed. Rotas were altered and routines upset, and from day to day none of the remaining three was quite sure whom they would be serving and where. Luckily they had had experience at holiday times and during sick leave of meeting this kind of emergency and to the rest of the staff the tea trolleys seemed to be running perfectly smoothly, except that they never knew which face would be behind the tea urn.

13

'There are certain things we can be reasonably sure of,' Joe Birch was saying. 'Fontaine was in his work area at five thirty on Thursday, 4 January when the other staff left Research and Development. He was never seen again. That night TC1 was locked up when a collection had been arranged. Both enough staff to load, and the security man, should have known about that but did not. An attempt was made to suggest that the collection had taken place. We thought this was probably normal cover-up behaviour to hide a clerical error. Fontaine's body was discovered in TC1 a fortnight later. I think that we can conclude from this – as a working hypothesis – that Fontaine was killed later that evening of the fourth and concealed in that pallet. We know that it was stored as one of a locked-in group which were to go to the top layer in a far corner of the warehouse and which would have been left undisturbed for a long time, if it had not been for the accident of the random sampling revealing a fault in handling.'

'It would need two people at least, don't you think so?' asked Bob Southwell.

'I do think so. Also it was most likely premeditated, in view of the fact that the TC1 staff were sent home at five thirty. The fact that a row of pallets was waiting on the ski run overnight – well, that probably often happens, but it was a bonus that four of them had lock-in bar codes. All that was necessary was to add a label with the same bar code to the Fontaine pallet, and hey presto! it was lost, if not for ever, at least for several months during which the murderers could decide what else to do with it.'

'You feel sure Fontaine was killed that evening?'

'Yes.'

'But why and how?'

'For why, we must go back to our original idea of industrial espionage, surely. This is a wider spreading affair than a maintenance man whose girl has left him and who thinks he can get her back by spending money on her which he hasn't got.'

'But he may have been involved?'

'He may, or he may not. We aren't going to get anywhere if we concentrate on him. We must take a wider look at the thing. We know that at least one big international firm had made Fontaine a good offer for his recipe, which he refused – he told Faith Benn as much. We know that a second firm, Brandt's, is interested in taking over Benn's. The situation is there in which someone might have decided to kidnap Fontaine to stop the process of development going any farther. They would not know that he and Benn's had already signed the final agreement. I feel that is significant. Faith and Hannah Benn both stressed how anxious Fontaine was to have the contract signed. This must indicate concern on his part that no one else got the recipe. The opposition would need to have agents in the factory, among this apparently very loyal work-force, to do this. It is likely – and I'm guessing here, Bob – that they did not intend to do him any harm. Kidnapping is a situation in which an unintended outcome often happens.'

'I can't see people who have lived in York all their lives and been associated with the industry as long turning traitor like that.'

'No. But we mustn't rule out that possibility. However, you did get a list of people who had joined during the last twelve months, didn't you? They might be more likely.'

Bob produced the list.

'That Swedish girl looks a bit suspect to me.'

'We've checked her out. Her CV is accurate, and everyone speaks well of her. None of the big league of confectionery manufacturers are based in Sweden.'

'The maintenance man was a York chap, wasn't he?'

'He was, which I feel is a factor in his favour.'

'This HGV driver from the Midlands . . .'

'Len? He was part of the cover-up for TC1's closure that night.'

'Not been here very long.'

'No.'

'You don't sound as if you feel he's a possible, Bob.'

'He might be involved. Doesn't seem to fit the role.'

'Several of the men are new this year. Surely it is a man we are looking for on this one? One of the electricians in this list – here only six months and came from Leeds.'

160

'The natural tendency would be to suspect anyone from Leeds,' agreed Bob, rather tongue in cheek.

'Oh, I don't know. I have an aunt who lives in Leeds and she's very respectable. There's a fitter come from Harrogate, your neck of the woods, Bob.'

'Even Harrogate might not be above reproach.'

'One of the tea-ladies has only been here eleven months.'

'Vi? Yes, she's newish. She comes in every day from Stamford Bridge. I gather her previous firm went bust and she was too old for most people to want to take on. Faith Benn carries on the philanthropic tradition of the industry and she employs older redundant people whenever she can.'

'Is she that little old wrinkly?'

'You could describe her like that.' Bob didn't dare add that she was the same age as his boss.

'You think I'm being rude about her? One of those competent middle-aged women, salt of the earth, Bob. More people should employ that type. Very under-valued as a source of reliable labour.'

'I agree.'

'Most of these new people are on production.'

'There seems to be a high turnover of women, sir. They marry and have babies usually, but I'm told they often come back after a few years and are welcome because they are trained. They have a refresher course. I've already had everyone on that list investigated.'

Joe Birch put the paper down. 'I'm sure that at least two people working in this factory are involved in this. One of them may or may not have been Kevin Marrish. Get a team on to checking the whole of the personnel again, Bob. You can have as many men as you need for as long as it takes, and don't miss anybody, from the Benns themselves down to the cleaners.'

It was the following Tuesday.

'Mother,' Hannah Benn said, 'I want to talk to you.'

'I'm here. Talk away.'

'No. Let's go out to lunch.'

Faith looked at her daughter in surprise. Go out to lunch today, with all these events stirring up the factory and unsettling the work-force?

161

'Please, Mother.'

'All right, then. I'll have a look at the Selection production before we go.'

It was only since finishing the Easter eggs that the production of the Fontaine Special Selection had begun again and Faith kept checking to reassure herself that all was well. Now she walked slowly up and down the ten lines, smiling and nodding at the operatives but scrutinizing carefully all that was going on and the amount of waste being produced.

The Alpine Truffle was causing some concern, and the Parisienne Cream which had a little squiggle on top was currently subject to a lot of misformed squiggles. 'Stop the line and have the fitters on to that machine,' Faith instructed. The Nougate Supreme, Pistachio Cup, Lemon Snow, Yoghurt Surprise, Café Delight, Mint Bombe and Curaçao Liqueur seemed to be functioning perfectly. The Marzipan Melody was generating an unacceptable level of waste and Faith paid it special attention.

'It's the consistency of the filling,' she was told. 'We've had words with them about it.'

'Them' was the team of men concerned with creating the filling which flowed into the production line in a smooth sheet. Faith went to have further words about it. Then she walked out, reasonably satisfied, and changed into her outdoor things so that she could lunch with her daughter.

'Where are we going?' she asked.

'Anywhere, as long as it is away from this place.'

From a Benn, and particularly from Hannah, this was heresy. The place they never wanted to be away from was Benn's.

They drove the short distance to a reasonable pub, settled into a corner, and ordered a simple meal. Hannah had a ploughman's lunch. There was a cheery gas fire with flames and they had the lounge bar to themselves.

'I had a talk with Bob Southwell this morning,' Hannah began without preliminaries. 'He says the crime must have been committed by at least two people and that one or more of them must still be in our work-force. We must trust nobody, who-ever it is.'

'There was that fuss over the switchboard,' remembered Faith.

'Yes. He says trust nobody, not even your secretary Ann. Not that there's anything wrong with her –' Hannah saw that her mother was about to splutter a defence of Ann – 'but we must not trust anybody at all. Walls have ears, he said. That's why we've come here. We must watch everything we say in the factory and even at home. He believes that someone has been paid to steal Recipe 179, or to put it another way, to stop us producing it.'

'We haven't got it until the analysts come up with something,' Faith interjected.

'They've finished their analysis. I received it this morning by hand and I didn't produce it in the office. Here it is.' Hannah took the envelope from her handbag and opened it. She pulled out the report and she and her mother looked at it together.

'I want to tell you something, darling,' Faith said. 'I have opposed you all along on your plans for Recipe 179 and everything that's happened did get on top of me. You know I don't usually break down as I did the other day. But I've had a change of heart over it.'

Hannah said nothing, waiting for her mother to go on.

'We're not going to be beaten,' her mother said sturdily. 'We must stand up to the type of people who will descend to such methods. I'm behind you, my dear, one hundred per cent.'

'So you will be ultra-careful of what you say and where?'

'I will. I was alive in the war, you know, when we had to be very careful. We are facing an enemy now, it is just the same. I have a plan for discovering this person.'

'Mother! Hadn't we better leave that to the police?'

'Do they know the factory as well as we do?'

'Go on.'

'We alter this analysis a little, so that it is no longer the true one. I will go to the firm myself and ask them to produce another version on their own notepaper, while you put this in our safe-deposit at the bank. Then we hold a meeting in the seminar room with all the managers and heads of department, a celebration – why not a glass of champagne? – and lay the false version in the middle of the table in full view so that everyone is sure we have got it. Then we await developments.'

'It certainly might bring some. But the analysis is useless to us, you know, as it stands. They can't give us the method used in preparation and that is as important as the ingredients.'

Joe Birch went in search of his DCI Bob Southwell with a piece of paper in his hand.

'A memo from Mrs Faith Benn,' he said abruptly. 'What are you doing, Bob?'

Bob looked up from the desk where he was sitting in the incident room at the police station. They had contemplated moving back to Benn's but had never done so.

'Going through everything again,' he replied. 'When there's a new turn of events notes from the beginning of the case start to take on a different aspect.'

'Well, leave it for now and come back with me. I want to discuss this away from the noise and clatter of all these blinking machines.'

'They do buzz a bit.' Bob was more accustomed to modern computer technology. As records were being kept manually there was not a great deal of mechanical noise in the room but some computers were switched on. They had their uses, but the atmosphere, as with all closed-in offices, was rendered less habitable by the machines which were emitting heat and vibrations.

'You need some plants in here,' Bob said in passing to Jenny Wren, who was still seconded to the enquiry. 'Gerberas are supposed to be particularly good at combating sick building syndrome.'

'I don't like gerberas,' she retorted. 'Or is that an order, sir?' But Bob had gone.

Once back in the super's office Birch explained Faith Benn's plan.

'She wants me to be present.'

'Does she expect something to happen immediately?'

'No, of course not, but she seems to think a trained observer can look round and spot from people's expressions whether or not they are guilty.'

'She's an optimist. I suppose it could work. Someone might get the wind up, seeing the whole object of the plot defeated.'

'You feel as I do about it. I did wonder whether to ask her not to do this, but as you say it might move things on a peg. I'd like you to come with me, Bob.'

'Do you want me to be in on the meeting as well?'

'No. That doesn't need two of us. But I'd like you there in the building. You could talk to the work-force, find out what they think of Faith's little plan – they're sure to know all about it by tomorrow.'

'Is that when it is to take place?'

'Yes. Ten o'clock.'

'Sir, I've been meaning to ask you . . .'

'What is it?'

'It's an awkward thing to ask for in the middle of a murder enquiry.'

'No, you can't have time off, Bob.'

'Only this evening, sir. It is Linda's birthday and I'd like to take her out to dinner.'

'If you were still in charge it would be impossible, but as I've taken over – yes, all right, but keep quiet about it. Everyone else is working their socks off.'

Bob arrived home at half-past seven on that Tuesday evening to find Linda absolutely ready and both children in bed. She was perched on the arm of one of their easy chairs in the sitting-room and talking to Tom Churchyard from next door, who was baby-sitting, or child-minding, which was the substitute word Linda had started to use to avoid domestic contentions. Bob, tired and feeling grubby, was struck once more by how attractive his wife was. It was unusual for her to be out of jeans and she looked very pretty with the new haircut modelling her hair to show off the shape of her head, and wearing the pink dress which she saved for high days and holidays. The neckline was deep enough for him to see the beginning of the cleft between her breasts and the full swirly skirt to mid-calf moved and swished in response to every slight movement she made.

'Hurry up, darling, we'll be late,' she said.

'You're very lucky I could get off.'

'Well, as you have got off, hurry up.'

The traffic was still thick as they joined it at the Clifton end of the bridge and turned right to drive towards Bootham Bar. There they went left down Gilligate and right on Lord Mayor's Walk and then left again along Monkgate and out of the city. Once they began to drive out the traffic thinned and the journey became much more pleasant. Bob had not yet lost his sense of delight and wonder as he drove round York, and the journey down Bootham towards the floodlit Bar and Minster still gave him that authentic thrill, even though by degrees he was noticing them less and the congested traffic more.

At the tiny roundabout at the end of Heworth Road Bob turned right and then abruptly left.

'You're taking a funny route, darling,' Linda said.

'I'm not taking a funny route at all.'

'This is Stockton Lane.'

'I know it is. I thought we'd drive past the house one of Benn's managers lives in.'

'They must do quite well. This is an expensive road.'

'So I understand,' said Bob, reading the house numbers. 'This is it.' He stopped the car. 'Do you mind waiting here for a minute, pet?' Without waiting for her answer he got out of the car.

'It is my birthday!' Linda sounded as annoyed as she could, but he had gone and did not hear her. She saw his shadow, thrown by an old street lamp, slide across a massive brick gatepost and a mass of laurels and then nothing else. Her little evening watch said eight o'clock and that was the time of their booked table and they were several miles away yet . . .

'Hmmm,' said Bob ten minutes later when he arrived back at the car.

Silently Linda showed him her watch.

'There isn't far to go.' He switched on the ignition and to her surprise drove back down Stockton Lane, left through Heworth and down Melrosegate. 'Quickest up the Hull Road,' he explained and put his foot down on the accelerator.

On a weekday night in midwinter the Corn Mill, which had a lot of seating, had been able to hold on to their table for them without a problem. There was a jolly party taking place in one area of the dining-rooms and the rest had enough diners to create a friendly atmosphere without being uncomfortably crowded.

They sipped a pre-dinner drink and sat near the enormous old waterwheel, looking down at the mechanism through an area of toughened glass in the floor, then to eat moved near a window table, where Linda opened the curtain nearest to her so that she could look out on the frost-bound mill pond far below.

'Winter's rather fun,' she said.

'You think so?'

Bob did his best. He smiled tenderly at her and ordered a bottle of rather sweetish wine, of which she would have to drink the bigger share. One thing he had no intention of doing was driving while over the limit. He enjoyed the food and being on their own, which was a thing they managed only too rarely nowadays.

Everything was right for the romantic evening he knew that Linda wanted, something to remember during the humdrum days which came so often through the year.

It was not Bob's fault that he could not forget the murder of Pierre Fontaine. Most of his mind was not under his own control at times like these; he had spent the whole day carefully rereading through everything he could on the case, and had managed to reabsorb a tremendous amount. Now the computer in his head was busy assimilating and sorting that mass of information and only a small part of it was free to deal with normal matters.

When Linda glanced lovingly across at him she usually caught that abstracted look she knew so well.

'The soup's here, darling,' she said clearly, and he came to with a start and said, 'Oh! Yes! Splendid. That looks very good,' but within two minutes his spoon had stopped moving and before long she was saying, 'Your soup will be cold, dear,' and some courses after that, 'The sweet trolley's at your elbow, Bob,' and he jumped again and said, 'Lovely! Now what is that one?' although the waitress had told him the names of all the sweets a moment before.

'I don't know why I bother,' she said on the way home.

'Why you bother what, dearest?'

'Why I bother going out with you. A tailor's dummy would be better company.'

'I'm sorry . . .'

'It's all right.' She sighed. 'We'll go out again when this case is over.'

Faith had organized the meeting in the seminar room on the Wednesday morning, exactly a week after the discovery of Pierre Fontaine's body. DS Birch was present, and Bob Southwell had come along as back-up. Bob intended to walk around quietly on his own through the busy factory, hoping that something would occur to bring a fact to his attention which would help them to a resolution of the case. Both the detectives were unhappy with the state of affairs at present. They knew that a lot remained to be uncovered and there seemed to be no way of grasping a handle and discovering the mechanism behind the crime.

Also present at the meeting were Faith, Hannah, both their secretaries, Ann and Lena, and most of the heads of department.

Faith took charge.

'Ladies and gentlemen,' she began, 'you all know what has happened in our firm, the tragic death of Monsieur Pierre Fontaine, inventor of the Benn's Bars and the Fontaine Special Selection, and of Recipe 179, potentially our new mass market commodity. We have all felt a great sense of loss over the last weeks and more particularly since the finding of his body. But today I don't want to talk about that; I want to talk about the positive aspects of this situation. In fact, this meeting has been called more in a spirit of celebration of achievement than as a wake or an inquest. Pierre Fontaine was a creative man who achieved a great deal in his lifetime and many lives are richer as a result. There are many small moments of happiness in the world as people give themselves a treat with his Selection, or stave off hunger on a journey or on a mountain walk with one of the bars. Benn's intend to continue and build on those achievements with our future production of the new Recipe 179.'

She paused there, having ended on a ringing, rising note in her rather penetrating and cultured voice. No one in the room dared to break the silence.

At last, with a dramatic drop to a lower register, she went on, 'The analysts have now produced for us, from the samples prepared by Monsieur Fontaine, *Recipe 179!*'

At this Faith picked up a folded sheet of paper, unfolded it impressively, waved it in the air and then, every tiny movement impregnated with significance and drama, she bent right forward and laid it down in the middle of the long conference table.

Her audience could not resist taking a collective indrawn breath.

14

Bob's mind had been working overtime ever since that Wednesday morning of the previous week. By now he was so obsessed with the case that eating, sleeping, everything else was subordinated, but he seemed to be no nearer a breakthrough. He knew though that soon it would come, if he could only put himself in the right place or situation for things to fall into a pattern. He had been through this process before, this kind of agony, feeling he was getting nowhere, and then suddenly pieces would come together.

Gradually his thoughts focused on Fontaine's body in the pallet, and he decided to look again at the packing and warehouse areas.

He remembered being shown round the factory when he had first come to see the Benn women, and, taken into TC1, standing on the balcony of iron trellis and looking across the strange building.

Approaching one of the fitters, he asked for the loan of the keys, knowing that the entrance doors into the ground floor of TC1 were kept locked, access to anyone other than the staff of the building itself being restricted to the balcony across one end.

'What do you want to walk round for?' the fitter asked him. He was a pleasant, friendly man and Bob answered frankly that he didn't know really, but as that was where the body had been stored he wanted to get to know the place better.

'Nothing happening in there just now,' the man said. 'We're waiting for some more stuff coming through. There was that electric cut yesterday afternoon put us back a bit.' He hadn't the authority to forbid a detective going into the place, and didn't see why the chap shouldn't go if he wanted to.

Bob Southwell let himself into TC1 through the two locked doors, doors marked STRICTLY NO ADMITTANCE and KEEP CLEAR FOR EMERGENCY ESCAPE ROUTE. As he entered he saw a row of hard hats hanging up, and out of the habit of setting a good example he took one down and put it on.

At present the four tall yellow cranes were silent, standing in line next to the entrance side of the vast building. Bob had seen them at work on his previous visit, from the vantage point of the balcony.

Looking up now at the openwork metal of the balcony he remembered how the cranes with their orange lights flashing had moved up and down the alleys between the huge metal-framed storage racks, each crane on its own tram track let into the floor, and how they had each returned after every task to the balcony and come to rest near it with a kind of dipping whistle, gliding into line like a row of cygnets from *Swan Lake*.

It seemed strange that the place was silent and not still vibrating and shaking with the swishing movement and the dipping whistles and shining with the orange flashing lights. There was only the gleam of stainless steel tubes in the working light provided by fluorescents. The atmosphere was always eerie, but it was even more eerie now.

As these storage places went, TC1 was not large; not nearly as large as the comparable area at Rowntree's. It was as tall, the height of eleven pallets, but only two thirds as long at seventy-four pallets and two thirds as wide at sixteen pallets. Bob remembered he had been told that old Matthew Benn had allowed for expansion and had put larger foundations in so that extension would be a simple matter when the time came.

Apart from the yellow cranes it was a colourless world. The large packages referred to as pallets were made up usually of many boxes of brownish cardboard, but sometimes of a single large box with a lid. All were shrink-wrapped in clear plastic film so that they made a kind of dull neutral gleaming all along the tall racks. Southwell wondered what the purpose was of all the stainless steel tubing in loops and coils and was grateful that he was not an engineer. After the central heating of the offices and the general warmth of the factory and the cold of the outside world this place struck a strange middle note, for it was a controlled atmosphere of thirteen degrees Centigrade and sixty-five per cent humidity. Bob Southwell did not know whether to shiver or feel warm, but on the whole he felt that the constant draughts which the temperature controls caused to move through the building were something he would rather be without.

He reminded himself that he had not gone there to stand still and contemplate. Contemplation was to be done in your own time and not that of the CID. He had gone there to have his mental processes prodded by being in the place where the principal thing, the secret thing, had been discovered. There might be something else to be discovered, that was what had brought him here on his own, but it must be in the recesses of his own mind.

He moved past the resting cranes and set off down one of the outer aisles, looking intently all around him. The farther he went from the entrance side the more dim and mysterious TC1 became.

He reached the place where on the highest rack Fontaine's body had rested and stood there for a while, hoping that the longed-for breakthrough would come to him. Apart from feeling strangely moved, oddly emotional, nothing happened. Some five minutes later he thought he might as well go back again, and he began pacing down the long alleyway farthest from the door through which he had come, looking down at the single tram track, placing his feet on either side of it.

He had almost reached the more open area under the balcony when the crane ahead of him came alive, its orange lights flashing. He had not realized before now how huge they looked when one was down on floor level. His eyes travelled up the great machine to where it almost touched the roof of the warehouse, and he noticed the ladder fixed to the side of the more delicate top structure, from the roof of the solid cab-like part at the bottom.

In the cab he could see a human figure, and was surprised until he realized that it must be one of the fitters checking the machine for some reason, because normally their movement was automatic, controlled by computer. Vaguely Bob thought that when he reached the crane he would shout up and speak to the person there.

That was before the crane began to move.

Bob was quite close to it now, within feet, almost at touching distance. The great thing, with flashing orange lights and whistling noise, was getting into motion and sliding towards him.

'Hey!' he shouted good-humouredly. 'Watch out!'

The figure in the cab did not seem to hear him. Bob moved back a little. The crane still came on.

Looking to right and left, Bob saw that he could not sidestep to safety; the crane filled up all the space between the two racks except for a few inches' clearance on either side. There was no way those few inches could accommodate a human being, even a thin one such as Bob. He stepped back, and then stepped back again a bit more smartly.

It was then that he realized he would have to go more quickly than that if he was not to be run down, and there was no clearance under the thing where he might lie flat and let it go safely over him. He was strangely reluctant to turn his back on it, convinced that it would rush at him, but walking backwards was a slow process.

Turning round, Bob began to walk quickly down the length of the alleyway, glancing over his shoulder. The crane was moving faster and faster and soon he found himself breaking into a trot as he looked for an opening in the racks through which he could slip. There was one, the escape route to the fire doors for use in emergency, but he had passed it before noticing somehow – his attention was fixed at that moment on the crane.

It would be all right, he told himself. He remembered that he had been told the cranes had an automatic ray a little way from the end of the warehouse which slowed them down ready to stop at the buffers which projected from the end wall. Those buffers, as seen from the balcony, projected quite a way from the wall so that he would be safe once there, standing between them or at one side.

He reached the end of the warehouse not far ahead of the crane, panting and wary, turning to see it slow down for the buffers . . .

The crane did seem to take a momentary check but the figure in the cab moved the controls like lightning and the enormous thing picked up speed instead of losing it and came straight for the buffers and Bob. At the last possible second he leaped sideways into the gap at the end of the racks between them and the wall, escaping by the skin of his teeth as the crane crashed at full speed into the buffers and the concrete blocks of the wall.

Bob did not stay to speak to the figure in the cab. He thought that whoever it was would have to climb out now from the damaged vehicle and there was only one way to leave the warehouse. He told himself that he would issue a severe reprimand for such dangerous behaviour when they were both out of this terrifying place.

He was reckoning without the superior knowledge of the driver of the crane. Looking back, he saw something in a green overall and a hard hat running after him, and they were both a long way from the entrance. Now was he to stay and speak, or fight, or run? The figure emitted a high continuous scream and Bob changed his mind about the dignified reproof. This must be a madman. Madmen should not be confronted alone in an empty warehouse unless that was a last resort, certainly not when within yards there were men and women behaving normally . . . Something was the better part of valour, thought Bob, wishing he could remember what it was and quite frankly turning his back on the figure and running. With his long legs he knew he was likely to be the faster runner. Discretion, that was it. Discretion.

Then behind him he heard the clang of an opening door coming into contact with metal racking. Turning, he saw that the figure was escaping from the warehouse. Running back as fast as he had run

172

forward Bob found that it was a special fire door which had been opened and that the figure was running round the buildings of the factory already well ahead of him.

At once he too went through the fire door and after the figure, shouting now, 'Catch that man!' in case there was anyone to hear him.

The pale winter daylight and the remains of the night's frost did not help in the pursuit. Bob fell over a pile of discarded boxes and slid on a frozen puddle while the figure ahead skimmed round such obstacles. The two plunged through the narrow neck where TC1 was only connected to the main building by the packaging area. In at one door and out of the other, Bob crying out, 'Catch that man!' and the few workers who happened to be there looking stupefied with amazement and doing nothing.

Once out in the works yard Bob sensed that the figure would be making for a car and shouted once more, 'Catch that man!' amazing now the drivers, dispatch staff and general warehouse men who were unpacking raw materials and sending them up in a hoist to the top floor of the main building.

The only person to take action was James Jester, who had just parked a police car and was walking towards the factory entrance. He heard and came dashing round the corner in time to run slap into the overalled figure in the hard hat and grasp it, falling together with his captive on to the frozen asphalt surface of the works yard.

They were both winded but before Bob Southwell could come panting up James had found a pair of handcuffs in his pocket and slipped them on to the wrists of his victim. Holding the arm of the figure firmly he scrambled to his feet, helped the other, and both turned to find themselves face to face with Bob.

'Jesus,' panted Bob, 'it's Sally Binson.'

The hard hat had come off and her hair had come down. James Jester felt awkward. This was one of the management at Benn's and a woman and he'd hardly been gentle.

'You tried to kill me,' Bob gasped out. 'Lord, I didn't think such a little bit of running would wind me. I must be out of condition. You're coming to the station, young woman. I want to get to the bottom of this. Bring her round to the car, James.'

173

She was a strong, muscular woman and struggled wildly to escape James Jester's hold but Bob Southwell came back to help him and took her other arm. It was no use fighting against both of them.

Faith Benn had intended, hoped, to provoke reaction from the traitors in her camp when instead of a gauntlet she threw down the analysis of Recipe 179, but she had not thought it would happen as quickly as it did.

The awe-struck silence round the conference table was broken by the door opening and the tea trolley appearing, pushed this morning by Vi. The note of comedy produced by this intrusion into Faith's high drama relieved the tension and people visibly relaxed in their chairs.

'Tea only this morning,' Vi announced brightly. Ever since Polly had gone off work they had been offering tea only to the directors, because the coffee machine took extra time and trouble and there was enough of that already with only three of them on, wasn't there?

'Tea will be fine for everybody, Vi,' said Hannah. 'We won't get up. Use those plastic cups you've got underneath the trolley this morning, and take them round the table, if you don't mind.'

Vi put a bowl of sugar and some spoons on the table for those who wanted sugar and quickly began to move round serving everyone with plastic beakers of tea. It could not be said that they were fragrant or even hot but they were welcome.

It was as they all began to attend to their cups of tea that Lena Lindgren got up from her seat at the side of the room, where she had been taking shorthand notes on a pad resting on her knee. She came over as if to take one of the teas but instead reached out over Paul Change's shoulder and picked up the paper bearing Recipe 179 from the centre of the table.

'I will take charge of this, I think,' she said in her beautifully articulated English.

'It is all right on the table, leave it there, Lena,' said Hannah Benn.

'I am leaving you, Miss Benn,' said Lena. 'This is what I came for, this Recipe 179. I will say goodbye, everyone.'

She began to move towards the door but before she could walk out of the room Vi acted. She snapped open her handbag which as usual was perched on the end of her trolley and, knocking aside the hare's foot and the black cat, she drew out from the bottom a Smith and Wesson 38.

'I don't think you are going anywhere, Miss Lindgren,' she said firmly, and whipping the paper with Recipe 179 out of Lena's hand, she herself backed towards the door. 'Sit down, Miss Lindgren,' she ordered, waving the revolver towards Lena, and when she was slow to move a bullet exploded over the heads of the astonished company sitting round the seminar room's conference table.

Lena sat abruptly, with blood beginning to stream down her arm.

'I'm sorry about this, Mrs Faith, Miss Hannah,' went on Vi. 'But I'm a good shot and I will not hesitate. If anyone comes after me for the next two minutes they get it in a more vital place than she got it.'

Snatching up her handbag, she went backwards out of the door, pulling the trolley after her so that it wedged inconveniently in the way of pursuit. Vi had her Metro parked expediently near the front entrance. Before anything could be done she was in it and away, ripping off and dropping as she went the orange mob-cap worn by Benn's tea-ladies, to reveal her usual woolly knitted hat.

Detective Superintendent Birch had been as much taken aback as anyone when Lena made her move and once Vi produced the Smith and Wesson he was as powerless as anyone else, but the second she and her gun were out of range he whipped out his portable telephone and rang in urgent orders to the station.

'How does she travel?' he asked. 'She must have had something arranged.'

No one had noticed how Vi arrived at the factory each day.

'Is there a bus from Stamford Bridge?' someone said in a vague and stunned manner.

'Mode of transport isn't something we put on record officially,' Hannah answered him like a zombie. 'Her workmates would know.'

Birch was looking ill. His face appeared drawn and a curious grey colour. When he tried to get up from the table he moved like a man who has grown suddenly old. He clutched at his chest.

'Bob,' he said. 'Bob Southwell. He's somewhere in the factory. I'm not at all well.'

15

Bob Southwell had had to take charge of the case again, because Detective Superintendent Joseph Birch was in intensive care after a massive heart attack.

'He's going to be all right,' Bob told the rest of the force. 'They're very hopeful that he will make a complete recovery, but it's doubtful if he'll be able to resume duty before his retirement comes through.'

Meanwhile Lena had also visited the hospital for treatment to the bullet wound in her arm.

'Are you going to arrest Lena Lindgren?' Hannah had asked Bob, and about her had been the suggestion of a banked-down volcano. He sensed that she was in a fury and that it was taking all her considerable force of character to remain in command and not explode.

'There doesn't seem to be much I can arrest her for,' he said mildly.

'She wormed her way in as a spy and then attempted to steal Recipe 179.'

'She failed in the attempt, though, didn't she? And was shot for her pains. Isn't that enough punishment? Do you want to pursue her out of a sense of justice or hurt pride?'

Bob had not failed to hear how, when the ambulance arrived for Joseph Birch and Lena Lindgren, Lena had turned on her employers and informed them in no uncertain terms that it was time Hannah and Faith began to live in the twenty-first century and that they had no idea what the world was really about. For a modern go-ahead young executive-type like Hannah that must have been galling, nearly as galling as discovering that she was not such a good judge of an employee as she thought she was.

'Hurt pride, I suppose,' Hannah answered him.

He looked at her with renewed respect. Not many people would have admitted that. He had discovered much more about her character in the last weeks; he still thought she was one of the most attractive women he knew but he had realized that she was far more complex than he at first thought, more complex a woman than the average man would want to take on in a permanent relationship, more dominating than the average man could cope with. In some ways Bob frankly admitted to himself that he was an average man, and, even if he had been available and in the running instead of being very happily married, Hannah would not have suited him.

'Anyway, what have you found out?' she asked, and there was a weary note in her voice.

'I think we've found out everything. Suppose I call round and tell you and your mother all about it?'

'Please do.'

'What time would suit you?'

'Strange as it may seem, we still have a factory to run, with three hundred people depending on us for their wages and countless retailers expecting prompt supplies of our products. We can't spare working hours. I have to interview applicants for the post of personal secretary as a matter of urgency. We have had to give temporary promotion to a stand-in to be in charge of Dispatch and that is not very satisfactory – we will have to do something about it very soon.'

'In the evening, then?'

'If you can come at that time, we would be grateful. Could we give you an evening meal, or anything?'

'Perhaps you could give me a coffee. I will come after you've eaten.'

'I appreciate the trouble you are taking, Mr Southwell.'

Bob stood in the darkness of the winter's evening where some weeks before PC John Clark had waited to be let in as the Benns' First Foot. There was a little more light than there had been then. Above him he could see the stone underside of the pretty wrought-iron-fronted balcony which stretched across two thirds of the house, making a shelter for the front door as it did so. He had already pressed the bell.

Once in the softly lighted sitting-room he looked around and thought that he must try to remember this to describe it to Linda. The curtains showed him that this was a double room, and that they were in the inner part. There was a beautiful oriental carpet on the floor in soft pastel shades. The walls above a white-painted dado were an unusual turquoise blue, and carefully spaced on them were a number of original paintings in old gilt frames. The fire burned in a surround of white marble and white-painted carved wood and the armchairs were drawn cosily up to it. The wooden occasional furniture was obviously antique, well loved and cared for; there was a small but pretty flower arrangement on the walnut semi-circular table at one side, and some colourful china in a glass-fronted hanging wall-cupboard.

'Do make yourself comfortable, Chief Inspector,' said Faith, lifting a coffee pot. 'Do you like white or black?'

'White please.'

Then both Faith in a chair by the fire and Hannah on the sofa looked at him expectantly.

'For a long time Sally Binson would not tell us anything,' he said. 'She refused to speak at all until we told her that Vi had stolen the Recipe and apparently got away with it, and that we were about to search her own house on Stockton Lane. She's under arrest so we don't need a warrant. I think it was the search that did it. You see, Vi had been blackmailing her.'

'Blackmail?'

'Binson is into something called bondage. She was convinced that if you knew she would be dismissed.'

'She thought correctly, Chief Inspector.'

'So as soon as she knew that we were to search her house, she realized that this would be found out and that you would learn of her activities, so the whole point of the blackmail then lost its validity. She knew her job was lost anyway and decided to save her skin as much as she could.'

Bob took a sip of his coffee and found it very good, but hot, so he went on, 'Your friend and colleague, Pierre Fontaine, had become friendly with Binson when he was here for a while some five years ago. Undoubtedly they had a sexual relationship, but they were so discreet that no one seems to have got wind of it at all. However, during the last eleven months while Vi Ayton has been working at Benn's she acquired knowledge of Binson's private behaviour, but don't ask me how. All I will say is that Ayton has a son who is not only a spendthrift but a very shady character. I would suggest that it is Vi Ayton's love for this son, who constantly needs rescuing from financial straits, that led her into participation in criminal activities. We have no record of anything against her until this, but plenty of intelligence information against him, though we didn't connect them as he doesn't live at home. He might well have known about Binson and passed it on to his mother.'

'This is awful,' Faith said. 'Pierre was our friend. He lived in our house. He asked if Matthew could go down and spend a holiday with him.'

'Don't blame him too much,' said Bob. 'As far as we can see it was his only vice and he doesn't seem to have indulged very often.'

'How would examining Sally's house have made a difference?' Hannah asked.

'Quite simply. She had a room kept specially for entertaining her . . . friends, let us say, and within it were a number of whips, dress-up gear in shiny black plastic and leather, chains, handcuffs, torture implements . . .'

'What? Torture?' Faith sounded both horrified and uncomprehending.

'Not for actually hurting anyone, of course. She wouldn't have gone as far as that, I feel sure. It was a matter of being pleasurably frightened on the part of her customers. Perhaps a little whipping. Definitely constraint, in the form of shackles, hoods and so on. In the interests of sexual arousal,' he explained.

Faith shook her head. 'I have heard of such things of course, Chief Inspector. But the idea of actually having known and worked with people who had such strange desires and practices . . . it is incredible.'

'She is exactly the type, I would think. Strong and with that impassivity which one could imagine in a fantasy gaoler. You mentioned her hands to me, Miss Benn. They were noticeable, beautiful, firm, capable. Ideal for such a sexual practitioner.'

Hannah shook her head in a gesture very similar to her mother's, indicating amazement and non-comprehension.

'Again we think it may have been the son who put his mother, Vi Ayton, in touch with people who wanted a spy inside Benn's, for money of course. Once the contact was made she proved a very satisfactory agent. Do you realize that your receptionist cum switchboard girl, Elfrida, tells her Aunt Sue – who worked with Vi – everything that she picks up during the course of her work?'

'Elfie? I can't believe it!'

'That is what we have been told in written statements and what people are willing to state on oath in court.'

Hannah buried her face in her hands.

'Now I know why you told my daughter not to telephone from the factory,' Faith said bitterly.

'I had no evidence at that time against Elfrida. It was only a sensible precaution, as there was obviously far more in the whole thing than met the eye.'

'So, you have told us – do drink your coffee, Chief Inspector – that one of our tea-ladies was blackmailing our head of Dispatch, who was – I think I quote you correctly – "into bondage", and that the said tea-lady was at the same time a secret agent for some other manufacturer . . .'

'Correct,' said Bob.

'Also that our very trusted switchboard operator was in fact not to be trusted, but was as sounding brass and a tinkling cymbal?'

'That is a very good description, Mrs Benn.'

There was a pause during which Bob tried to drink his coffee quietly and was offered a second cup, which he accepted.

At last Hannah asked, in a very low voice, 'But how did Pierre Fontaine die?'

'The way Binson tells it is that he asked her to come to see him at going-home time one evening and she fixed the Thursday – the fourth. She went to his work area soon after half-past five, when the staff had left. The purpose of this visit was apparently to talk together, to see whether both were willing to resume their former relationship after the five-year break, and if so, to make arrangements to meet for that purpose.'

'And?'

'And Vi was also involved. She told Binson that this international consortium had offered her an immense sum of money, which she would share with Binson, in return for ensuring that they got hold of Recipe 179 and that Benn's were not able to produce it. Vi devised a method and made Binson go along with her. In case you begin to think too well of Binson –'

'There's no danger of that,' said Faith.

'. . . she agreed quickly, lured by the money. The plot was partly hers. She suggested that instead of only talking about future meetings, she begin a little sexual play with Fontaine, persuade him to be tied up and hooded, and that they should then take him to her house like that and keep him there in her special room, which has security blinds and can be efficiently locked. A simple and workable plan. She had her own parking place for her car in the works yard outside the entrance to Dispatch.

180

The nights are dark and the watchman was under pressure due to illness reducing the number of security staff, so probably not doing his job as well as usual. It would have been easy to carry out. So that there was no risk of interference she sent all her staff home at five thirty. She intended later to put Fontaine, bound, in the boot of her car and drive round the building and out through the front gate, remarking to Stan that she had stayed behind to do some paperwork.'

'Not telling the driver, Len?'

'Forgetting about notifying Len. That was her only mistake. Had she sent a message to him that he would not be able to collect that night, and altered the record sheet, the tracks would have been much better covered. As it was we began to wonder about the bona fides of Dispatch.'

'She is usually such an efficient lady,' mused Hannah.

'Yes. Even the most efficient are not perfect. Everyone makes mistakes, everyone. She must have been under strain.'

'So she went to Research and Development, talked to him, involved him in a sort of game, for which he was tied up and a hood put over his head −'

'She put a plastic carrier bag over his head. That was a bit of would-be clever planning. She intended the game to seem spontaneous and unplanned. To produce a purpose-made hood would have shown that she had planned that it should take place.'

'And?'

'And that was when Vi Ayton took a hand. She had been waiting outside. Binson may have been aware of that, I don't know. She could have taken him down to her car on her own, I would have thought. Perhaps they anticipated trouble from him. In any case, Vi entered Fontaine's work area once he was tied and hooded with this makeshift hood. Vi gathered up the slack of the hood behind − this appeared to Fontaine, I suppose, to be all part of the game. He was asphyxiated, of course, very rapidly, and was unable to struggle because of his bonds.'

There was no sound from anyone. They all felt rather sick, even Bob, who was hardened to murders.

At last he went on. 'They discarded the carrier bag once he was dead. I expect they took it off to make sure it was over. Binson seems to have been upset by seeing his face. Then they took the body down and packed it into the container, in the empty packing area. Even though they are both strong women it took two of them

181

all their time to do it satisfactorily. Then they left him in the line on the ski run to be stored next morning. Binson had all the know-how required.'

'Yes, of course she had.'

'But there are other things, Chief Inspector!' cried Faith. 'There is Lena Lindgren for one, and Sally Binson chasing you in the warehouse for another, and Vi suddenly showing her hand like that and snatching the recipe and shooting Lena.'

'I have talked to Lena, although at present we are not charging her with anything. That may come. She has a strong dislike for violence, an almost pathological fear of it. As soon as Fontaine's body was found she began to realize that someone else was working as an agent in the factory and that they were not as scrupulous as she is. She began, to put it bluntly, to be afraid that violence would occur again and that she might be involved, as in the event she was. When she saw the opportunity to snatch the recipe she took it, desperate to complete her mission, leave Benn's and be safe.'

'What about Sally Binson chasing you?'

'I am sure now that she saw me last week when, on my way to take my wife out for a birthday dinner, I parked the car by Binson's gate and walked round her house, trying to make out what was happening inside.'

Nobody asked what had been happening inside; they felt they would rather not know.

'Once the body had been discovered both Binson and Vi became very nervous. They had intended it to be hidden for several months, by which time the trail would be thoroughly cold, even if it was discovered then. They thought they would be able to work out a plan for permanent disposal during the time it was hidden. You can imagine that Binson was nearly beside herself when she saw that Research and Development were examining some of that same day's production – for 4th January. She must have gone away after speaking to them very much on edge and chewed her fingernails to the quick in her own office, unable to do anything except hope that they had not retrieved that particular pallet and would not be opening it. Then later I went round her house, and next she found that I had asked for the loan of the keys and gone into TC1. Attacking me was a crazy thing to do. I think she was nearly out of her mind with worry. Don't forget her plan had been to keep Fontaine captive in her house, not to kill him. As far as Vi goes, it must be said that she took to crime like a duck to water. Perhaps her son inherited a hidden tendency. She also felt nervous and anxious to finish the business and claim her reward. We are hoping to pick up the pair of them if they attempt to leave the country.'

'And was Kevin Marrish involved?' asked Hannah.

'Not at all, according to Binson.'

'That's something, anyway. Nor Polly?'

'Nor Polly.'

'We had two enemy agents working in our factory,' mused Faith. 'Lena and Vi. Surely, Detective Chief Inspector, they must have been collaborating – they must have been in cahoots?'

'I am absolutely positive that they were not,' replied DCI Southwell.

'There's one thing I would like to make quite clear to you, Chief Inspector Southwell,' Faith Benn went on. 'Vi Ayton is not a York person. I would like to make that quite clear. I'm not sure where she came from originally, but she is not a York person.'

16

DCI Robert Southwell was sitting at home at his ease and had totally stopped thinking about the case of Pierre Fontaine. He stretched out his long legs to the fire and gazed appreciatively at his wife, who was knitting a jumper for their daughter. It had an elaborate pattern on the front in bright colours.

Linda felt his eyes on her and looked up. They gazed at one another for long seconds and then she said, 'You're back with us again, then, are you?'

'You could put it like that.'

'Till the next time.' Linda dissolved a slight tincture of bitterness into the remark. 'I hope it isn't my birthday next time you have a case like this one.'

Bob considered this. After a while he said, 'What can I do to make up to you for it?'

'Nothing.' Linda concentrated on knitting-in a differently coloured ball of wool.

Bob didn't think she was really angry with him. If she had been she would have been storming about or throwing saucers by now, not sitting intent on her knitting. He took up the paper and found the columns of forthcoming weekend attractions.

'I see there's a special event at Harlow Car Gardens this Sunday,' he said in a normal conversational tone. 'They are running conducted tours round the Winter Garden, talking about what plants they chose and why. Would you like to go? We could take the children to have Sunday lunch out in one of the Harrogate hotels and then join the 2 p.m. conducted tour. What do you think?'

'Not a bad idea,' Linda responded cautiously at last.

'We might plant a few winter-flowering things.' Bob was weaving a subtle web. 'A jasmine nudiflorum next to the front door, do you think?'

'A hamamelis mollis where I can see it through the kitchen window,' put in Linda.

'Harlow Car should give us a few ideas, don't you agree?'

'What would you like to drink, darling?' asked Linda, getting up. 'Tea, coffee, Horlicks? Let's have an early night. I'm tired of struggling with that knitting.'

Bob had achieved his object. He stretched out again, luxuriously. 'Whatever you're having,' he said.

'We're going to have two weddings among the staff,' Faith said happily.

Hannah glanced at her. She thought her mother was sentimental about weddings. All this business of dressing up the bride-to-be like a maypole . . . Marriage seemed to be a sad, disillusioning business most of the time and often the rewards didn't seem worth the punishing work and grinding routine involved, at least for working-class women. She felt that she ought to produce a better response, to sound interested.

'Who is it?' she asked.

'Two of the tea-ladies. Polly, who must have been very upset by that horrible experience with Kevin, and Betty. They are marrying two of the drivers, Brian and Leonard. I really think it is a case of *all's well that ends well.*'

'If you think so, Mother.' Hannah stirred her tea. 'I'm glad for them,' she added at last.

'They both want to stay on, so that's all right.'

'I don't think we ought to recruit any more tea-ladies,' Hannah said. 'The bars production line was going to go over to a drinks dispenser as soon as Vi retired, anyway, so they may as well switch now. Maintenance and the fitters go to the canteen for their breaks. The most isolated workers, taking longest to wheel a trolley to, are TC1. We'll give them a dispenser. Sue and Betty and Polly can manage the rest between them if they try. We could give them a bonus.'

'What about during holidays and sick leave?'

'One of the canteen staff would probably be glad of a bit of overtime.'

Hannah wanted to see Matthew. This was a permanent condition with her if her son was away for more than an hour or two; but after the stress of the last weeks the need had become urgent. It was almost as though he were the parent and she the child, for in his presence she felt she would find reassurance and peace.

The school she had chosen for him was near Heptonstall on the Pennine spine of the north country. It was isolated and rural, plunged half-way down into a quiet valley which had once resounded with the clatter and bustle of a now-ruined woollen mill. She had chosen it for the good reputation of the headmaster, the small size, and the fact that it gave a very traditional education. There was time in the rest of life to be trendy. The little boys – it was a prep school and took mainly very young boys – started Latin at the age of seven, had constant testing in maths which they seemed to find great fun, and read or absorbed somehow most of the children's classics from English and world literature very quickly. The only objection she had had from Matthew was to the school uniform, which she admitted was behind the times. It was grey flannel, which he didn't mind, but the shorts, worn with knee-length socks, were his abomination.

She had rung first to say that she was coming, and asked permission to take Matthew out for lunch and a walk. Matthew himself had come on the phone a little later to stipulate that he wasn't going to be taken anywhere where people could see him in his school uniform and he wouldn't come unless he could wear his casual clothes. Then she had to ring the headmaster again and obtain his agreement.

'I think we will have to change our uniform,' he said thoughtfully. 'We are considering allowing long trousers next year. They would still be grey flannel, of course.'

'It would be a great improvement,' Hannah assured him with heartfelt enthusiasm.

The next day she was swinging her car off the main road on the high open moorland and dipping down the narrow track into the tree-lined valley. Drawing up at the back of the long low stone buildings, she left the car and went in search of the authorities and her son. Within ten minutes she was carefully reversing and driving in second gear up the bends of the track.

'Where are we going, mater?' asked Matthew. He always sounded very polite and well-spoken after however short a time at school. Hannah enjoyed it, but then she enjoyed Matthew most of the time, whether he was acquiring the latest slang from Orlando Trim or being ultra-formal as at present.

'Hebden Bridge? Or if you feel like the great metropolis we aren't many miles from Halifax.'

'Hebden will do,' and Matthew sank back with a sigh of content.

He was too absorbed in looking out of the window to talk much and that suited Hannah, who wanted to have all her attention on her driving. The fact that he was with her was enough.

They found a hotel which did good hot or cold lunches. Matthew went for roast beef and Yorkshire puddings and Hannah made a careful selection from the enticing array of salads on the cold table. For a while they exchanged small news, mostly from Matthew with his mouth full, about school and the other boys and the masters.

'What about a walk?' suggested Hannah. 'Here round the town, or back at school and along the side of the valley, or up on the tops?'

'On the tops.' Matthew was unhesitating.

They drove half-way back and stopped at an enticing sign which said *Bridleway*. Up here the snow, which never reigned long in the vale of York, was still in full possession. Hannah was glad of her high boots and that Matthew had brought his wellingtons as well as his best shoes. They drew great breaths of the moorland air which blew keen about them and pulled their ski hats down and their cashmere scarves up. At first Matthew ran wildly in great circles round his mother but soon he calmed down and they trudged enjoyably along together.

'I told you about Pierre,' Hannah said at last. She felt that if Matthew was worried about the events in the factory during that January he ought to have the chance to discuss them.

'Yes.' For two seconds Matthew's face looked sorrowful and then he asked, 'Who gets his Rolls?'

'His brother took charge of that. The police were able to release it because it wasn't needed in evidence. I was very pleased when they took it away for examination. I didn't like to see an expensive car out twenty-four hours a day in all weathers.'

'No,' said Matthew, who obviously hadn't reached the age of considering such things. 'I wanted a Ferrari anyway.'

'It could never have been yours,' she said gently. 'All his property was left to his family in his will, apart from a few small bequests to his friends down in Hampshire. His bridge club got his rather nice card tables and his gardening society his gardening books. His housekeeper had a financial thank-you and so did his gardener.'

'What happened to Paddy, his dog?'

'His housekeeper is to have Paddy. She's very fond of him.'

They were silent for a while and then she added, 'We have our memories of a good friend, Matthew, and the Benn's Bars, and the Fontaine Special Selection.'

'And Recipe 179,' added Matthew.

'No. No Recipe 179.'

'Why not? You told me you'd signed an agreement, Mummy.'

The 'Mummy' signalled a return to home speech from school speech.

'We did. We had the analysts on to it and they've given us the ingredients and proportions.'

'That's all right then,' said Matthew. 'Utterly brilliant.'

'It is the method which is proving impossible to duplicate.'

'Oh, well, it is tricky,' said Matthew condescendingly, leaping up and knocking the snow off a branch of a wind-twisted hawthorn tree.

Hannah pondered this for a while.

'What do you know about it?' she asked.

'He taught me, didn't he?' Matthew said in a dismissive tone. 'You remember, Mummy, I was with him twice when he was making Recipe 179. He told me he'd make a chocolatier of me yet. He made me do all the processes after he showed me each one.'

'I don't suppose you remember very well.' Hannah refused to raise her hopes. She had abandoned the idea of ever being able to produce Recipe 179.

'It will need modification for mass production, of course.' Matthew sounded lofty.

'Tell me what you remember.'

Matthew screwed up his eyes, fixed his wellingtons with a narrowed gaze, and began to recite the process of making Recipe 179. It was as if he had a tape recording in his head. Phrases of instruction which were recognizably Pierre Fontaine's sounded strange in Matthew's childish voice.

Hannah knew all about that kind of memory, because she had it herself. When she had been at school she had never needed to swot because she could always turn back, as it were, to a lesson they had had and run it through in her head. It was not until now that she was aware that Matthew had inherited this capability. People with it did not realize they were unusual, at least they did not realize it as children. It tended to be borne in on them later when they assumed everyone was like that, and found that the assumption was not true.

Hannah turned round and they began to trudge back to the car. She thought she had a notebook. Even though her memory was still excellent she was not going to rely on it now, nor on Matthew remembering for any longer than he had already.

They settled in their seats again and once the wind was shut out the car seemed delightfully cosy. With the notebook on her lap, Hannah said, 'Come on, now, Matthew, let's go through it all again and I'll write it down.'

'Oh!' he said. 'I've just done it!'

'Once more, Matthew.'

'Utterly boring!' he said.

'If we are going to produce Recipe 179 we need everything you can remember. Pierre's remarks to you, the things you were doing wrong and how to do them right, everything.'

'I didn't do anything wrong,' Matthew grumbled. 'He said I was a very good student.'

'So you are, my darling. Now, from the beginning . . .'

'Is there anything to eat in this car?'

'There's some Special Selection waste in the glove compartment.'

Matthew opened it and groped about, finding a strong paper bag and pulling it out.

'Goody,' he said. 'Alpine Truffles and Café Delight. My favourites.'

'Not my favourites if we go on getting so much waste on them,' retorted his mother. 'I had to send three tons to the pig farm.'

'Good for the pigs.'

'Come on, Matthew. Help me write all this down. It is important, you know, and you can't be hungry after that dinner. You can have that waste to share with your friends.'

With a mouth full of misshaped Alpine Truffles Matthew complied.

It was as she drove home that Hannah Benn began thinking about Matthew's father. They had not seen one another for five years, but from time to time she sent messages through an intermediary to tell him how Matthew was doing, and in return she had news of him. He was happy and successful in his career, still married to the wife he had refused to divorce for Hannah. Over in America, at the top of the scientific tree in the confectionery industry, he seemed quite content to be without her. So be it. She knew that was the situation when she conceived Matthew.

'If you've hit on a winning recipe,' she thought, 'why change it? But all my eggs are in one basket with Matthew. He means too much to me. What he needs is a brother or sister, and I need to see my man again . . .'

A short holiday, she thought. Somewhere within reach of him so that he could come to her easily. Just a few days, a few hours of his time. She knew she could command that; he would not fail her.